Stay H

About the Author

Ava Pierce lives in Kent. *Stay Home* is her first novel.

AVA PIERCE

Stay Home

HODDER

First published in Great Britain in 2020 by Hodder & Stoughton
An Hachette UK company

This paperback edition published in 2020

1

Copyright © Ava Pierce 2020

A CIP catalogue record for this title is available from the British Library

Paperback ISBN 978 1 529 34994 8
eBook ISBN 978 1 529 34987 0

Typ
Printed

Hodder &
and rec
forests
confor

Before

It hadn't been supposed to happen as it did. But a push grew into a shove, and then without quite meaning it to, the shove became, well, something else.

And for an instant, just for a moment, the earth seemed to halt on its axis.

With the bright sunlight dappling the floor and dust motes playing in the space between them, everything shrank to just those two people staring at each other with, what might it be? Confusion? Certainly. Horror? Maybe.

Whatever it was, it seemed that neither could pull away from the gaze of the other, and somehow the moment of silence grew and swirled to feel almost as if God was in the room alongside them both.

Then one crashed to the ground gasping and groaning until, with one last thrash and tremble, it was all over. The other crouched to stare, unsure at that moment quite what had just happened.

A surprised tear began to slide from the still-open eye, hovering just above the floor.

A finger caught it before it had a chance to fall, and a tongue slicked across the finger, faintly tasting salt.

There was a slight creak to the knee and a step or two back, with a solemn look at the consequences of bad behaviour.

It was the closest a person could ever be to another, and yet the most distant.

It was the worst thing anyone could do in the world. And there would be no coming back from it.

Footsteps to the door, and a final look over the shoulder.

No, perhaps it wasn't the worst thing one could do, no, not at all. A smile devoid of remorse crept across the killer's face.

Late

Caitlin

'Twat.'

'Leave it, else I'll tell Mum about you dis—'

I really hope she's not actually going to tell me.

'You're fat and you're ugly,' her brother cuts her off. 'And you know it.'

That won't irritate Ellie in the slightest, even though Harry sounds more tetchy than usual. Whatever she is, she's definitely not ugly. And she's still at the age when nothing she eats hurts her model-trim dancer's figure, when it's all angular hip bones, and short shorts are not yet the enemy. I expect she is now lifting one slender leg honed from hours and hours of street-dance classes high into the air to prove it to her brother.

I don't have the energy for this, and I don't think their hearts are in it either. The edge of heat that thrums their words when they're on the verge of really going for it isn't there.

Ellie hasn't quite given up yet though, although by her standards it's a weak counter-attack. 'You MIA bum-wipe.'

'Oi! Stop it, both of you . . . idiots,' I interrupt, as I open the door and stick my head into the den. I always try not to swear as it seems so coarse and unimaginative, but sometimes I only just manage to catch it before it slips out anyway.

Not swearing seems rather harder these days. I think we're all fraying a bit around the edges, aren't we?

7

At fifteen, they are at that age when bad language feels creative and daring, but James and I have decided not to comment too much about this as we work hard at not stifling them. So, although I can't help cringing sometimes at what they say, I look on it more as a recreational activity temporarily enjoyed by my children, more intended to spice up their day than make real waves.

To be honest, I'm a bit surprised that they aren't being more vocal right now.

'Mum,' says Ellie in the voice she always uses to dob her brother in, 'he—'

'Hey!' I stop her there.

Ellie looks quite shocked. I usually listen patiently to whatever she and Harry have to say. But I just can't handle them today.

'I'm not interested in what's going on, and Dad's on a Zoom and so he doesn't need a fuss making. You need to tone it down,' I add, trying to make my voice more reasonable.

My eyes flick to Harry's brand-new dayglo-stripped trainers. His feet must be huge now, I realise. At this age, my children appear to change and grow almost daily. Looking harder at Harry, who seems intent on the game on the telly screen and has his laptop open beside him, I think how he looks like a curious mix of the child he was and the man he will become, always dressed in oversized clothes that look the same to me but which will have a logo or a zip that only he can see, and with as many forms of technology as possible close to hand.

I have zero idea as to whether James is actually Zooming. He'd not been beside me in bed when I woke and this meant I didn't get the usual morning run-through of his itinerary (although I'd be betting it's the same as yesterday, and the day before that). I'd drifted off again and haven't yet got as far as going down to where he works.

Instead, when I finally roused, I'd flopped down in front of my own laptop upstairs, still in my pyjamas, fiddling about with an idea for promoting my knits-importing business that I named 'Caitlin Calling' when I set it up a couple of years ago before realising how egocentric that made me sound. James and the kids had joked at the time that I should get over myself, but the name stuck. I never can work out if I'm a serious businesswoman or not. Sometimes, most definitely; then others, not so much. Put it another way, it's probably a good thing that James is more diligent in funding the family than me.

Still, before I knew it, I'd spent an hour tapping away in the boxroom upstairs which has been my office since we moved into this house.

The twins silently mime rude actions, Harry angling his vaguely in the direction of that rather odd room near the front door that we've never really known what to do with, where James has set up his temporary office.

I'm not immediately sure of the best way of censuring them and so I act as if it's perfectly acceptable.

In theory I try to be a good parent, and I know this means setting boundaries. But my urge to be the approachable, always-chilled mum, the sort of mother that all their friends wish they had, very often feels overwhelming and gets the better of me. I yearn to be the type of mother rarely shocked, or rattled, or concerned about loud music or whether games and films are age-appropriate, and who makes sure there's always enviable mountains of food and drink. The parent I promised myself I'd be, back when James and I first met.

This last intention has taken a bit of a dive in recent weeks though, I admit, with everyone so bonkers in the shopping aisles.

Anyway, what's the point of me making a fuss, really? It would be like shouting down a well to stop Harry and Ellie squabbling and pushing the limits, and once the twins are older and out in the real world, I expect they'll tone it all down.

Everyone else learns to do this once they're out in the workplace, and so why shouldn't they?

Rather than herd immunity, I think it's like herd behaviour, the way teens behave. And I feel they should be cut a bit of slack now that every day is the same and normal routines have been shot to smithereens. I mean, who'd want to be cooped up at home twenty-four seven at fifteen? As far as I can see, school has a major advantage of wearing them out a bit. And in giving them an education, of course.

But, like everyone else, Ellie and Harry are confined to barracks, where they spend a significant portion of their time bickering over nothing in a horrifyingly repetitive order. By the second week of listening to them, in what has come to feel like the background hum of the house's fabric, I can tell what time of day it is by the tone of what I hear coming from the den. It might be potty-mouthed and designed to shock at times, but very little of it is serious, I'm pretty sure.

I love Harry and Ellie to the point I'd happily take a bullet for either, but this doesn't mean that I'm not feeling a bit bored of motherhood and rule-making at the moment. In fact, I think it would be fair to say that I'm enjoying this home-schooling malarkey a whole lot less than the twins, even though I know I should be taking an interest. And so should they. But it's not a GCSE year, and there's talk of postponed exams anyway. The Easter holidays are soon, and so I guess we'll review it all next term.

When I'd said to James a couple of days ago that we should maybe be pushing them harder, he told me to give the kids a break, and that I should imagine what it was like being a fifteen-year-old in the midst of lockdown when, as he put it, they should be out larking about alongside their friends, 'getting with' all the wrong people and drinking alcohol purloined from the remnants of our final Waitrose delivery that squeaked in before normal life had to stop. So that is what I'm doing, giving them a break.

I hate it when James deliberately uses teen-speak such as 'getting with'. Worse, as he'd said it, he'd even made quotation marks in the air with his fingers.

At that precise moment I'd seen James as a classic trying-too-hard man increasingly worried about any signs of a paunch (there aren't any), receding hairline (his is actually enviable) and where his life is going (chugging along very nicely, thank you). It was a fleeting moment though. Maybe it's true that I can't remember the last time he surprised me over anything – that's hardly the crime of the century, and there are so many other things about him I adore. I don't kid myself that he doesn't find me irritating at times too. Some days he can be quite short with me, and occasionally when I make a joke it seems as if his smile doesn't quite reach his eyes. But I'm sure he loves me, like I love him.

He has got wonderful eyes, nobody could deny him that. I still remember the first glimpse I had of him. It was at a party when we were at university. He was taking on a shots-drinking challenge and, entranced, I watched his throat swallow as he looked back at me through his lashes, the bob of his Adam's apple making my stomach flip and dive as I decided Yes!

Love at first sight is real. He's so good looking! Who is he? I must meet him. So, I did and, as they say, the rest is history.

But although James can be firm at times, I don't think he's ever done anything to make me change my mind much from my first impression of him. And I wouldn't want a total push-over to be my partner as, well, who'd want that? We're still having regular sex, which is more than a lot of my long-term-married friends are these days. I try not to feel too smug.

I guess I have the grumps these days largely due to having to spend too much time at home.

Home is supposed to be a place of comfort and love. And it is. But it's also a place where I quite often can't help feeling invisible to my family, other than when somebody wants something. I try, most days, to look around our lovely home and garden, and at my handsome husband and coltish twins, and I tell myself firmly that I have everything a right-minded person would want.

I do, I know I do.

It's just that somehow I can't quite shake off the feeling that when I was the age of Ellie and Harry I'd expected more out of my life once my thirties were trotting over the hill, although I'm at a loss to say what that 'more' really was.

With each demand from one of my loved ones for a drink or something to eat, a little more of the gloss of my life feels scuffed. There are precious few times when anyone says to me 'Caitlin, sit down and let me do it'. With each day that passes I feel there's a little less of Caitlin left for any of us, me or them.

I wish I could find a way to help them all understand this, but I don't seem able to.

With Harry and Ellie now, I settle instead for an overtly dramatic sigh, with my eyebrows pointedly raised, as if to tell them I've heard and seen it all before.

'Butt-hole,' I think Ellie mouths at Harry, who responds by looking at his sister through narrowed dark eyes as he flips an even ruder gesture back to her.

Loudly I sigh again and cast my eyes around the rest of the room. I'm not sure when I had last properly entered it, but now that I notice the depressing state of it, I realise it must have been a while ago.

The den looks wrecked. It had once been our dining room, but since the arrival a couple of years back of our lavish kitchen extension with its huge skylight and the ridiculously expensive table – twelve, it seats, with ease! – and the benches and Perspex chairs I've placed around in a pretty much failed attempt at encouraging family time, it has been all-change for this space.

Our redundant dining room has given way now to what I lovingly imagined would be a teen hangout. A place where they'd loll around with their friends, and I'd be invited in to share confidences over Ben & Jerry's Cookie Dough ice cream, laughing together and sneaking in the odd bottle of illicit lager without their dad knowing.

The picture before me of what the den has spiralled into, is not how I thought it was going to be. And how I hate the phrase 'the den' now, as I suspect does everyone else in our house. When I'd christened the room, I truly believed 'the den' brought to life a cool but deliciously arch US-TV-show-of-the-1980s vibe, whereby James and I could smile knowingly at each other in a private-joke kind of way whenever either of the children uttered 'the den'. That has never happened.

But filthy or not, this room is where Harry and Ellie pass the bulk of their daylight hours. I banned them from spending all day in their bedrooms after my friend Shona drunkenly insisted, with far too much graphic detail, quite what it is that teenagers will do for hours given the opportunity of endless 'me time'.

Even through the Zoom gallery thumbnail, as Shona chugged from her glass of expensive wine, I could see that she had that annoying know-it-all look on her face that I remembered from university. I hadn't liked it then, and it certainly hasn't improved with the passing of the years. But her words must have stayed with me nonetheless, as I've at least been strict about them getting up before the school day would start, and spending their time downstairs.

Behind the twins, the plush cushions from the Habitat cobalt velvet sofas look as if they have always lived on the floor. Used cups and plates and pizza boxes litter the room, and there's just stuff everywhere. And a pervasive smell too, a malodourous mix of fetid unwashed teen boy, and Ellie's too-strong eau de parfum.

Actually, that's my perfume, I realise. She's obviously found where I had hidden it.

The only pristine areas I can see are the two desks I installed for Harry and Ellie's home-schooling sessions. With their matching chairs tidily tucked under and a faint bloom of dust on their surface, these two desks remain as virginal as the day I had them set up against the wall.

My son looks to be busy playing Call of Duty: Black Ops 2 on the large telly. I think he varies this with Fortnite and Grand Theft Auto (I'd be hard pressed to name his favourite version of GTA), and goodness knows what else. I get the feeling that he's quite secretive about some of the stuff he's into that he thinks I might not like. I remember not wanting my parents to know everything I was up to at his age, and so I'm cool with that.

I exaggerate slightly – there has been a tiny bit of me that gets suspicious at times over the detail Harry can click into occasionally when he is provoked into talking with me about games or what else he is doing on his battered laptop. When I get him to pull his head away from his various screens or his phone, that is. I can remember acting similarly when I was younger, in order to distract my parents from all the other, more illicit stuff I was trying to hide. But I don't honestly believe that my Harry has the guile to really get up to anything properly no good. The little boy he was still peeps back at me now and again, and he was such a sweet little thing. Even now the very sight of him can make me melt with the physical sensation of love, just as I did back then.

Ellie meanwhile has her laptop propped open on her belly as she flops on the floor, a huge and half-eaten bowl of popcorn beside her, and I can see that she's paused an old episode of *Say Yes to the Dress*. I suppose watching something fluffy and hopeful on weddings is verging on an act of deliberate provocation right now on Ellie's part, especially as she knows my views on both reality telly and shows that keep our fires of feminist debate raging.

It seems that sexual stereotyping is clearly alive and well in London's E8, I sigh to myself, with Harry and his make-believe violence and techy online stuff, and Ellie getting ready to fall in love with the idea of being married in a long white gown. Hello, the 1970s are on the Trimphone and they want their attitudes back.

It's obvious that schoolwork is definitely not on the agenda.

I know I should push them harder to keep up to the time-table the school has emailed us, but I don't really see how I can do this with any likely chance of success, especially while trying to run my own business and keep on top of all the things I have to do.

Home-schooling is fine, I guess, if your kids are of primary school age, or swotty. But mine only ever do the bare minimum, even when school is running, and it's already caused too many arguments since this all began. I daresay Harry and Ellie can make up any lost ground later, even if we do have to bring in some private tutors. I've too many other things to think about.

'Look, just keep it down, guys,' I say, and then I could kick myself as the once-hip-but-no-longer-thus 'guys' slipped out unintentionally, and I know it will have them rolling their eyes with amusement at my expense.

I shut the door swiftly so I don't have to see.

We have some fairly new rules in the house. These came about after I had a meltdown on the second day we couldn't go out, when the kids were being iffy about loading the dishwasher.

Ellie suggested at this point that it would be a good idea if, as a family, we put together a plan of the new way of doing things, and I agreed this was a good idea.

The result was that we had a family meeting sitting around the kitchen table, at the opposite end of the table to where I've set out my 18,000-piece Ravensburger 'Evening Walk in Paris' jigsaw – yup, 18,000 pieces! £146.08 with nearly £20 delivery on Amazon, about which James had joked that the pandemic was more likely to kill me than I was to finish the puzzle.

The upshot of this four-way pow-wow was that we agreed the following: no arguing; and in the wake of not being able to have our cleaner the usual three mornings a week, everyone should clear up after themselves and pull their weight in terms of general housework; and everyone should do their own clothes washing. Oh, and we would all respect each other and our opinions.

I'm probably the best out of the four of us in sticking to these rules, but that's only because I can't bear the clean lines of our minimalist kitchen and equally Spartan day room area not looking tidy, or the dishwasher waiting to be unloaded, or crumbs on the kitchen work surfaces, and so I keep those areas going, much to the relief of everyone else.

However, I am sneakily proud that I have forced myself not to pick up the dirty crockery abandoned in other rooms, or sort out anyone's discarded clothes. It means that each day I have to kick James's rumpled tees and sweats from the day before under our bed so that I can't see them, but he seems fine with that, and now that I have given myself a stern talking to, I am too.

But, in fair disclosure, the house slowly sliding towards bedlam with sticky floors and dust bunnies running rife doeo rankle with me, as it means the others are – as my granny would have said – swinging the lead.

I'd rather cut my tongue out than comment though, purely because to give in to this impulse means that I'd lose all moral high ground by having fallen at the 'no arguing' hurdle.

Moral high ground is important, I always think.

Naturally neither Harry or Ellie have put the washing machine on once. It sits white and serene in our utility room, a foreign territory to the twins. Their clothes live on the floor, like their father's (well, Harry's probably don't as I think he wears the same outfit every single day, and in fact he probably sleeps in it too), interspersed with Ellie simply ordering new stuff online to keep up her normal three changes of outfit a day. I suspect she is using my PayPal account, thinking I won't notice. Actually, I'd better check on that.

There is one thing though that makes all of this tedious nonsense worthwhile as we muddle through lockdown.

I have a secret. A thrilling secret.

No.

A *thrilling* secret.

As if on cue, my telephone vibrates silently in the hip pocket of my pyjamas.

My belly gives a little fizz, and I see a flush of goose bumps rise on my arm as I turn around and walk to the pantry to read my WhatsApp in private.

As I stand looking at the stacks of tins, I know what I need to get me through the next few days, and it's not to be found anywhere in this house.

I have a fleeting sensation of his breath on my neck.

Disappointingly, the text is from James, who wants me to know that he could do with a coffee. Physically, he is no more than forty feet away from me, but at this moment it feels an ocean, which saddens me.

It's a momentary sensation though, over-ridden by one much more selfish. I try to push the thought away, but I can't.

After I reach for the cafetière, the kettle heating on the Aga, I go into the utility room, where there's still a faint whiff of the perfume that Ellie sprayed so lavishly on herself. Opening the hidden door to one of the cupboards, I dig out and pull on my running kit, chucking my pyjamas into the washing machine.

I have tried so hard not to give in to this impulse that I've surprised myself.

I declared it was over – and very much meant every word I said. At the moment I said it.

There were tears (mine mainly) followed by a serious talk during which we agreed that during the coming lockdown it was only right and sensible that I should concentrate on my family.

But I'm buckling.

I'm not sure why right now, but all I can say is that it feels as if I have a pulse deep and insistent within me demanding that I still it.

Perhaps if James had got up to make his own coffee, I'd have felt stronger today. But he didn't, and I don't.

I am ashamed of myself, of course. But not ashamed enough.

'Be there in fifteen,' I type.

We always message, and never phone.

My message isn't to James.

I pause in readiness for the reply, but there's no answering vibrate back.

It's usually immediate, and I feel a flash of unease. Surely I've not been forgotten.

Then I smile at myself. I know what he and I have together, and it's something rare and earthy, and he's not going to be forgetting about it, that's for certain.

While I tap a foot impatiently as the kettle takes its time, I check the highlights in my hair under the spotlights – not too bad yet, which is a relief, and it looks as if that new shampoo I'm trying is making it admirably shiny. I stuff it into a scrunchie, before applying a slick of my favourite nude lip gloss and a squirt or two of the scent he gave me.

It seems prudent of me to keep everything to do with my secret separate from the rest of my life. Consequently, the utility room and the privacy it affords me has proved a godsend for this, what with all of us now at home.

As finally the kettle makes that noise it does before it starts to whistle, I tip my head to one side, pleased to see in the mirror that even with my fortieth birthday not far away now, my neck and shoulders, and the rest of me actually, are still enviably tight and slim. I'm trim but definitely not scraggy – I'd hate to be somebody without curves in the right places.

I've thought before that if I were a man, I'd think I look good, even perhaps as much as a decade younger. I don't see anything in the mirror today to disabuse me of these notions.

I don't much like the fact that my appearance is a bit too important to me, but I'd be lying if I pretended otherwise.

And then I wrench the toggle a bit tighter than it needs to be on my running shoes, as if I mean business, which I suppose I do.

Before I return to the kitchen to make James's coffee, I give myself a final once-over.

I breathe in as I look sideways at my reflection in the mirror, standing on my toes and then plucking at the waist-band of my running tights, ignoring the glint of my wedding ring. I could never remove my wedding ring; I made a promise all those years ago to James that it would be a symbol of our marriage, a marriage I am very much committed to still.

But that doesn't stop me taking a last peek at the curve of my buttocks nestling snug in their Lululemon extra-firm Lycra. They look inviting.

Then, as I'm not feeling proud of what I'm about to do, I open a packet of biscuits and arrange a few on a plate for my husband, and I nip into the garden and snip off a few early blooms which I stick in one of the jam jars I bought online for just this sort of off-the-cuff moment.

As I position this pretty tray with James's elevenses on his desk, and he lifts his blue eyes away from his Zoom to smile at me in thanks, I grin back.

It's a genuine grin on my part as this sort of look from my husband can always brighten my day.

And of course the thought of what I'm about to do not too far away would make anybody with a pulse grin stupidly too.

'Just leaving,' I type a minute later.

Ali

Even by my slatternly standards, I am a mess.

The face staring back at me from the splash-pocked bathroom mirror does me no favours.

A boy at the school bus stop once told me, rather cheesily, I had dancing eyes. That was more than twenty years ago, and I assumed he'd been trying to make me look a fool, that he'd have laughed if I'd seemed to believe him. The next day his mate swore he fancied me, but by then I was too shy to do anything about it.

A lot of water has passed under the bridge since then. Nobody would claim there's a shadow of anything dance-like about my eyes now. The whites are bloodshot, a maze of tiny lines crazily multiplying deep in my skin around them.

It's a look that makes me seem much older than my thirty-eight years.

Worse is the flesh on my neck, which I see is beginning to resemble the ruches of an Austrian blind. Whoever has Austrian blinds these days? I ponder, and then I recall there is a blue one at the window to the rear of old Mrs Grave's house down the street. She's one of my subjects-in-waiting, and so I must remember her when I'm next at Mehmet's.

Earlier, I awoke with a start from a bad dream of somebody trying to batter my door down. And now the pee I've just taken smells cloyingly sweet and that, with its vibrant burnt-caramel hue, tells me I'm dehydrated.

It was the same colour when I'd peed a couple of hours back, and I realise that, although I'd meant to have a glass of water before going back to bed, my attention had been diverted by my subject across the street.

I could see him gesticulating, talking on his hands-free earpiece, at one point pulling his murky green tee-shirt from his dark grey shorts before tucking it in again. And I must have been so absorbed in my snooping that I forgot to drink my water.

The drinking glass rattles between the tap and the porcelain of the bathroom hand basin as I empty and then refill it.

I sip tentatively, but then I'm overwhelmed with thirst and I can't help but gulp huge mouthfuls.

A mistake, as in a whoosh all the chugs of water come right back up again, my stomach not yet ready for such an assault.

There's a minute or two of me staring down at the hand basin as I hold on to either side of it. Grimly I gather my feeble reserves of strength and stare accusingly at the glass now lying on its side near the plughole as I will my stomach to settle.

It takes a while but then I am able to gingerly pad across the grubby beige carpet, navigating around my piles of books and bits and bobs, to my seat at the cluttered round table in the bay of my front-room window, overlooking the street. As I sit down an unbidden sigh escapes my mouth. It sounds like *ouf*. Only old people or very worn-out people make that noise when they sit. And I'm not old.

The effort of all this movement makes my head thump, and I have to close my eyes.

It's a while before I can look out of the window. It's how I spend most of my time now.

Our building has four flats including the basement, but we are all either too poor or too tight to spring for a window-cleaner, not that he'd be able to come to us at the moment.

In this sea of gentrification that's changed my area almost beyond recognition since I moved in, in fact I'm verging on proud of the fact that we are by far the grubbiest and most run-down house in the street. It feels almost a badge of honour – so blatantly a refusal to follow what passes for Hackney living these days, in my street at least, an attitude I like to tell myself is sparky and bristling with character. I've always embraced a sense of 'outsider'.

It was familiar to me when growing up – my parents making sure of that, what with our constant moves and new schools for me – and it's probably a factor in why I don't push harder for the rest of the residents in our building to club together and give the outside a spruce-up.

But dingy kerb appeal of our house or no, I am glad for what I have.

I grew up ricocheting through an endless array of crummy rentals as my parents struggled to make ends meet and weren't averse to the occasional midnight flit if things got really tough. By the time I came to sit my GCSEs I think I'd attended nine different schools in various parts of London. I was used to never asking my schoolfriends to mine, which always felt terribly shabby compared to what I saw when I visited their houses, and I knew I couldn't rely on my parents not to embarrass me. The constant attention of being 'the new girl' was murder for some-one naturally introverted as I was, and I can't really remember a time I didn't feel awkward and shy, feelings that have never really left me. Safe within my tiny flat now, I get a little respite.

Hackney is lively these days though, and so it surprises me that it's become the place I feel most at home. But my time here has given me a stability I've never experienced before. This flat has been good to me, a little peeling paint on the window frame notwithstanding, and sometimes I dread to think what would have become of me if I hadn't found it when it was even more dilapidated and rundown than it is now and, to my joy, actually affordable to buy.

I'm tobogganing towards glum thoughts and so I force myself to sidestep this well-trodden path away from how I could have ended up, and concentrate on nicer things instead.

It's cold out but the sun is bright. It's my favourite time of year as the large tree rooted into a small patch of bare earth between the paving slabs outside our front garden is coming into leaf with its caterpillar-green new growth. It's this verdant sprouting, when combined with the patina of grime on both the outside and the inside of my window, that convinces me few people going about their business in the street below will be able to see me. I like this feeling. Another month and the leaves will be so big my view will be curtailed, which won't be so nice. I tell myself that at that point I am going to do some cleaning and make that window sparkle. I've let things slip far too much these last few months. I wonder if I should have spoken to my doctor. I've been a little hazy for a period. Not quite myself.

But I never did, and perhaps my laziness has turned out to be a good thing as, without me really trying to, oddly this morning I feel clearer headed than I have in weeks. Certainly up for a bit of rigorous 'sit and stare', as I keep an eye on everyone from my first-floor eyrie.

Since I was 'let go' from work a while back, my scrutiny of the other lives in my street has come to feel probably more like an occupation than a hobby than is wise. Especially when it comes to Daniel. He has been promoted recently from vaguely interesting to a definite project.

Watching having become my primary occupation does bring me down a little if I think about it too much, as once I had been, even if I say so myself, rather a good teacher.

But then I allowed things to fall to pieces. I'm sad about that, but possibly not as sad as I should be. Although I'm nosey by nature, getting way too involved in the lives of my poor neighbours feels, at the moment, necessary. But also just a little peculiar. Still, I am nosey. And not ashamed to be so.

I perk up when I hear the clink of the original Victorian metal gate to the garden of the house opposite opening and closing, and the slight creak of its hinges.

I dip my head to get a better view through the branches and, snatching up my binoculars, I catch a jarring close-up glimpse of some hideous accident-in-a-paint-factory-coloured calf-length leggings stretched over a pert derrière, while expensively streaked hair in a ponytail sways jauntily from side to side as its lithe owner trots down the path away from me.

She looks the shiny personification of the phrase 'spring in her step' and she very much appears as if she feels that she deserves to be there, as if she is about to be rewarded.

This can only mean one thing, IMHO.

In my humble opinion.

I had had to look up IMHO when I noticed it on Twitter for the first time a few years back, and since then I've been planning to slip it into a conversation, at the right time, of course. Until now the opportunity has never arisen.

I digress. That one thing causing such a bouncy stride has to be sex, the impressive level of bounce suggestive of someone who knows more than a bit about it.

I have only had sex with three men in my life, and the liaisons with two of those were little more than a slippery fumble during Fresher's Week at university (and the noun 'men' may be an oversell for those).

It's not much for my lifetime to date, I know, but I tell myself that I should feel positive. At least I'm not a virgin.

I have fonder memories of a female colleague's lips on mine. We were escorting a school Geography trip down to the granite tors on Dartmoor and, late one night when the kids were in bed, my heart beat faster than I ever knew it could as we kissed more passionately than I'd dared to imagine. That was as far as it got though, for when I went to sneak a hand near her chest, she got cold feet and we never talked about it again. I like to think of myself as someone who may be pan-sexual – it seems so bold – and just about ready for anything. The problem is, I've found, that anything isn't ready for me.

Opposite, I see the shiny woman briefly jogging on the spot, her ponytail a frenzy of swingyness, outside the main front door to the expensive terraced, double-fronted house. Number sixty-six contains two separate apartments – the top two storeys being a rental with a revolving door of well-heeled tenants, and the bottom two belonging to Daniel Horne.

The woman shoots a final look around before she adroitly sidesteps to her left, hurrying down the steps to Daniel's basement maisonette. Presumably she's satisfied that she's not been seen.

She's a local then.

She's not fooling anyone, least of all me.

Daniel looks to be in his late twenties, and he alternates a rather old-fashioned City suave of Brooks Brothers clothes, with an off-duty look that has enough of the hipster about it to merge seamlessly with the young people around here who probably wish they could afford to live in Shoreditch.

I've walked down these steps several times myself, although after I watched his disaster with the cauliflower cheese, and me then leaving him a small cauli and a packet of cheese sauce to encourage him to try and make it again (both of which later I found in his dustbin), I haven't been back there recently.

Despite this, I haven't stepped away totally from Daniel.

He caught my eye when he moved in. I think it was the casual way he bossed the removal men about as he stood watching them lugging his possessions around that first hooked my attention. Most people his age rely on mates and a borrowed van on moving day, but not him. I didn't find his stand off attitude endearing in the slightest, and those removal men weren't impressed either to judge by the looks they were shooting each other when Daniel's back was turned. I don't think he tipped them either.

Conveniently, I can see into a lot of his home from my window bay – the developer had spent ages on this property a few years back, 'opening it up' in estate-agent speak. It belonged at that time to a young couple, until the husband was caught playing away. To judge by the endless skips outside prior to Daniel moving in, I think he then ripped out pretty much everything the developer and the young couple had done, including any original features, and started again with some quite extensive renovations.

Aside from what I think must be a bedroom on the upper level at the back that probably overlooks his garden, and a bit beyond his kitchen I'm curious about on the lower level, I feel as if I can see pretty much everything.

Certainly, I've had lots of opportunity to keep tabs on Daniel over the last couple of months in his lair as he rarely employs his blinds or shutters, which makes me think display of all kinds is important to him.

We couldn't be more different, I often muse as I look between the clean, empty lines of his home, and the stuffed-to-the-gills bookshelves and unruly cupboards of mine. Maybe this is why I find him so fascinating.

It makes me smile to think that there was a time when I nearly gave up on him altogether. There was none of the drama of that previous couple, which I definitely missed, and in comparison I thought him simply too boring.

But, my opinion has changed. Now I think, yup, Daniel is certainly criminally dull, but there is something intriguing about the sheer level of dullness he has achieved that I find compelling. And of course it helps that I can sit in my window and study him to my heart's content. It sounds lazy, and it is, but convenience has a lot in its favour.

It must have involved a heap of hard work on his part to manufacture such a deathly persona, a task that to all intents and purposes Daniel has pursued with diligence, almost as if competing in an extreme sport of being a man with virtually nothing about him to recommend other than a superficial handsomeness. And as I saw him faffing about in front of his biggest mirror trying to fluff up a small patch of thinning hair the other day, I suspect even his looks might be short-lived.

I am a natural-born cynic though, and so I keep giving him the chance to prove me wrong. So far he hasn't even come close.

I had several abortive attempts at door-stopping our regular postie while I sought his name, who, surprisingly for such a dozy-looking man, gave me short shrift. But pay day came when the John Lewis man couldn't deliver some crockery (well, that's what it sounded like to me when I took the box in and gave it an exploratory shake), and I was able to learn my young neighbour across the way goes by the name of Daniel Horne.

A high point of my early surveillance was a girlfriend he had. She looked a decade older and quite often extremely peeved with him. They had a slanging match in the street more than once, the loudest of which only ended when an Uber arrived and he bundled her into it before stalking back inside. I've not seen her for quite a while, and so presumably his plea during the spat of 'for Christ's sake get a grip, Nikki, and just bugger off' had the effect he was looking for.

What I do find odd in these days of online transparency is that there's surprisingly little I can discover about Daniel. He doesn't seem to do Facebook (well, few young people do these days, I guess), or Instagram, or Twitter, or any of the other platforms that I can access.

After a fair bit of digging, I have been able to locate his date of birth though – 1 June 1995. I had been just on the verge of concluding in frustration that he must have created the Daniel Horne identity when I found this piece of the puzzle, and it wasn't long afterwards that I could trace him to a fairly mediocre City job with a fairly mediocre stockbroker. I was even able to track some of his trades, although they didn't look impressive to me.

Perhaps I'm being mean – after all, he's managed to scrabble together the cash to buy nearly two thousand square feet of prime E8 real estate on the expensive side of the street, which is a lot more than I have.

The property on my side of the street is much more moderately priced and most of the houses and flats are significantly smaller, although the money even they go for nowadays still seems eye-watering to me. Certainly, I wouldn't be able to purchase here if I were hoping to buy anything now.

Another thing I find fascinating about Daniel is that he's not living the Hackney dream that pulls many folks in their twenties to our area of London; I believe the word is 'vibrant', according to the estate agents. He's not a big goer-out and I've never seen any sign he's gay, and he doesn't seem to have any mates who call around, or a regular girlfriend since Nikki, or a string of visiting casual lovelies. 'Vibrant' certainly wouldn't be his middle name.

And I can't help but ask myself why this is the case. The more I know about him, the less I know, if one takes my drift.

What I can say though for definite is that Daniel Horne is the sort of man who thinks a lot of himself, and when he's not working – which he only seems to do for a couple of hours each day – he spends an inordinate amount of time staring at his reflection in a mirror.

I've not seen this Miss Ponytail woman here before. If she's an early bird, or comes very late, then I suppose there could be windows of time when I'm not yet at my post, so it's not necessarily her first visit, or that she is his only female caller. I'm not yet so far gone that I spend all my time at this window.

Anyway, there are worse hobbies than taking an interest in the neighbours, aren't there? From what I can make out on his screen, Daniel spends hours looking at amateur pornography. Although in fair disclosure I should also point out that he spends a lot of time online gaming, too.

Now that I've treated myself to a stronger pair of binoculars on Amazon I can spy what he's pulled up on his laptop if the angle is right, which it usually is when he sits in his favourite chair in the window.

I have a quick shufty through my notebook of observations to date and remind myself, not for the first time, that he's oddly stupid but also full of confidence. I don't know whether to be irritated or impressed by his continual triumph of hope over experience. Whatever, frankly I'm riveted by his pernickety manner for one so young.

For instance, he always lays out every single item of what he's chosen to wear on his bed before his shower; I throw on any old thing. And virtually every day I see him carefully reading the labels on the wine bottles arranged in his expensive freestanding wine cooler, although he always places the bottle back inside.

(Note: Daniel's kitchen of expensive burnished copper and its bespoke units with their terrazzo worktop in multi-hued chips of chocolate-brown glass is dominated by a statement black Haier WS53GDA wine cooler, with its swanky Dual Zone Temperature and fifty-three bottle storage – the two temperate zones providing optimum conditions for both white and red wines. I've caught him lovingly running a forefinger across the nameplate on the wine fridge on more than one occasion.)

One thing that has nabbed my attention is that I think his wine, together with the spirits he keeps on a retro table at one side of the room, are there merely for show. Show, can you believe! I'm yet to see him drinking anything stronger than a double espresso (from a Gaggia Classic Pro – no surprise there then).

I wonder what it feels like to be as controlled as he seems, to be such a living contradiction of a young person's life.

At his age I always loved to push the boundaries, and for a while I savoured the contradiction of living the most slovenly life I could, yet always feeling able to hold my own in just about any discussion. I don't suppose I've changed over-much, though as contradictions go, it all seems sadder now than it did when I was twenty-one.

And there's something about Daniel's essential aloneness that makes me see a kindred spirit. I realise that what held me back in my personal life in my early years of adulthood was only me – plenty of people have triumphed over far worse, but I gave up the struggle to join a happy sort of life very early on. My fear – I guess of being unlovable, combined with a conviction that anyone who cared for me was neces-sarily and irredeemably faulty in some way – has led, ironi-cally, to me building unbreachable barriers and instilling boundaries all around myself, rather than breaking them down as I once thought I was destined to do. The last laugh has been at my expense, hasn't it?

All I've done is make myself an island in a sea of humanity. It might seem safe in theory, but the older I get, the more vulnerable it makes me feel. It's no wonder I like the bolster-ing effect of a little wine now and again.

I've never spoken with Daniel, and so I don't know whether I'd like him as a conversational adversary. I suspect I wouldn't a whole lot as we have little in common. Just about everything catches my attention on some level, while it appears he's not interested in very much at all. He'd be horrified to know he's caught my attention in the way he has!

But although I'm predisposed not to respect him much, I can't stop wondering about what it must feel like to be Daniel.

To him, does his mind feel as barren as it seems from where I sit? I may be wrong, but to me there was something in that ponytailed woman's preoccupied expression that hints she feels similarly curious about him.

At the thought of her, I have to smile.

Miss Ponytail's running tights are so hideous and garish that they are most definitely exceptionally expensive. Nobody on a limited income would dare to sport anything so repulsive, and I appreciate this woman's unspoken reminder to me that having money doesn't mean you necessarily have good taste. I sense labels arc important to her too, so perhaps she and Daniel are a good match. Or to put it another way, I doubt she'd be wearing those leggings if they camc from Primark.

I consider the brief glance I snatched a bit more.

Am I imagining it, or was there a furtive look about hcr, perhaps hiding in the slight crinkle of skin I fancy that's around her eyes? I think there was. I conclude it's very possible she's married or otherwise committed. And while I didn't have enough time to be sure, I think she may be older than Daniel.

IMHO.

Bad girl. Bad woman.

It's nice I can step up and on to the moral high ground for oncc. Sadly, it's not a feeling I can enjoy legitimately too often.

He certainly goes for a particular sort of lover, does Daniel.

Miss Ponytail and the one I saw him arguing with that while ago – Nikki – are similar both physically and in the way they present themselves to the world. All athleisure, tanned limbs and generally a look that can only be described as glossy and pampered, with their lustred cheeks and gentle pigment tones peeping through the balm of their lip products, set off by their squared gel nails and expensive hair.

But the day is moving on, and I need to file Daniel and his acquaintances for another time.

I run through the various bits of my body, and note there are a few after-effects from last night hanging about still. It makes hard work of concentrating for too long.

This is because I'm currently in that nervy state where I'm poised between moving to sober or needing to go back to topping up my blood alcohol. The second of which being generally what I choose. But who can blame me? Lockdown makes me edgy, and so these days it's extra-nice to soften the edges.

But before I quite pull my thoughts away from the path to Daniel's lair, I notice my inconstant cat Pusshkin stalking down the garden path with his faithless tail straight up in the air, following purposefully in the footsteps of the woman with the swingy hair, bold as brash.

Brass

Not brash.

But, come to think of it, just a little brash too.

Hell. You know it's bad when you slur your own thoughts when thinking about your cat's intentions.

Damn, I need a drink, to get back to my not-so-new normal.

This is not good. I know that.

And so I promise myself that tomorrow is the day I'm going to clean up and stop wasting my life, drinking away hour after hour. I need to get outside more – or I would if we weren't in lockdown – and I definitely need to stop obsessing about Daniel for no reason at all. This new normal isn't doing anything for me, clearly, and it needs to stop.

But I'll just have something today first to level myself out, so that I can gather my strength for cutting back.

*   *   *

Back when I was a run-of-the-mill English teacher at a secondary school, before I was head of department and everything became Academies, naming a cat after a classic author and being able to shoehorn a pun into the name at the same time tickled my funny bone.

How easily I was amused.

And how the world shrinks around us all.

In what seems almost a single heartbeat, Pusshkin is fifteen years old now, and my career is shot to pieces.

I was let go following an unfortunate incident one parents' evening, after a secret nip or two of vodka may or may not have been involved.

A colleague recently tried to suggest to me that the school has used COVID as an excuse for a reorganisation, gently implying that this was what happened to me and I was a casualty of the new order.

I didn't have the heart to say that I was well ahead of the curve in this respect, and my 'reorganisation' was squarely because of me shooting myself in the foot with a poor choice of behaviour, quite a while before we all started really to believe in the pandemic.

Since then I've had a lot of time on my hands to think, and I've realised that the parents' evening debacle was, to a large extent, intentional. I'm not that much of a drunk that I don't know the difference between me setting a chain of events in action, and being caught up in someone else's.

I never thought I would fall out of love with teaching as I have. But standing in front of a class and telling teenagers a lot of things they're never going to need when out in the big wide world increasingly came to seem crazy. What is the point of it all? I began to question this, and once you do that as a teacher, you're dead in the water pretty much. I could have taken the honourable way out and just resigned, I know, but that seemed to lack a certain punch about it that my abrupt fall from grace provided. In hindsight, I suspect that deep down I just wanted to make dead certain I'd never be asked, or tempted, back.

At first, I tried to keep my hand in with some private tutoring.

But I was emotionally bruised and unready for this; I'd under-estimated how jarring it is outside the cosy world of the teaching system. This aside, if one has to bring one's fledgling self-employed tutoring career as a crammer crashing down in a single afternoon, I'd say the most certain, and arguably the most entertaining way to do it has to be with a session for two dim teenage boys in the fresh air of London Fields, when I tried to get them thinking about poetry as if poems were songs. However, the boys and some strong cider produced precisely the messy results that anyone used to sixteen-year-olds and the effects of potent alcohol would predict. The boys' parents were not impressed, and I can't say I blame them.

In the cold light of day, I berate myself often for my natural inclination towards drama. And recently I have had the odd brief flash of understanding that a little of Daniel's undramatic attitude would be good for me, while my need to create a wave or two might be beneficial for him too.

Moreover, I accept that definitely I shouldn't have encouraged those lads I was tutoring to start drinking as it was totally irresponsible on my part, but it was only then that they had started to listen to me at all. And, as I have learnt many times before and since, it's hard to stop once you've started. Self-sabotage could be my middle name. IMHO.

Secretly, I think the pressure of being out on my own and self-employed turned out to be way more scary than I'd expected, a fear of failure that has fed itself over the years in many ways in my life, and proved to be more deeply rooted within me than the brazen manner in which I left the school. I probably just took a short cut to catastrophe before fiasco sought me out as surely it would have.

Still, I'm too young to put myself wholeheartedly on to the scrapheap, and therefore I have picked myself up and I am trying again. In order to bulk up my rather weak and one-dimensional 'portfolio CV', I am putting myself out there as a techy nerd for hire, doing computery things for others from the luxury of my window bay. I don't plan to be particularly scrupulous that the demands of my clients need to be one hundred per cent legal, and I know I have a grittily relentlessness that is good for this sort of work. However, both of these attributes remain untested as I'm yet to get any commissions, which is serving me right for trying to do this in the midst of a pandemic. Still, if anyone needs mild stalking of celebrities on the web, say, then I'm your gal.

All of which is my way of acknowledging that these days I am way beyond punning fun names for pets, such as my dear Pusshkin's moniker, or in fact doing anything that's of much real use to society.

It's a choice I make readily, I repeat to myself, as I try not to remember the friends I now avoid, or the students who gave me thoughtful gifts at the end of the year.

I'm always surprised on the odd occasion when I recall that once I was rather popular, both as a friend and a teacher. Those with happy families (my former friends) or glittering careers (my old students) have become an unwelcome example to me of how far I've slipped.

Now, I can see there was no need for me to cut myself off in quite the way I did in those early days of my imposter syndrome. Instead I should have worked at building my confidence rather than assuming always I needed to protect myself from a world that's hell bent on going all out to bring me down and then stab me with hurt. What a stupid attitude I've wasted years on.

In some ways a pandemic is good for someone like me. It teaches us all that we're mere dots in the cosmos, just trying to get from day to day the best we can. Life's not a personal insult, but something that is often tricky and hard to negotiate, and it's the case for everyone – it doesn't mean that, like me, one should give up at the first hurdle.

It's a shame it's turned out as it has, but it's too late for me to go back and do it all again differently.

Instead I try to embrace my apparent bottomless capacity for never getting bored with the limited confines of my life, even though if I had to describe to anyone quite how the hours of my days race by so rapidly, I'd be hard pressed.

I look behind me and over to the work surface at the other side of my 'bijou' living-room-cum-kitchen. It's twelve by fourteen feet in old money, with a little bit more added on for the window bay.

There're several centimetres of vodka left in the bottle I've been trying to ignore.

I'd placed my two empties from the wine I'd bought yesterday in front of the vodka as a distraction, but literally and metaphorically I've seen through them. It's too early for vodka. It's too early for anything other than a cup of coffee really. But at least if I drink it now it might chase away my hangover. And then there will be no more alcohol in the house, so I can concentrate properly on what I need to do.

I can't find a clean glass, mug or cup, and so I pour the clear spirit into a vessel that has dried-up dregs of coffee encrusted on the bottom and go to glug it back in one.

But at the last moment I pause. It suddenly doesn't look as good as it should.

Ironically, although I don't drink what's in the mug, the smell means I still have to blink away the tears that shoot instantly to my eyes. It seems as if my body is experiencing the combo of neat vodka and my acid reflux that gives such a unique kick of pain, it always leaves me reeling.

I almost laugh that I've conditioned myself to such an extent that today the vodka itself is irrelevant. What a joke on me.

Still, time to crack on.

I scrabble around for pen and paper – I'll make a shopping list first. I'll stick to my budget, and that will be my first win of the day.

It's surprising how cheaply you can live if you rarely go out and you don't need to socialise, and you never go on holiday or follow fashion or buy lotions and potions. My careful watching of the pennies over the years has meant that I could pay my mortgage off in full a while back, and since then I've squirrelled away a small stash of savings.

If I'm frugal, I can go on as I am for a while yet, provided I stick to my budget. That doesn't allow for the roof blowing off, or Pusshkin needing a massive operation, of course, but I'll deal with those catastrophes as and when, should they occur.

COVID is showing me on a daily basis that many others are MUCH worse off than me, and I should be grateful.

Frankly though, quite often 'grateful' can suck. IMHO.

Although, now and again, when I consider my mortgage-less little corner of Hackney and the love my dear Pusshkin gives me, or I look at the optimistic hue of the soft green of those new leaves unfurling on that tree outside our gate, grateful feels rather gratifying.

On the news websites there have been in recent days psychologists extolling the virtues of everyone sticking to a routine in these grim times. Apparently it helps when there is a crisis, and if a pandemic isn't a crisis, then I don't know what is.

I agree about the value of routine.

I always stick to mine.

I get up quite late as I'm usually to bed only once the small hours have arrived. Then, rain or shine, I head to the corner shop run by Mehmet to buy my day's food and two bottles of Sauvignon blanc. (I drop off the previous day's empties in somebody else's recycling en route, ever since I heard the bin men joke about my 'impressive' box(es) of glass bottles.)

A few weeks ago, the shops put a limit on buying more than two bottles of wine at a time. I don't disagree – it's best to have a limit and at least I know this will ensure that I get out once a day. I try not to touch the wine until four o'clock, as I think this is a respectable hour, even if not quite over the yard-arm. Sometimes it's been difficult to stick to this. It's hard to know how often I manage it.

It's good to have a goal. Repeat the next day. And the next. Ad infinitum.

I'm not kidding myself what would happen if I didn't have my regular sojourn as part of my daily routine. It wouldn't be pretty.

I've had to avoid the larger shops in Hackney, now there's queuing.

Mehmet is always understanding, and his shop is usually quiet. I like supporting a local small business too, with the added benefit that Mehmet knows where I live in case I ever need help getting home. Which has only happened the once, I hasten to add.

I learnt the hard way that standing in a queue outside Sainsbury's in the glare of the sun is very hard to handle when hung over. Even more so when a cheeky guzzle has already happened.

Sincere apologies to all those I shouted at when The Great Toilet Roll Crisis was at its height and making everyone very tetchy. But how was I to know there was actually a meandering queue, seeing as how it had wig-wagged around the corner of the supermarket?

It Was Not Obvious.

IWNO. Perhaps I could start my own online acronym, although that would mean I'd need to start joining in, I suppose.

I'm more of a watcher than a joiner.

Generally my shopping at Mehmet's is pretty simple. I eat a daily single meal of pasta six nights out of seven, adorned with a knob of butter and a twist of black pepper. I've never been hugely into food, and for some daft reason I'm pleased I can still wear the same clothes – literally the same clothes – as when I was doing my Masters and the first half of my PhD, at which point I gave up my own studies.

Mehmet is always watchful when I am in his shop, but I would be too, in his position. It can't be easy running a corner shop – or convenience store as I hear the trendier clientele call it; I know this is a nod towards a recent popular book title but I don't have anyone to show off to about what I've read – and I don't flatter myself that Mehmet watches me more than anyone else.

I don't care for his other customers though, and a while back I got to thinking that a lone woman with only alcohol in her basket looked more than a little sad.

I was standing there, minding my own business and probably, to be fair, looking a little worse for wear from the night before, when I saw the stuck-up woman from number thirty-two shooting me a dirty look. I was on edge anyway, and the look of what seemed to me to be barely disguised disgust filled me with a familiar despair that got me reaching for the nearest shelf of canned goods.

At first it seemed as if this hideous woman had made me a victim, but then I decided to do something positive with the extra cans. I left them on the doorstep of the nice couple with the little boy that has, I think, cerebral palsy; I don't think they've got much spare money, if the worried way they hover their bank card over Mehmet's reader is anything to go by.

Since then, I usually add a few unnecessary items that peep out of the top of my basket, perhaps disguising the pitiful sight of my two bottles of Mehmet's cheapest Sauvignon. Accompanied now and then by the chink – no, a higher sound than that – the tink (that's the sound, precisely) of one or two spirit miniatures, which I like to keep in reserve just in case I need a little extra lift on the days a bottle of vodka seems too much. I limit myself to a single bottle of vodka a week. It might sound foolish, but it's all become part of the routine. And we know how important routine is. All my purchases at Mehmet's are carefully chosen and within my budget, naturally.

And so my routine has stretched to allow me to give away these extra items I've bought. I vacillate between being kind (carefully chosen gifts) and mean (mainly to score a point).

I try to be nearly always kind, but occasionally I swing the other way.

Mehmet never comments on whatever I add to my basket – though I thought I saw his curiosity flicker on the bucket of Halloween pick 'n' mix I added the day lockdown was announced (it was from the autumn before and was in the discount tub) – and we rarely say more than the basic pleasantries. He is always polite as clearly he has a vested interest in keeping me coming back for more. He doesn't need to know I've been banned from all three of the other corner shops within easy walking distance.

(Note: Incidentally, I chose the pick 'n' mix for the grumpiest man in the street, Neil, who is a notoriously bad-tempered old fart. I hoped my gift might soften Neil a little, and encourage him to be a bit nicer. And if it didn't, at least I tried – I'm not a wholly horrible cow. Afterwards I watched his door with my binoculars, but even though they are strong, Neil lives too far away for me to be certain as to his feelings when he found the bucket.)

(Note: And double incidentally, on my seventh night of the week, I keep my diet varied with a jacket potato, topped with the obligatory knob of butter, and black pepper. Mehmet did once incline his head very slightly in the direction of his display of fresh vegetables and fruit with a questioning raise of a single eyebrow, but after I blinked solemnly at him, the subject was closed.)

Caitlin

I'd first noticed Daniel when the weather turned warm enough for outdoor swimming last year, and actually I hadn't thought much of him.

He was boy-band good looking in an obvious way that Ellie would probably describe as buff, sure, but as I sat with my best friend Dukie I decided he was annoying. And an inch or two too short to be a hunk, and possibly even a bit shorter than that. Whatever, he's certainly not tall, although I've found that when we're lying down he seems as lofty as the next man.

For the record, my oldest friend Dukie is also annoying (oldest as in we've been friends for the longest time, not in how old she is, although she was born a year before me). This is because she is really called Dulcie, which is a perfectly acceptable and already quite unusual name. But when we were in the last year of A-levels she decided that Dulcie wasn't unusual enough, and so from then on she wanted to be known as Dukie (to rhyme with pookie), and somehow it stuck. If she and I get drunk enough together, I occasionally say to her that Dukie sucks as a name, and then she tells me I need to 'grow one', which I've never quite understood the meaning of. And so, even if there is no alcohol involved, I make sure to call her Dulcie now and again, if I feel she's getting a bit bumptious.

47

Anyway, it was a warm and sunny morning early last summer when I was sitting on my yoga mat at one end of London Fields Lido, with Dukie at my side. What an age ago such an intoxicating freedom to do whatever we wanted seems, now that everything is shuttered and closed, perhaps for ever. Grim times.

But that day at the lido was when I first spied Daniel. My attention was caught initially by the way he was so keen that people notice him. Promenading. There was simply no other word for what he was doing.

Actually, a lot of people were behaving similarly, probably because, as my other book group girlfriends tell me, the lido is a great place for pick-ups, as it legitimately allows for lots of opportunities to show off the wares.

But as I watched, Daniel felt to me just a tad more determined as he went about it than the others, and so perhaps it was this that caught my attention.

And there was something eye-catching about him as he paraded about, swimming a couple of lengths now and again, and then climbing out of the water for a quick catwalk, after which, once we'd all been reminded that his washboard abs are spectacular and his shoulders to die for, he'd get back in the water for another couple of languid lengths, as if everyone then was meant at this point to admire his swimming skills.

It wasn't long before I couldn't decide if I thought him more eye-catching or vexing.

There were plenty of women who were looking on in open admiration though, I was vaguely irritated to see as it clouded my unexpected hopes that he was doing all of this just for me.

Perhaps I was susceptible as I have been very faithful over the years to James (well, apart from on that hen do a couple of years back, but that was just a mild and unimportant peccadillo I've almost forgotten). But as I stared at Daniel, I became aware of a little buzz of shuffling among the women around me that vibrated between us every time he climbed out of the water and reached for his towel, which was that little sort you wring out when it gets wet, the ones the professional divers use between dives. Occasionally he'd have a little rummage down in his swimmers, just in case we weren't already thinking of that part of him.

I noticed how he had a natural kink to his rather splendid dark hair, which he would draw attention to by running his fingers through it and then he'd give his head a little shake so that the droplets of pool water sprang from it, just to remind everyone he was there.

I smiled as I decided it looked like he was enacting a television advert for men's razors, and privately I nicknamed him Mr Gillette.

'What a ponce. But I would, wouldn't you?'

Dukie's words in my ear made me jump slightly, I'd been so deep in thought.

'Pardon?'

'Him.' Dukie tossed her head in Daniel's direction. 'The short-arsed one you can't take your eyes off.'

'I don't know who you mean.' I was pretty certain my hat and dark glasses hid the direction of my gaze.

'Liar! You do too.'

I didn't deign to answer, but instead I ostentatiously ignored Dukie as I smoothed some more sun protection on my legs and arms and quite a lot on to my décolletage, and then I lay down and placed my hat over my face.

What felt like a mere second or two later, I opened my eyes. I realised I must have dozed off as my legs were in the shade of quite a chill shadow, although the rest of me was still in the bright sunlight.

Dukie was speaking. 'And the Sleeping Beauty beside me snoozing on the job is my very good friend Caitlin.'

There was a little sound of acknowledgement, sort of midway between a tut, a grunt and a guttural growl, that I thought almost sounded like the throaty hum made by a large cat. But I knew it had emanated from a man.

It was a sound that was unbearably sexy somehow and I felt an answering rumbling thrill between my legs.

I took my hat away from my face and as I lifted my body on to an elbow, I angled my head towards the pair of them.

Dukie had managed to persuade the man with the sculpted abs to sit alongside on her towel. She has never married or lived with anyone. I used to think she envied me, but over the past couple of years she's been outspoken about the downsides of marriage, and just occasionally a little critical of James and me.

'Daniel,' he more or less purred, extending a hand towards me.

'Hullo,' I'd replied, a bit sulkily as I didn't especially appreciate waking up to find him quite so close to me, as it felt like he was invading my personal space. Fortunately, with my strategic hat over my face he wouldn't have been able to see if I was napping with my mouth open. I'm trusting that Dukie would have given me a prod if I'd been snoring.

I hadn't been going to shake this man's hand when he offered me his, but when he realised this, he smiled with what to me looked like a spark of bravura in his eyes. He reached forward with a quirk of an eyebrow, and then, tantalisingly slowly, pulled my hand towards his mouth. With velvety-feeling lips he then – I can only describe as grazed – the skin across my knuckles. It certainly was something different to a kiss.

For some reason I thought there was a soft, quivery quality to his lips slightly redolent of the curved top of a Portobello mushroom. With that one unusual move of his, coupled with the strange sensation of his lips, I was hooked.

My body thrilled intolerably to his physical magnetism and that feeling has never lost its intensity. Although now I have the added bonus of knowing him as a person.

Less than an hour later Dukie had been called away to deal with an urgent work crisis – there has to be a God after all! – and Daniel and I found ourselves in a multi-sensory, windowless room down in his basement level having frantic, and then just energetic sex on a huge circular platform that wasn't quite a bed and not quite a sofa but which felt ridiculously exotic as I was ravished upon it. That is absolutely the correct word: ravished.

Three times.

Somebody once said to me that if you want great sex then you need to find an ugly man to have it with, as they work harder than the good-looking ones.

I'm proud to say that I've never had sex with an ugly man – and back in the day James was simply devastatingly handsome – but I think much the same could well be said for a shorter man.

I'm sure Daniel would be delighted that I give him an A* in the categories for enthusiasm, technique and stamina. And although he is not quite as tall as average, it's not by much.

If anyone asks themselves how affairs begin, in our case it was as easy as that. I hadn't been looking for it, not especially, but when it happened I didn't say no.

I suppose I'd been caught in that halfway house of watching glamorous single friends enjoy a freedom that occasionally I envied, feeling a little over-encapsulated in a long-term relationship where at moments I felt invisible other than as a mother or chief bottle-washer.

I hadn't been thinking of straying, but when Daniel arrived in my life it seemed a gift.

At first I wondered why I had so little guilt about our liaisons, and no panic at the thought of being caught. But then I realised that with Daniel I existed wholly in the moment with him. It never was a threat to my life with James and Ellie and Harry. It certainly didn't mean that I loved them any less, but just that I had more love to spread around, enough for Daniel too. And I was so organised about the time we spent together, that the chances of us being caught seemed negligible.

Even though James will reassure me during sex how adored I am and how great I look, the truth of it is that even so it doesn't seem quite enough. And so I couldn't help myself with Daniel, although I've made sure that I keep thoughts of each man as separate as I can.

The truth of it was that even as I'd whisper back in the dark to James that I loved him too – and I've meant this every single time – there has been an insistent niggle in the back of my mind. When I turned thirty-nine on my last birthday, pointing out the big four-o would be the one after, it began to shout louder. I guess it was as if the clock was running and I needed to make my time count, as if every ounce of my desirability had a sell-by date I'd be foolish to ignore. And Daniel has been making my time count, big time.

Very early on as we lay post-coitally on the big circular

contraption – I always want to have sex in that room as it gives me the frisson of slight dungeon fantasies – Daniel claimed he really cared for me, and he felt we could fall in love. He'd look after me, and I'd look after him, he promised with a conviction I found naïve but sexy.

And although I've never yet quite responded likewise, I have recently begun to wonder if indeed I might be in a bit further than I intended.

The hook has been, more than the sex, that there's something about Daniel that I find, well, encouraging. From virtually the moment we began to see each other I heard myself saying things to him that I simply couldn't imagine saying at home.

It goes further than sex, for me.

Daniel has the capacity to listen to me, really listen, and I love that about him. In fact, show me a woman of almost forty who wouldn't.

It's highlighted to me that somewhere along the way James and I seem to have lost the knack of how we once spoke to each other, when we really concentrated on what the other was saying and it was confessions whispered into the ear, and lying in bed for hour upon hour as we tried to make each other laugh.

I think kids, and work, and just life all eventually get in the way in a long relationship. I mean to improve our marriage, I do. But it's so much easier just to pretend, in the moment, that all is fine. And actually a lot of the time, it is fine at home. More or less, with much more emphasis on the 'more' bits than the 'less'.

And even though Daniel rarely offers much of an opinion on what I'm confiding to him, or what he thinks I should do in any given situation – a bit like the Samaritans, I've joked with him – this under-estimated quality of just listening is something amazing about him, and I've wanted more and more of it.

It makes me feel valued, and through this I'm a better, stronger person than I used to tell myself I was. It's also an attribute that is definitely an aphrodisiac.

The fact that Daniel fancies me has also done wonders for my confidence. Aside from all the younger women his age who are ready to throw themselves at his feet, he could have his pick too of all the other yummy mummies around here, and so I always get a frisson when I remember anew that he chose, out of all of them, me.

I asked him once what drew him to me. He replied it was my sophistication. And my hot bod.

I'll take that.

And as my time with Daniel is limited, James reaps quite a lot of the knock-on benefits as my liaison has definitely perked our marital love life to the point I've rekindled a desire for my husband that I admit had fallen somewhat dormant over the past few years.

Still, prior to lockdown I had begun to feel uncomfortable about my duplicity, which was why I decided I absolutely had to put the brakes on seeing Daniel. My behaviour hasn't been wholly nice, has it? And I would definitely feel awkward if I had to tell Dukie or Shona what I've been up to, and I'm not used to this. The affair has been making me feel a little grubby and selfish recently, if I'm honest, and I tell myself this might be no bad thing.

It was how much the idea that perhaps Daniel and I have had our last time in his basement has torn me up that made me truly see that I have gone too far and too deep into this relationship.

I know it has to end, for the sake of me and my family. And the sooner I can do this – and stick to it – the better for all of us.

But today, I don't know, I just can't not see my lover. I'm weak, and needy. Right at this moment he feels like my drug, and I badly need a fix. These days I feel more sexually charged than normal, I've realised. I guess it's Nature's way of coping with a natural disaster.

The permitted daily exercise of an hour outside is a godsend as far as I am concerned (and, I'm sure, similarly for a lot of other adulterers across the nation).

'Taking up running' – even though I've never previously done anything much more lively than a snappy stroll to the fridge for more Prosecco – in theory gives me a fair amount of leeway with my nearest and dearest for early-morning absences from the house now everyone is at home, while my running gear should offer a pretty much watertight alibi for any nosey-parker neighbours who might wonder what I've been up to.

I know I need to be hyper-vigilant. I'm used to hours on my own in the house, unwatched and un-thought-of, and I need to make sure this hasn't made me sloppy.

I grew up locally, and James and I have lived in various places in the area since we began our married life immediately after uni. Once you have children your mummy network grows year on year as well, and so I don't want any awkward questions from anybody if I can avoid them.

Although for a long while I felt the tiny risk of discovery was worth taking, now I'd be mortified, simply mortified, if James, or the children, were exposed to my deception. Life is all over the place at the moment, and they need me home and making sure they are all safe. It's none of their faults that I've just been needing something a little extra.

Daniel's no threat to anybody, and the release I find spending time with him at his has been a way of keeping me calm at home. That's what I used to tell myself.

But these days I can no longer kid myself that there is any such thing as safety. I can hardly bear the news or the statistics about the virus, and I'm sure others feel the same. And one doesn't have to be Einstein to know that secrets are dangerous.

Too dangerous. Far, far too dangerous. Almost as dangerous as COVID maybe, and on the days when I really feel the danger, then I'm happy to stay at home all day. But on other days, from the moment I wake I'll be looking for a window of time, usually before the twins are up and James is doing his Peloton class, when I could sneak to Daniel's. Until now, I've managed to hold off, and keep those visits in my head. But not today.

Even though the more my secrets have grown, and the harder I've fallen, the more I know I must keep Daniel locked away in the deepest corner of my heart.

Secret from my family.

My friends.

Everyone.

Almost a secret from myself too, in fact.

It doesn't take me long to jog to where I need to be. I look around and I can't see anybody, although for a moment I have that uncomfortable shiver one gets just before you glance behind and realise that someone is watching you after all.

But there's nobody there, and so I tell myself my imagination is just working overtime. I don't take much convincing, my urge to see Daniel so strong as it's been three weeks since I was last here.

I nip down the steps and give our secret knock at Daniel's front door, but when there's no answer I tap in the code to the keypad.

Daniel has never actually given me the code to his front door, but on that first day I memorised the eight-digit number and letter sequence I watched him use. 112299ZA is hardly difficult to remember.

Once I'm inside it's to be greeted by total silence, which is unusual as Daniel is one of those men who loves sound surging in the background.

Indeed I've never been here without music, or the latest movie, and once, thrillingly, a looped few seconds to a pumping beat blasting out from all six of his televisions (in the basement, kitchen zone, downstairs lounge, gym area, bedroom, and upstairs living room – I know because I checked them all) of a clip that shows me stroking my own breasts that since then he's sent me every evening at nine o'clock.

In fact, this is something I want Daniel to stop doing. The other day I noticed James looking a trifle pointedly at his watch when my phone pinged in my pocket, although he didn't comment. And should he ever mention the regular messages to my phone, I plan to say it's from 'a client anxious about home-workers meeting their deadlines'. That should quell all interest.

To be on the safe side though, I've since made sure I keep my phone with me at all times, on silent nearly always, and I keep changing the passwords on my laptop and desktop and iPad, just in case.

'Daniel!' I call, ready to smile at the sight of him, as I pause with the door open and listen.

There is no 'Caitlin' back to me.

Before I shut the front door a fluffy grey cat scampers through the gap and into the passageway.

I've never noticed a cat before, but that could be because Daniel takes up all of my attention. The cat certainly seems to know its way around as it canters silently up the stairs to the upper ground floor as if on the way to an important meeting.

The quiet feels almost muffled.

'Daniel?'

I hear a tremor of impatience in my voice. I haven't realised quite how worked up I must be at the idea of seeing Daniel.

Still nothing.

I pass the kitchen, and I check where he keeps his gym equipment. And the downstairs bathroom, and the large room at the back with the massive bi-folding doors out to the garden, which are open, and the second downstairs loo. And everywhere in our special place downstairs-downstairs, of course. He can't be far as there is a coffee cup out on the kitchen counter. He never leaves old cups or glasses out to sully his spotless flat.

He must be outside, and so I call through the gap a sing-song 'Dan-i-el!' At the back of his house I'm not so paranoid about someone recognising me from my voice.

But Daniel is not in the garden or anywhere in the clean and always-tidy lower ground floor, and I can see through its large windows he's not in the posh shed to one side of his garden.

He exercises at home, and has food delivered by one of those healthy meal delivery services. I can't think of any reason why he'd have gone out.

I go up the stairs to the upper ground floor.

He's not in his bedroom though, or the upstairs bathroom.

The upstairs area at the back is slightly dim as the slatted blinds have been left more closed than open, which is unusual.

Daniel has a touch of the show-off about him, and he's taught me to love the risk of frolicking in what may or may not be plain view. I have a silk scarf I keep here to wrap around my face as a disguise, just in case anyone seeing us might recognise me.

I notice suddenly an odour up here that is faint but a little pervasive. Well, in some ways it's a familiar-feeling aroma, but it's one I can't immediately place. I turn to watch the cat coming back down the staircase with its tail lowered and an intent look on its face.

I enter the living room, and it's at that moment, with that thought of the predatory slink of the cat foremost in my mind, that I find Daniel.

And the teasing look of desire I'd made sure was pasted across my face, fades in an instant.

He's quiet, and very pale.

And quite, quite dead, lying on the floor on the other side of the room.

If I doubted his deadness, a fly buzzing close to an open eye presses home the point.

Somebody has killed him, shouts his swastika of angled limbs.

Somebody hated my Daniel enough to do this to him.

He was a fastidious man and, stunned, I lean down as if I'm going to mop up the pooling dark and gluey liquid beneath him. Daniel was a fastidious man and I know he would have hated lying in a mess like this.

I realise that what I could smell is Daniel's blood, and for an instant it's almost as if I can taste the iron of it filming my teeth.

I notice then how the iris of Daniel's open eye is becoming very faintly cloudy. It's peculiar how alert my senses are at this minute, how much I can see, I can't help thinking. It's peculiar too how the shock of finding Daniel has just at this moment cauterised all my responses. I can't feel anything, but I can see – usually I'm all about feeling, while I struggle to notice much, or at least that's what James tells me. But now it's as if my brain can't make sense of what has happened, and so instead is thrown out of kilter as it insists on focusing on the little things before me. The sight is so vivid I know I'll never forget a single detail.

Many episodes of *Silent Witness* and the *CSI* franchises have primed me. Immediately I recall that a smoky-looking cornea means Daniel has been dead in excess of two hours.

Perhaps when I was just waking up for the second time this morning, somebody was killing Daniel. I was doing something I'd done thousands of times before, while he was being done to death.

There are no obvious defensive marks on his arms or hands. I think he must have been surprised by his attacker. Perhaps it was someone he knew. What a thought.

Still, I don't shudder.

I'm frozen, motionless. I want to feel desperate, shocked, sad or something. But I feel nothing at all. It's all so senseless, it almost feels a joke.

I'm not prepared for how death looks in reality, even though I understand it's an obvious consequence of an absence of life.

What's before me is stone-like. So bereft of the living, breathing person I know as Daniel, it's almost awe-inspiring in its desperate finality.

I'm not a believer, but if I were, this sight would convince me we live in a Godless world. Daniel isn't, wasn't, perfect, and neither am I, but he hasn't deserved this. And those of us in glass houses – by which I mean pretty much everyone – shouldn't throw stones.

Daniel is on his back, with his head angled right over to one side, a saucer-sized circle of blood under his head, oozing into the wood of the newly laid flooring, the planks fanning hipster-diagonally across the room.

There is a tiny four-padded half-footprint in blood about a metre away from Daniel's head made by the intrusive grey cat, and I see a corresponding wrinkle in the shiny film topping the jammy-looking puddle.

Daniel's eyes are staring right at me, imploring me to make him whole again, yet his uncomfortably spread limbs announce the impossibility. I notice then that blood has soaked into his tee-shirt too. He would have hated that.

It's a bit feeble, but all I can do is just stand there, looking at him.

It's a while, but at last self-preservation kicks in. It feels disturbing, the sensation that I must look after myself suddenly indelibly taking over my mind, pushing thoughts of Daniel – my Daniel – aside.

But in this moment what I understand quite perfectly, without the faintest shadow of doubt, is that I can't – simply *cannot* – call the police to report what I have found.

I know it is what I should do, of course.

Others, faced with this, might try to work out a way to alert the authorities anonymously.

But if I were to do the right thing, the risk of my life crashing down around me is just too high a price. Of that I am in absolutely no doubt. It cannot be discovered that I have been here.

And what is the point of jeopardising everything? Now that Daniel is dead, me behaving as I should is hardly going to bring him back, is it? All my feelings for him count for nothing now – he's beyond my feelings, and so must I be.

Persuasive as I am, even I wouldn't be able to explain away convincingly to James and the twins how it came to be that I found a dead body in a strange flat when I was supposed to be out jogging around London Fields.

And the twins are at that difficult, suggestible age where to have a mother touched by a violent death might have horrifying repercussions. I'd hate the thought of them being bullied, or worse, by their friends, offended by something monstrous that would then be for ever connected to my name. Fifteen would be a very difficult age at which to hear these allegations. I don't want any taint to come the way of Harry and Ellie, especially in such a generally hideous time. As Ellie said at breakfast, whatever has pissed off 2020 so?

I love my husband and my twins, and my life. Truly I do. They, and it, are everything to me. Well, almost.

I think of the time Daniel and I had spent together.

It's just not enough for me to risk everything over.

Is it?

I feel a clench of something in my chest, painful, as if I can't get enough breath.

I know that it's inevitable Daniel's body will be discovered at some point, although who by, I'm not sure, as his cleaner and his personal trainer are no longer able to come. After he is discovered, in time the police will trace me through our messages. But the longer he lies undiscovered, the better this is likely to be for me.

I mustn't touch the body in any way. This can't be traced back to me, and I don't want to damage any evidence which would link to the actual killer. It would be awful if the real murderer couldn't be brought to justice because of something dumb I had done. And it would be even more awful that if through being stupid, much as I yearn to stroke Daniel's cheek a final time in goodbye, I managed to do something that would implicate myself in the crime.

I have a moment that feels out-of-body, as if I am staring across at me and Daniel, caught in the dance of death. Me, still and uncharacteristically icy-calm, and him looking as if he is still desperately trying to clutch on to the last moments of his life. I've always been a panicker, yet to see before today a real disaster before my eyes. I find it's such a shock that my emotions feel momentarily quelled by an over-riding composure I've never had before, as if there's comfort to be found in routine and planning and thinking things through, and if I cling to this, it might save me from what I see at my feet. I didn't know I had it in me.

It's time for me to go. I feel a cold heartless dry-eyed bitch as suddenly dizzy I skulk backwards from Daniel, the soles of my running shoes giving baby-mouse-sized trills as I move on the wooden floor.

But although my mind has made the decision to retreat, my limbs are more reluctant.

I look at Daniel once more. I want to say something to him that's incredible, and momentous.

All I can manage as my lips tremble is 'Goodbye, my love'. It's not enough, but I don't have it in me to do better, especially as I'm starting to shake all over as devastation overwhelms me. It is sinking in that a man I think I loved is dead. We'll never kiss again, and the longing for just one last time breaks my heart.

Somehow I make it down the stairs and then career through the lower ground level, ricocheting from left to right and back again. I stop and gather myself, and once I've wiped the inside of the front door with my running jacket, I slip out of the bi-folding doors and nip as silently as I can around the side of the house, where I key the same code into the security gate at the side so that I can make my escape. Once I've wiped down the keypad and front door with my jacket.

I make my way to the pavement, checking I have my phone with me still, which I do. I realise my running sunglasses have been clutched in my hand the whole time. And – shit! – I remember I've not heard the click of the security gate shutting so I may have left it ajar. I hope that isn't setting off an alarm somewhere and I dither about going back to check.

But as I ram on the sunglasses, a shabby woman almost lurches into me, and I realise I can't now go back to the side door and pull it shut.

It is the crazy woman from across the street. She is an apology of a person, all knotty hair and a wild expression, and with a look to her eyes that's slightly too knowing for her own good.

I've seen her a couple of times in other people's front gardens, and Daniel and I once spied on her as, clearly under the influence (in early morning, no less!), she staggered down the path to leave on the doorstep to Daniel's flat a tatty plastic bag with a seen-better-days cauliflower and some totally unknown and very probably revolting packet cheese sauce of the type one can only find in Hackney corner shops. Goodness knows what that was all about, and then Daniel joked about her being a crazed crone driven nuts through her single-dom, and I'm ashamed to say that I laughed. Later though, I felt a small pang just below my ribs as we threw the bag away, as I thought what Daniel had joked about could just as well describe Dukie, and I'd hate people to laugh at her in this way.

64

Thoughts of the sad woman from across the road, and my loss of Daniel, and my shock, are pushed out of my mind as I'm suddenly consumed with thoughts of, though I'd wiped them from the door, my DNA and my fingerprints being splashed all over Daniel's flat. It's more than three weeks since I was last there, but I suspect that's not long enough for all trace of me to be erased. There's nothing I can do though, I could never clean up everywhere. I must make my peace knowing that there will be little remembrances of me there everywhere, I've visited so often.

I need to get away, and it takes all of my energy to force myself to calm down, get a grip and keep walking.

I have no criminal record, and nor have I ever been interviewed by the police, I tell myself. Never had my fingerprints taken or DNA swabbed. That doesn't necessarily put me in the clear as far as the police will be concerned, of course, but it is a plus rather than a minus, no?

It's not as comforting a thought as I'd like. I'm not sure why.

Damn.

Damn.

Ali

On the way back to my flat from Mehmet's, I risk a quick couple of slugs from a miniature of brandy I added at the last moment in celebration of my restraint with the vodka. But it's still a win, as it will definitely mean I can keep my wine for my four p.m. deadline.

What I am striving for is a happy state of constant mild inebriation that lasts from lunchtime onwards, tipping into neither sobriety nor belligerent tipsiness. It's a tricky tightrope to navigate, one that's easy to miscalculate.

I have a confession – I don't even much like the taste of alcohol.

And I hate how fucking boring alcohol makes me, both in how I talk and think when pissed, and how I fixate on all sorts of things I don't need to be thinking about. Boring, and bored when I look at the bottom of an empty glass. That's me.

As I get close to home, my attention is caught by the antics of a small brown bird. With a liveliness I can only imagine feeling, this bundle of feathers is making the most of a half coconut shell filled with some lardy gunk that's dangling on a string, and so I stop and watch for a while, rather envying the sheer abandon with which the bird is feeding.

Maybe we should all make ourselves like birds, I muse. Or, better still, cats; they have the art of doing exactly what they want down to a tee.

A stumbly noise I wasn't expecting comes from across the road, and so I turn around to see the woman in the horrible running tights heading slowly towards Daniel's garden gate across the front garden.

She must have come around from the back of the house, but there is something wrong. The confident way she was previously moving is no more, and she looks clumsy and ungainly. Interesting. Daniel doesn't normally come around from the side; I've only ever seen him use his front door.

Already, she's leaving? That was a quick visit.

Immediately, I realise this is even more intriguing.

Perhaps Daniel has tired of her and she has gone the same way as Nikki.

The confident way Miss Ponytail jogged down the steps to see him hadn't made me think she expected to be in and out so quickly.

I barely have time to think about what I'm doing before I find myself bolting across the road to her side. I have an over-whelming desire to get closer to this woman, to see exactly what is happening and who she is.

Thank goodness I don't have to look out for cars as I am barely paying attention, but practically no one has driven up or down our street for days now.

She pauses just outside the gate, seeming not to notice that I'm less than the obligatory number of feet from her as I halt and then try to take a casual surreptitious gawp.

Up close, she's at once prettier and yet plainer somehow than I had expected.

Prettier, as despite the manicured nails and expensive perfume that wafts over me and her whole exercising ensemble being perfectly matched, even down to her laces, there's something about Miss Ponytail that seems to me to be, oh, I don't know, innocent somehow.

I have the impression that in spite of her shiny veneer, in actual fact she's more vulnerable than she wants to seem. She's standing still on the pavement, blinking rapidly as if she's not really focusing on anything, as a hand distractedly pulls at the soft hairs on her arm. I think it might be shaking, the hand, I mean, and not the arm.

I guess that she has to be in her late thirties, so as old as me, although much better preserved.

A woman of her age, who appears to revel in the safety of her world, looking so at sea is, in my experience, unusual.

From the look of her, I'm guessing she is, best-case scenario, about to find life just a teensy-weensy bit irritating. In the way that a pair of shoes can fit in the shop but once you're wearing them outside you realise they pinch, and before you know it, they've sloughed off a bit of skin to reveal a painful blister. Worst-case scenario, well, how long have you got?

The longer I gaze, the more I feel I can see what her face must have been like as a teenager. It's there, lurking just beneath the surface. A time when everything probably went her way.

For some reason, I can just tell that she was one of those passive-aggressive type of teenage girls, always insisting you borrow their favourite jumper or try out their new mascara, whether you wanted to or not. The ones I never particularly liked – they wore themselves out with trying too hard, casually but deliberately showing you up and revealing themselves as all about control.

I see a pulse just below one of Miss Ponytail's eyebrows. Maybe what she's thinking feels a worst-case scenario to her, but I'd bet it's probably something insignificant to people with real problems in their lives.

Although she is attractive, she's not quite beautiful, a plainness manifesting itself in a lack of focus around her eyes and a somewhat corded neck, almost as if she were lifting a heavy weight. This adds up to a slightly vacant, or possibly it's a vaguely insecure look on her face as she fiddles now with her sunglasses against the bright light of the endlessly sunny days we're having.

I feel I'm missing something, something important.

And then I notice a paleness to her face that's at odds with the expensive tan on the limbs on show beneath her runners, although whether this honey-coloured flesh on her legs is from winter sun, or a sunbed, or an all-over spray tan, I can't tell, not having tried those myself.

It could be that she rubs in sun block too thickly to her face, but I doubt it. To me, this woman seems the type to know exactly how much of anything to apply.

I think I hear a tiny sigh of a supressed moan.

Then she seems to come to, moving past me with a gait that has a robotic feel about it and none of the joy it embodied when she'd arrived. She barely seems to notice I've been so close, standing and watching. I don't think she even registers my existence as she moves slowly away, stopping every now and again with her hand on a garden wall for support.

I move towards my own front door, and decide that, as I'm up and about, I'll deliver the little gift I bought yesterday for Daniel's neighbour Dodi, though my mind is still lingering on what I've seen. The gift is waiting on the table where we pile all our mail, so I scribble a postcard to go with it, and enter the garden next door to Daniel's house.

It's a polythene-wrapped pack of six SlimFast milkshakes, chosen to counteract all the bad things that Dodi, who lives on the upper ground floor, must eat to keep her wobbling rear-end so large. The other day I couldn't help but notice, as she lumbered down the pavement in front of me, that her lockdown diet wasn't going so well. I don't think Dodi ever takes up her full hour of exercise, and frankly she looks like a tank. I'm sure she'd say it's not her fault, but that it's her metabolism. Either way, this should give her a hint. And if she takes it wrongly, then I really don't care. She shouldn't have barged in front of me in Mehmet's last week, as if I didn't exist.

I set down the SlimFast pack on the doorstep with the anonymous card tucked on top that tells her to enjoy it and see it as a way of kick-starting a new regime.

Not all my gifts are of the sort which could be taken in the wrong way like this, I must point out.

I do try hard to pay a little kindness forward each day as well. Recently I left some treats for the nice family at number thirty – sweets for the kids and some bubble bath for the mum, who is somehow managing to be both a nurse as well as a single mum of three! – and I went out of my way to choose some nutritious ready meals for that elderly gentleman at number fifty-four who doesn't ever seem to get any visitors. I popped in some Liquorice Allsorts too, as I know he's fond of them. Lingering in Mehmet's really can tell you a lot about the neighbourhood. And I've worried about the Polish lesbians who are both office cleaners, as it seemed like their work has dried up, so several times I have left some food parcels on their doorstep. I know they were thrilled, as they pinned a little note of thanks telling me so, right where I leave my presents. So, I'm not all bad.

Until the day in the shop, I had been going to drop a note of a very different kind into Dodi's, saying I'd fetch her shopping if that was helpful. But I changed my mind after she was so rude, and although the SlimFast is a little cruel of me, I can't help but feel that she deserves it.

As I re-cross the road back to mine, thinking my thick cardie was A Very Bad Idea in this bright sun, I see, far in the distance, the blonde woman running fast now, almost as if the hounds of hell are hot on her tail.

I look upon the frantic beat of her bouncy ponytail and wonder then if the look I'd seen on this woman's face had perhaps been closer to one of deep shock, rather than that of a lover spurned, or of discovering that young and healthy Daniel had been hit with the virus.

Has this woman done something she should be feeling very, very ashamed about perhaps?

I can't tell. But the wink of the coloured rubber of the trainer soles, shrinking as they disappear into the distance, seems to beat a panicky Morse code that's screaming out all isn't well.

Caitlin

Once I'm standing in the road outside Daniel's, I'm not quite sure what to do – I can't return home yet as my run will have been too short and I must make sure that I am seen to be acting normal, since I don't want to raise suspicions at home. The cool and practical me of earlier has well and truly fled. The me of now is a jangle of nerves, and fear, and sadness, and horror. I don't think I can ever remember feeling so bad, and it's manifesting itself in me feeling cold, shaky and unbearably sweaty.

So right now I certainly don't feel like 'allocated exercise' either.

I dither, and then I speed as fast as I can to London Fields, where I try to find a secluded bench to sit on to gather my thoughts.

This proves to be easier thought than done.

There are jobsworths all over the place warning me that if I intend to sit down for a second on a bench, or even on the grass, I'll be arrested. I'm sure most of them have good intentions while out on their hour of exercise, but it doesn't stop them being supercilious and interfering, and I feel very cranky at their attitude.

'Shit,' I mutter, kicking at the tufts of grass, as I find myself unable to move forwards or backwards. Standing here, talking to myself in the park, I have the sensation that I'm standing under a house of cards poised to come crashing down around me. I quake apprehensively in a way that I couldn't when I was looking at Daniel splayed on the floor, and now my mouth and throat are dry.

A police car enters the park with a loud-speaker and officers ostentatiously tapping at their watches to get everyone moving on and returning to their abodes.

Instructions to 'Stay Home' blare from a loud-hailer, and I can see reluctant people faffing about with their dogs and leads, trudging towards the exit.

At the sight of the police car I feel a pang of guilt, even though at this minute I'm not doing anything wrong.

Other than trying to cover up a murder. And having broken my marriage vows for the past year.

With a huge effort I retrace my steps to the park's entrance, trying to saunter along in a manner that any fool would think incredibly innocent.

From there I go very slowly home pretending to check an important message on my phone, just in case anyone I know sees me. I need time to go over in my mind what I have seen as best I can.

There is a moment when I struggle to recall what Daniel even looked like and I'm shocked.

It's like a dream.

It all seems so unreal.

I don't at this minute feel bereft, or even sad at his loss, but I sense I will before too long.

I'm consumed by listing all the things upsetting me.

There's Daniel's death, obviously. I still can't actually process this; it's not believable and so it's not yet properly hitting me.

What is believable though is my conviction that I am a changed woman since finding his body.

Then there's the generally fucked-up background to all our lives at the moment – and by this I mean everybody's – as these days it's all depressing news reports and daily death counts, and a lingering sense that we could all be doomed. We're like ants in the path of a flood, and there's not much we can do other than wash our hands or keep away from one another. No longer do I look at the news or keep up to date with the daily briefings, and I'm sure many will be feeling likewise.

Then there's the virus itself too, of course. It's a horrid, insidious, terrifying thing, that's for certain.

But maybe what is most disturbing of all is the way all of this jumbles together into something that seems remote and hard to bring into sequence.

It feels like a kaleidoscope.

And the heightened sense of unreality is continually magnified by it being such a lovely sunny stretch of weather at the moment, with day after day of unbroken glittery sun and azure skies, but none of us allowed to enjoy it on our own terms. It's all boiled down to essential shopping and daily exercise.

And while I understand the need for lockdown, and the shopping and exercising rules, and the disinfecting everything and washing our hands – of course I do! – it seems we're only a heartbeat away from a co-operative feeling of mass desperation and, when I think of the no-shit-taken police car I've just seen, combined with my desperate feelings over what I've seen at Daniel's, I feel as if I am about to burst with the pressure of it all.

But of course I don't.

Nobody is the slightest bit interested in my return home. Music is thumping in the den, and I can hear James on a Zoom, or maybe a Teams. It's very mundane. And comfortingly, boringly normal.

For a moment I despise everything, the sheer safety of it. And my James and my Harry and my Ellie, and my lovely life and wonderful home.

I pull off my trainers and hurl each of them as hard as I can into the shower cubicle off the utility room. I yank off my scrunchie and throw that on top of my shoes. I want to scream aloud, but I bite it back.

How could something so momentous happen to me, yet be something so utterly ignored by everybody else? It seems so unfair.

Then I tell myself as forcefully as I can that what I have arrived home to is perfect, quite literally perfection.

My family's distraction will protect me. Better they live wrapped in their own wants and needs, than just now they pay the slightest attention to mine.

I am numb to my core, and so it feels incredibly dreamlike as I plod upstairs. In my bathroom I put four soluble Solpadeine codeine tablets in a tumbler with some water and when dissolved, swig it down. It's way beyond a recommended dose, but I need something strong to quiet my screaming nerves.

It's only once I step into the shower in our bedroom's en suite that I notice I've gnawed off peels of my gel nail polish on one of my thumbs, and I've bitten the tips off two other nails. It looks horrible.

But there is relief: in private at last, I can begin properly to unspool the last hour. Perhaps this is because taking a shower the moment I come in from seeing Daniel is what I'm used to, and this replication of something I've done so many times remains a link with normality, an unspoken and now desperately broken contract between the old me and the gone Daniel.

Whatever, as the hot water pounds the top of my head and then my torso, the enormity of what I've seen hits me like a sucker-punch.

My lover is dead.

Dead!

My lover.

I loved him, I feel perhaps more powerfully than ever, and I don't know that I can manage without him.

How could this have happened?

Somebody hated Daniel enough to kill him.

Somebody hated him enough to leave him dead, with his eyes open and his blood oozing across the floor.

Somebody hated him enough to leave his body for me to find.

And now that I've thought this, I can't unthink it. I feel contaminated by all the detestation.

I'm washed through with nausea and light-headedness, and suddenly my knees tremble uncontrollably.

And I slide my piebald nails down the wall of the tiles and sink my body downwards until I am crouching on the shower tray with the water raining down on me, as I start to half heave, half howl in despair as silently as I can into a large sponge.

I don't know how I should be, it's all such an alien experience, and after a while I find my arms have snaked around my legs in a weird inverted hug, and then I surrender to the moment and in despair I just lay my forehead on my knees and try to will the whole wide world to fuck off.

After a while, there's the inevitable mumble of a voice outside the bathroom, accompanied in a beat or two by a loud bang as someone raps smartly on the door.

My nerves are clearly unravelled as the sudden brutal sound feels unbearably violent, and this makes me fling my head painfully back against the white tiles of the shower.

'Mum!' shouts a grumpy-sounding Ellie from the bedroom, as I lift my hand to press against the bit of my head I've just hurt. 'Hurry up! What's for lunch? We're starving.'

To be disturbed by something as trivial as this feels cruel.

'Mum?' Ellie's grumpiness gives way to an unattractive nasal whine at my silence. She's used to me jumping to attention at her every beck and call.

I swallow and take a big breath, and letting it slowly out, I try to make my voice sound as ordinary and as dull as she expects.

'Sorry, Ellie, I had shampoo in my ears. Shall we all have beans on toast? Do you want to be a hun and start getting it ready and I'll be down in a min?' I say as I stand up and turn off the shower, in a voice that to me sounds not too far from what I believe I usually sound like.

Hun is shorthand for honey, a word I've noticed Ellie is very fond of when talking to her friends, and so I hope this will divert her attention enough with embarrassment on my behalf that she won't think any further about me and whether I do sound a bit strange.

She doesn't say anything else and I take this to mean that my daughter has gone down to the kitchen. She probably won't much like having to make lunch, but I don't think it's going to kill her.

I get out of the shower and dress quickly, deliberately putting on light and cheerfully-coloured clothes and, in just a few seconds, a slick of tawny kohl and a hint of lipstick in an effort to appear what I need to be, somebody with few cares in the world. Hopefully it will do the trick of making me seem like Mum, like the Caitlin they hardly notice.

Perhaps if I can just keep doing this, keep dressing and talking like a normal woman, I can one day forget that I have seen the body of my murdered boyfriend on the floor. And that I walked away without a word.

I notice my towels and running gear heaped on the floor and I make sure to bundle them into the laundry basket. Just like normal.

I look in the mirror – I see I've made up my face to look like the old me.

It's a me I hardly recognise.

I wonder if I ever will again.

'Right, who's for a Coke?' I say brightly as I breeze into the kitchen, although possibly a bit too brightly, as James glances at me with a surprisingly penetrating look. Usually I police everyone's Coke intake. 'Let's spoil ourselves,' I add as I sit down.

Everyone stares glumly down at their beans on toast, and I think that maybe 'spoil' isn't the best word I could have chosen. Ellie has overdone the toast, and the beans look sorry for themselves, and even the most upbeat person in the world would find it hard to say that our lunch looks especially appealing.

I need to watch all of this, I think as I force myself to eat a mouthful. Harry is so glum in fact that he doesn't look up at all. I can't say I blame him.

I don't want it to be the little things that trip me up. Or a moment's inattention.

I've got to plot and plan, and think about each tiny nuance, and every possible ramification. And then go through it all over again.

Stay home, stay safe, I tell myself. And keep in character.

'So, Cat, how was the run?' asks my husband.

'Oh, you know. Fine thanks. How's work been? That tender still a problem?'

'You know. Fine.' I stare at the bubbles of Coke on the side of my glass as James goes on to describe the highlights of his morning's calls, and I feel the effects of the Solpadeine softening slightly the edges of this hard world.

Business as normal, I think, and then I repeat that to myself. 'Business as normal' is going to be my mantra.

The codeine and the shock I've had make it hard to eat, and in fact I feel a little woozy. But then the twins start to argue and James steps in as peacemaker, and I wake up a bit and suggest we make some pancakes for afters.

Business as normal. Almost.

My heart seems to scream the Government's instructions at me as it pulses the blood around my body – stay home, stay safe. I feel almost deafened by its urgency. And then I realise that for Daniel, home wasn't really very safe at all.

Ali

The day perks up.

Back at mine I cram the two bottles of wine into my small fridge, as I wonder about the two levels of coldness with which Daniel keeps those bottles I've spied in his expensive cooler. I doubt very much that he purchases his wine from Mehmet's.

Then I do some washing up, and after I've made a cup of tea, I angle my chair so that I can keep a watch on whether Dodi has collected her SlimFast.

It's perfect timing.

I fiddle with the focus of my binoculars as I observe Dodi's slow progress along the pavement as she shambles back from the supermarket (she's been given away by a spanking-new bag-for-life clutched in her hand), and then she halts and looks around suspiciously once she's hefted her huge behind up the steps to her front door. She's noticed what I've left her.

She puts down the carrier and lifts up the vacuum pack of diet meal replacement to examine it closely, and then with a look behind her, she takes both it and the card I wrote inside, and then she comes out again for the carrier. I am reminded of a spider pulling in a fly to its larder.

I was right.

I had pegged Dodi as the sort of person who wouldn't look a gift horse in the mouth, no matter what the gift might be.

Haven't lost it, have I?

Back when I was a teacher, I was ridiculously proud of my sixth sense at reading people, and my colleagues envied me. A welcome consequence was that my pupils were normally very well behaved without me having to do much at all to deserve such a smooth ride. I had a reputation among them for being able to identify a wrong-doer almost from the moment the thought even entered their head, let alone before it was acted upon, and so the pupils gave me the respect this talent was due. It wasn't that I was a brilliant teacher, but more that it wasn't worth their while not to behave when I was around. There was something about my no-arsing-about approach that quite often led to my students getting good grades, which kept everybody happy. They saved up all their naughtiness for the probationary teachers, and this was okay by me.

I read once about the small tells that people give away to others without realising. These minuscule expressions and gestures are a gateway shouting their state of mind. It fascinated me, and since then I've always insisted to myself I'm good at decoding tells. But it's difficult to build this seamlessly as a skill into a CV, I have to admit.

I turn on my laptop. I'm determined to get my Daniel notes into order and transferred from my notebook, and so I have a busy afternoon ahead. And I really should think about putting a bit more effort into trying to find some proper work, I suppose, although I can't say that is the most thrilling of thoughts that I've ever had. Actually I think I'll park this for when everything is back to normal, as I'm sure I'll feel more like it then.

But then Dodi's face as she stared down at my gift pops into my mind. The way she nestled it to her expansive chest.

I suspect she might not get many presents, and that she's lonely. My self-congratulation becomes dust in an instant. And my heart goes out to Dodi in a silent mutual recognition of someone as adrift as I am. Suddenly I feel seared and contrite.

What a callous person I can be at times. Now, I hate it that I behaved this way, as there really was no need. Dodi hadn't really done anything to merit me being quite so nasty. What does this say about me? And where is my tolerance and sense of humanity for others these days, in these times when kindness should be our first impulse and we all should be looking after one another?

I stand up to go to my fridge to get a bottle of wine, suddenly not much caring just how much I vowed to do today.

But then I decide I don't deserve it. I want to have a glass badly, very badly in fact, but in atonement for how I've hurt poor Dodi, I make myself suffer by refusing to open the bottle, almost revelling when my hands tremble with withdrawal.

I spend the next few hours trying to distract myself, musing on the past while keeping an eye on the opposite garden path for a sighting of Daniel.

But I still haven't seen him, which is odd, as I almost set my watch by him most days. Usually, at noon, he very reliably saunters out with a demitasse of coffee to stand in his front garden and admire his pride and joy. Several times a day even, quite often.

The object of Daniel's affection is a dark and dully burnished scooter, which at first sight might not seem like something a Hackney hipster would be proud of. But now that I've done some checking on Google, I know there's more to this beast than meets the eye.

Daniel owns a Vespa Sei Giorni. To the uneducated this might look just like a run-of-the-mill Vespa.

Wrong.

Very wrong.

Underneath a black cover that is carefully removed and tidily folded each inspection, Daniel has outside his home a 300-horsepower machine that is so powerful that the rider needs a motorbike licence to take it on the highway.

The Vespa is so top-end, it even has a USB port inside the rear shield locker, and the dull charcoal colour with a slight mercury tinge in certain lights smacks of an expensive bespoke respray even though the model is the very latest. I know because I lifted the back end of the cover one day to have a peek, as I was so curious why Daniel should spend such a lot of time looking at it so rapt. Ironically, I am yet to see him do more than turn the engine on for a thrum or two. It must have the lowest mileage for any scooter in London.

In fact, all these secondary attributes that Daniel so adores about his extravagance will, I strongly suspect, mean that he's merely fast-tracked it to getting filched-to-order very soon. I know there's a lively black market in especially nicked luxury cars and bikes.

But until that happens, Daniel delights in strolling out every day to admire his baby. If it were made in chocolate I think he would lick it, he loves it so. I'm pretty certain that the only thing in his life he worships more than his Vespa, is himself.

But it's now early afternoon, and there is resolutely still no sign of him today.

Unusual.

But no matter how long I sit and stare, the windows opposite, and the garden and the street around remain completely Daniel-free.

The Vespa looks droopy and discombobulated at being ignored. It's not used to such inattention.

By dusk, I know I have to go and investigate. Something might well be up. Daniel lives alone and anything could have happened, after all.

In the final twenty minutes of daylight I fortify myself with a small glass of wine as I think I've punished myself enough by now for being mean to Dodi, and I sneak over the road and, once I'm certain no one is walking about in the street, down to Daniel's front door where I ring the doorbell.

The possible whereabouts of Pusshkin shall be my excuse, who I actually haven't seen all afternoon. I've called him several times, but he has remained as absent as Daniel.

There's no reply elicited from my stab at the doorbell's button.

I press it again.

I'm pretty certain Daniel hasn't gone anywhere. He's always there these days, as we all are, and I've not seen him leave. More convincingly, to me as I stand on his doorstep, it feels as if Daniel IS inside.

Not On My Watch has he left, I'm certain.

NOMW.

I look around. The street is eerily quiet in the fading light.

Before I have had time to really think about what I'm doing, I'm punching in the numbers on Daniel's keypad. His door code was one of the first things I noted when I was trying out my new binoculars. At the time I never thought I would actually use it. I may be a bit of a snoop, but I've never actually gone into one of the neighbours' houses before. But, I remind myself, something might have happened to Daniel. So obviously this is the right thing to do.

And then I'm inside the flat, where my presence is acknowledged by Pusshkin, my faithless furry companion, who is sitting on the bottom step of the stairs to the upper level. He stops washing his face long enough to give me a friendly chirp of hello, as if it is perfectly acceptable for me to be in Daniel's home. Pusshkin narrows his eyes as he looks at me affectionately, passing his raspberry-coloured tongue around his lips, and so I wonder if Daniel has given him a snack.

The flat seems empty though, and I pause suspiciously. Not that I have ever been in here at any other time, but still, the atmosphere feels off. I'm not sure that everything is as it should be.

Unexpectedly, as I stand still and silent right inside the front door, there's a click from somewhere in the flat and suddenly lights flood down from upstairs, and then under the kitchen cabinets lights up.

My heart gives a large whump of adrenaline that courses around my body, even though I am yet to hear a sound of anyone moving about. My sudden guilt at being somewhere I shouldn't bubbles uncomfortably beneath my skin. Then I experience another fizzle of adrenaline when I think of the shame I'd feel if Daniel suddenly happened upon me. Pusshkin's whereabouts or no, me being here would take a bit of explaining.

I stay stock still, and it's an age before I understand that Daniel must have set his lights to be triggered by a timer. He must be out, even though somehow it doesn't feel like that. I breathe out with relief, and for a moment consider leaving without investigating further.

Then I realise there's the silence of a mausoleum swirling across and through the flat, and I experience a flutter of distinct unease.

My inquisitive nature wins out over good sense. It's only now that I fully understand why in horror films the young woman in the nightie always does end up going down to the dark and spooky cellar.

Taking another deep breath and wondering if I'm making a huge mistake, I call out a slightly croaky 'hello?'

Nothing.

My heartbeat is starting to return to normal. I must have just missed him leave this morning. Maybe he went to make it up with Miss Ponytail.

But now I'm here, it seems daft to let the opportunity go to waste. I know I'm not going to resist a quick look around. After all, it's been killing me not knowing stuff about this man. There's only so much you can glean from the window. Increasingly certain that I am alone, firmly I put out of my mind how I would explain what I'm up to if I were caught, and I begin to creep about Daniel's home.

I don't see much of proper interest at first, but I enjoy an exaggerated grimace at the equipment I see in his home gym in the back room. I knew Daniel would have instruments of torture like this! I guess one doesn't get a ripped physique like his without a lot of studied exercise.

As I wander around, I begin to notice there are quite a lot of hidden spaces here that I can't see from my flat, many more than I realised. Perhaps I've not been able to eavesdrop on as much of Daniel's life as I've thought. Considering what exactly this means, or if it means anything at all, I open a door I'd not noticed initially.

The lights that go on automatically at regular intervals just above the skirting board illuminate steps leading down to the lower level. It feels like an invitation.

Am I tempted?

Is the Pope Catholic!

I glance towards the door. Pusshkin is still sitting on the steps, as if we had all the time in the world. I promise myself that I will take a lightning quick look and be out of here. Five minutes, tops.

But this promise leaves my mind as I descend the stairs. It's a large room with, what looks to me like, a very strange set-up. There is, what I can only describe as a huge, ridiculous thing in the middle of the room. I sit briefly on its fabric-covered cushions that are quite hard and guess they are padded with some sort of up-market memory foam. I notice a book on yoga poking out from under a cushion and so it seems that Daniel does yoga and meditation here. Okay, that's normal enough for Hackney, though I've never seen him show an interest in yoga.

It's still a strange and not exactly hospitable space though, I think, as I stare around, not somewhere that looks built for meditation and relaxation. I notice four giant screens placed on the ceiling, and a mirrored wall, adding up to something that feels fur coat and no knickers. I spot a control panel in one of the walls and can't help myself experimenting a little. It creates myriad lighting effects, sounds and even fragrances, and I get up a picture of bright red poppies in a sunny field on the screens attached to the ceiling. I even manage to make the contraption in the middle of the room tilt this way and that – how ridiculous. I press another button and find that it vibrates, heats and chills too. Bonkers.

It's multi-sensory to a level I've not come across before, which is presumably the object, and so I park this under what I suppose the hipster generation probably sees as a Must-Have these days. I wonder how much this set-up cost.

In my day, this area would have been partitioned into a Scandi-style sauna at one end and a wine cellar at the other, both of which seem quaintly old-fashioned now. I give a rueful shake of my head; I'm only thirty-eight, so not totally over the hill, but I've been made to feel ancient in a matter of moments.

I find a wet-room to one side – of course there is! – and beside it, a door that exits on to steps up to the rear garden. I creep out to have a quick look.

Beyond the artificial grass and bushes and artfully arranged pots, the sunken seating area and the fire pit, I notice what may well be a back entrance to the garden, assuming that the gap between the terrace backing on to it provides an alley someone could enter by. There's also a summer house over in the other far corner that looks as unused as the fire pit.

The more I look at it, the more I am struck by how phoney and depressing it all is, and once I've thought that, it seems as if the rest of Daniel's whole place is too.

It's obviously had a shedload of money chucked its way, and everything is top-end and designer. But there is something about it that's just not right. Not lived in, not comfortable.

IMHO.

There's just no personality anywhere, and nearly everything feels as if it's pretending to be something else. Who lives in something so sterile? And can he possibly be as fake as his home?

I walk slowly back down to the cellar level, and make sure everything is locked and as I found it before I return via the internal steps to the lower ground level, the one on which I entered.

I move through the large kitchen space to the back of the flat and notice that the bi-folding doors have been left open. That probably means something, but I can't decide what. The level of carelessness doesn't seem to match up with the Daniel I know. But then, this trip is showing that maybe I don't really know as much about him as I thought I did.

Good with tells? Who am I kidding? It looks like I can hardly find my arse cheek to give it a pinch.

But before I can berate myself too much, my attention is diverted by something else.

I was right. Daniel's wine cooler is stuffed to the gills with quality bottles. I bloody knew it!

And the collection of spirits over on a strategically obvious table on the other side of his room comprises an array of things new to me: Amaro, Mr Black, Hibiki Harmony, Plantation Pineapple Stiggins' Fancy, Pisco, Biajiu, Soju, Feni, Shōchū, Berto Bianco and – yikes! – even Absinthe Verte.

A meow from upstairs distracts me, reminding me where I am. I've been in here too long. Time to grab Pusshkin and make our excuses to leave.

The expensively rebuilt wooden stairs don't give the tiniest creak as I climb them.

Not quite kidding myself that I'm only looking for Pusshkin, but at least managing not to linger, I take a quick gander into the bathroom and a bedroom with an en suite. It's all very tasteful and swish. And relentlessly totally, totally devoid of individuality.

In fact, the numbing sterility of all before me is incredibly dispiriting, and suddenly I feel in a little crack of heartbreak almost unbearably sorry for Daniel.

He has so little sense of who he is about him, other than perhaps an uncanny ability to fritter money on what actually increasingly looks to be a pretty shitty empty life, that it feels pitiful. There's not a photo or a book or anything personal that I can see anywhere in the flat. It's almost as if nobody really lives here. As if he doesn't care about anyone, and nobody cares about him.

While he's dull as a person, that's not the crime of the century. He's quite easy on the eye, and he should be seeking someone who can show him how to live life.

I spent a night in a police cell once and that certainly had more of a sense of humanity and occupancy than I'm finding here. Possibly my own fall from grace in life has given me an insight into the fact that having a proper place in the world is not a god-given right for us all. Certainly, I don't really have a place these days, and in fact I'm beginning to wonder if I ever did. But I did expect Daniel to have more of one, a proper place. A life that dents the world more than the 2D one I had constructed for him from my window. But, as I swallow down a lump in my throat that feels something to do with mourning lost opportunities, I'm not sure Daniel's life isn't sadder even than my own. That's quite a feat, and it definitely doesn't make me feel happy.

(Note: My arrest occurred after a staff leaving-do got rather out of hand. Three of us ended up in an Indian restaurant where a group of drunken louts were poking racist fun at the long-suffering waiters. It was the right thing to voice dissent, although wrong to resort to the stand-up screaming row. My cooling-off period in the cell was ultimately, in all respects, a sobering experience, and the only good thing to come out of it was that me and my two fellow teachers bonded. Oh, and none of us three teachers were charged or cautioned and I have never shouted in a restaurant since.)

I suspect that Daniel's addiction to his laptop and the Vespa and the dratted wine cooler could well be the only way of him finding more to life than what he sees immediately around him within these sterile walls.

Perhaps Daniel and I might not be so very different in how we deal with the world, after all. The miserable manner in which we choose to spend our time might be our warped way of seeking a shared something with a world we don't really much partake in.

Poor Daniel. Poor me.

It's at this point I walk into the living room area upstairs. And . . .

Well, words fail me.

It's Daniel. He's here after all.

He's alone, as usual.

But I guess that is no surprise, considering the state he is in.

I wince.

It's not the sight of his corpse that sets my nerves jingle-jangling so much as the sound – faint but still distinct – of Pusshkin's raspy tongue as he licks away with intense concentration at the edge of the dried and blackened patch of blood. It looks like it seeped from Daniel's head, or possibly from his neck, quite a while ago.

I must have made a noise as Pusshkin stops what he's doing to stare at me as if I should be proud of him and ashamed of myself, and I try to tell him with only my eyes that he's nothing more than a vagabond cat who too often verges on the thoroughly disgusting.

I make a split-second decision, cross the room and flip down the slats of Daniel's wooden louvred blinds to fully shut.

Oh yes, I can certainly see the irony in this, me shutting other people out from looking in.

It's only now that I dare to crouch and inspect what's lying at my feet more closely.

I've not seen a dead body before.

That blonde woman – Miss Ponytail – absolutely didn't appear as if she had it in her to do this.

But she must have done, as I'm ninety-nine-point-nine per cent certain that I saw Daniel alive and well first thing today, when I was watching him on the phone and I forgot to drink my water, before I went back to bed for an hour or two, though I suppose I can't be one hundred per cent sure that it wasn't yesterday I'm thinking of. My memories tend to blur a bit at the moment. Either way, I don't think anyone else visited, as with lockdown anyone walking about stands out like a sore thumb. It must have been her, I conclude, her bouncy ponytail flicking in fury as she went for him.

It was probably spur-of-the-moment, provoked perhaps by him saying something that unleashed a heat of emotion.

She absolutely hadn't seemed to be harbouring any murderous feelings when she arrived, not that I could see, and so I'd bet my bottom dollar that whatever kicked off must have blown up out of nothing very quickly, but decisively all the same.

When I'd seen her the first time she'd been happy and full of anticipation, I'm sure.

Respect is due to her for such a pivotal swing in the opposite direction, as that takes some guts. An example of how one shouldn't ever judge a book by its cover.

It's not often that human nature gobsmacks me.

As I rub my nose thoughtfully, I try to recall if that woman had any blood on her when I saw her in the street as she was leaving after she'd done whatever she'd done.

I think possibly she didn't, but it's hard to be sure as those foul running pants had such a riot of colour and pattern going on they would hide a multitude of sins. I put my head in my hands for a moment, trying to visualise the scene as she came out of the house. Trying to get a handle on what I actually, definitely remember. My sozzled brain cells try to snap to attention, but it's uphill work. I regret that glass of wine just now.

I had noticed that she did have an odd look on her face, enough to dash across the road to get a better view. The fact that I'd struggled to place exactly what was wrong with her is much more understandable now, I realise.

Goodness, what a turn-up for the books, regarding Miss Ponytail.

As the much-missed Aretha would say to her: R. E. S. P. E. C. T.

Socked it to him.

Just a little bit.

I gather that she's chosen not to call the police. Public services are stretched as they are all so busy keeping everyone moving along or dealing with other COVID-related issues, but even so, if she had rung them to report a murder, they would have been here a while ago.

She isn't planning on drawing attention to herself then. I wonder if she has left any evidence that she was here, or if she thought this all through?

*   *   *

I lose track of time as I stare at Daniel's body from every angle, trying to imprint every little detail on my mind. With a jolt of excitement, I notice the tiny tip of his earpiece with microphone poking out from under him, and this triggers a memory. Yesterday, Daniel receiving this new headset. I saw him answering the door to the delivery man in a mustard polo shirt then with navy chinos.

Now he's dressed in an olive polo with charcoal knee-length chino shorts. The light-top-half-and-dark-bottom combo I'd spotted that morning, proving that he was alive and well at around seven, I guess it would be, as that is when I normally surface for my first pee. I knew it! I had seen him as I'd got distracted from my glass of water. Then I went back to bed until around nine. It must have been close to eleven by the time I saw Miss Ponytail arrive, and not long after eleven when I watched her leave.

Interesting.

This jerks me out of my focus a little and I realise that I've been here far too long. It's time to go. I think about where my fingers may have been and retrace my steps carefully both upstairs and down, making sure I remove my fingerprints from anywhere I may have touched with my cardigan stretched tight across my elbow. The police do have me on record, and so I need to be careful. I make sure the bi-folding door is pulled almost closed, although not quite. I think this was how it was when I came in, I can't quite remember now, but I know that the houses to the back of Daniel's mustn't be alerted to what's gone on here. It would be very modern Hackney for someone with not enough to do in their life to ring the police to report a flat with an endlessly open bi-folding door. And I don't know why, but I want to give Miss Ponytail a chance to figure out her plan. I don't know what

Daniel did, or why, but there's something buzzing from deep within my bones insisting he deserved it.

I find myself pocketing two £20 notes I see casually lying on his breakfast bar and then I take a last look around, and as my eye falls on Daniel's glowing wine fridge I have a mad idea. The idea of not having a drink after everything that's happened here is impossible. I need to process and focus, and I wouldn't want to run out. And Daniel is hardly going to miss one, is he?

I start to rifle through drawers and cupboards, frantically rubbing away my fingerprints as I go. Eventually I pull out a holdall and then, one be damned, I grab six bottles from the cooler, which I muffle with two towels from the stack in the nearest bathroom.

Straightening up, I call 'Pusshkin', and for once he comes to me, his tail high and jaunty, a final stretch of his tongue around his mouth.

Very carefully we make our way home, Pusshkin padding along beside me as obediently as a dog, making sure nobody sees us.

It's fortunate that the maisonette above Daniel's home is currently between tenants. There is no danger of anyone noticing anything amiss from those quarters. The previous occupants moved out just before lockdown, and I guess the new ones have been forced to stay where they are until the situation eases. And Dodi's curtains next door are always drawn, as apparently she doesn't care for looking out on the street. I'll never understand that. Whatever, I'm sure no one will have spotted me.

Once safely home, I pour myself a glass of wine with a shaking hand from the bottle I'd already opened, not quite believing what has been done and, now, my part in it. My own very narrow life where nothing much ever happens out of my very limited routine doesn't seem so small any more!

I raise my glass, I'm not sure what for.

To my dead neighbour, perhaps. To Miss Ponytail, who stood up for herself. To Pusshkin for giving me a good excuse. To me for, well, I don't know, but to me anyway.

In short, I'm convinced I mustn't let this moment slip by without marking it in some way. It feels a big moment, and one to relish.

I turn on Spotify and start playing the Shangri-Las' 'Leader of the Pack' at top volume and on repeat for no other reason than it's the only song I can think of that comes with a motorbike as an integral part of the backing track, 'Motor Bikin'' rejected as too naff. Obviously.

Perhaps from wherever Daniel is right now, he will think that while the revving of the Shangri-Las' engine is not strictly comparable to the noise of his scooter, it's similar enough and therefore a fitting tribute from me to him.

And then a thought strikes me.

No, not that the fellow flat-owners in the house will be hoping that I stop endlessly playing the same tune, although obviously that's the case.

Instead, for the next few hours, I know I mustn't have another glass of wine.

Later

Caitlin

In my lifetime, I hope I never have to go through again anything like these first hours after I return home. I'm sure I've not been that wicked to deserve this.

As we finish our lunch, I feel terrible.

I'm hit by a huge wave of exhaustion that's perpetually washed with an unbearable heartache feeling of grief and a slow-wittedness from all the codeine. As experiences go, this is exceptionally gruelling to navigate while trying to seem as I do every day. It may well be a consequence of trying to live a totally vanilla life under lockdown when one has become used to having a secret, I decide. I suppose secrets mean adrenaline, and adrenaline keeps you energised, but only for a while. The adrenaline crash is not to be under-estimated, in my opinion.

And of course I've upped my secret quota exponentially, and clearly this has done nothing to instil any sort of calm or fortitude in my life.

If I thought my seeing Daniel in our illicit affair was a secret that could prove exacting at times, I find immediately that it's nothing to what the new secret I'm clutching close to me is capable of, with only me knowing Daniel is dead, murdered, and that it was I who found his body.

And my adrenaline crash escalates alarmingly quickly until I can't think properly. Within an hour of being home from Daniel's, even the smallest little thing seems to require an unfathomably huge amount of energy, and I feel flat and broken-hearted and physically in pain throughout all of my body. Hopefully that's not in a COVID sort of way, that's really the last thing I need right now.

The tiniest unexpected noise – the sound of a siren in the distance, say, or later, when I'm looking the other way, James suddenly turning up the sound on the telly for the daily Government briefing – has my muscles, muscles I didn't know I have, clenching and spasming with panic and fear. And the force of willpower that I need to hide this from everyone is just, well, something else.

I'm surprised to find that even though I'd not seen Daniel for a while prior to finding him as I did, I must have spent a lot of time thinking about not visiting, as suddenly I don't seem to know how to fill my time.

My thoughts segue endlessly on a loop between how I might alert the police to his death (but I can't imagine a way that couldn't be traced way too quickly back to me, and this would be foolhardy), what forensic or other clues to my identity might be lurking in Daniel's home (this is a hopeless train of thought, as I've been there so often that if the police can tie me to the crime through other means, then they'd certainly be able to prove I was a regular visitor), and what shall I say to the police should they arrive. (Do I look like a killer? I don't think so! is what I wish I was brave enough to retort.)

But it all comes down to one thing, and I arrive back at this point with increasing speed time and time again.

What I think incontrovertibly is: my own safety lies largely in not alerting anyone at home to my connection with Daniel; and if I can do this, then the result might just be that by then I might be able to convince everyone that I'm just a bit player in another person's nightmare, should it all come to light. I need time to get my story straight, and to try and work out what is going on.

I try not to think about our texts. Obviously the likelihood is that they will prove my undoing, but I can't do anything about them other than hope for the best.

And this is where all those earlier questions intruding upon one another in my mind inevitably end up. And then the whole depressing cycle of thoughts begins again.

It's shattering.

After lunch, I fancy James and Harry seem to be peering at my expressions with more attention than they normally would, and I see them catching each other's eye. If it were Ellie, whom I've always thought the most observant family member after me, I'd be more worried. But I tell myself that very probably the men in my life are just asking themselves quite when I'll fold, and start running around the house to clean and turning on the washing machine to take care of their clothes.

Or it could be a wholly mistaken impression on my part that I have inadvertently caused by paying too much attention to them, and suddenly my son and husband are looking back at me purely because I have been staring a bit too hard at them.

Or maybe I'm just a paranoid fool.

Hell, I've no idea, and so I tell myself to move on, and not ruminate further on it.

Sage advice, albeit impossible to follow.

I debate privately whether the Caitlin I used to be would have taken up yet the burden of doing all our washing again, or not. I decide that although she would surrender at some point, the chances are that she wouldn't today, and in fact not for a while. And so this means the new me can't either, for reasons of staying in character and being the solid and dependable wife/mother they expect, even though to keep this up leads to me feeling unbearably antsy at the same time as totally wretched.

Then at other brief moments, I feel a little more on top of my masquerade, and I try to reassure myself that I didn't know I had it in me to be so controlled, or that I could be such an actor. But it's all at a price, and I feel on a perpetual knife-edge.

At various points of the afternoon I make a bit of effort in keeping everyone well supplied with snacks, and as a ploy aimed at distracting everyone away from me this seems satisfactory.

Well, at distracting everyone other than me, I mean.

Increasingly, all I seem able to think of as the afternoon slips away is the sight of Daniel's body, and any time I'm not thinking about this, I feel overwhelmed by loss and despair at the thought we'll never be in each other's arms again.

Now and again I consider the killer and what might have happened, but this always seems something too dark and too abstract for me to contemplate, a puzzle I'm not equal to and, moreover, one that right now I don't want to be equal to.

I feel as if I've enough to handle, and any more will be too much.

I do my best though to rally, with the result that before tea Ellie and I make some very nice banana bread, and a delicious-looking coffee-and-walnut loaf.

I'm on auto-pilot, but I try to seem as if I'm standing back deliberately, in order to allow Ellie the space to take the lead in following the recipes; as if I trust her enough to make us something lovely without me butting in all the time.

It proves a surprisingly successful tactic, and I find these minutes as I stand at my daughter's shoulder are the most relaxing I have.

Actually, it's been a while since Ellie and I have done something mother-daughter together, I realise, and when I see how proud she is of what we make, I remind myself I should find a bit more time in my life to spend with her.

I've been, I know, a poor wife, and now it seems I've been a poor mother too, and all of this has to change, I decide.

I find I'm craving sweet rubbish, and barely care about eating as much of it as I like. It is the only food I want. It must be something to do with the sugar and comfort eating. Or maybe it's that I no longer have to worry about keeping as trim as possible for Daniel.

I must have fallen asleep as the baking cooled. I was slumped on the sofa and looked out of the window down the garden, trying to make sense of the nightmare. But on waking, I experience a moment or two of abject panic when I know something is desperately, desperately wrong, and for a horrible few seconds I am unable to remember if Daniel is dead; or alive, and I have merely had a terrible nightmare. As my heartbeat surges I have an overriding terror too that I might have been talking in my sleep, not that I have ever done this at any time in my life, I don't think.

And then I remember Daniel is dead. And it was me who found his body.

If I could have my way, I would retreat to bed, with a family-size pack of Kettle Chips and a bottle of chilled Chablis, as I nurse the hurt of where he has been wrenched so cruelly from my swollen heart. I want to sleep. I'm absolutely worn out. And I want to be on my own. And howl if I feel like it.

But none of this is what I can do.

Instead, I have to keep up for what feels like hours the pretence of 'me', and I decide that to avoid the running exercise issue which everyone will expect me to do as stupidly I've made too much fuss about it previously, I announce that I'm switching to Joe Wicks's morning workouts on YouTube as the streets around our house are getting too busy for safe social distancing on my runs. But, I say in as reassuring a tone as I can, I won't disturb anyone with my workouts as I'll do these up in the loft conversion.

Nobody offers an opinion either way on what I've just said as they are too busy in a debate of the merits of almond milk over oat milk, and then up in the loft I prepare the space for my 'workout session' in the morning while telling myself that I've just made a neat manoeuvre, as it means I'll have some time tomorrow to collapse privately on one of our Fatboy bean bags while the relentlessly chipper Joe Wicks leaps away in the background, with me making just the occasional stamp on the floor in case it's sounding a bit too quiet up here.

But this faint sense of triumph is quickly smothered. I remember my running is only a recent thing, invented purely to give me some designated free time, should I want to spend it with Daniel, which of course I wasn't allowing myself to. Until yesterday, that is, when I gave in to temptation. And nobody really expected me to go running in the first place. I'd talked about exercising more a lot over the years, but I hadn't really done anything about it, and I understand that this is something I'm rather prone to do, about all manner of things, and so now it's more out of character to have me and Joe Wicks in a stand-off.

I think about how one dishonesty leads to another, and before one knows it, it's easy to suffocate in a web of deceit.

I never used to have maudlin thoughts. The last few hours have crushed a whole lifetime's worth into my head. It feels very unfair.

As I bung some potatoes in the oven for supper, I have the shock of realising that although I feel dire, this is in large part because my negative thoughts are nearly always to do with me and what I'm feeling. And to think I've always believed I am one of those people who are never self-obsessed!

But to my disgust, I see that 'Daniel' himself has hardly entered my thoughts. To now, it's all been about what I've seen and the danger that finding his body has placed me in as I really don't want my marriage or my lovely life to disintegrate, or how much I'll miss him. And the sex with him

I am shame-faced as I stare out of the kitchen window and wonder what he might have felt in those final seconds. Remorsefully, I hope he wasn't too frightened, and it was painless and very quick. My dear, poor Daniel.

With the baking and rearranging of the loft space for 'exercise', I realise that I've managed to distract myself through the whole afternoon and soon my family will be demanding to be fed once again. I numbly begin to mix tuna with mayonnaise in a bowl, considering if Daniel has been discovered yet, officially.

As the potatoes bake, I scour every news website imaginable to see if I can find any report of his body having been found.

There is no news of him anywhere, not that I can find.

This is unsettling and not nearly as comforting as I thought it would be, and then as we sit around the table grating cheese over the potatoes or spooning canned tuna, with a crazy but compelling logic, my brain becomes fuzzed with a sense of it being really unsettling.

The more I think about that sight upstairs at Daniel's, the more I begin to doubt quite what it was that I saw.

After a while, I wonder in all seriousness if finding him was a dream, and that perhaps in real life he is still alive.

I don't think this to be the case, but I don't think it quite not, either.

I nip to the loo next to the utility room and use the opportunity to – almost – call Daniel, just in case. But as I'm about to tap my screen, I get cold feet and decide not to, silly notions of my electronic footprint intrude.

I have to go and check on him. I need to see again what it was that I saw.

Going back to Daniel's home makes no sense, other than I simply have to.

For a month now James and the twins have been ordering a heap of stuff online that has been delivered in dribs and drabs, with James unpacking the (usually giant) boxes, which he then carefully dismantles to have them ready for recycling. The final tranche has arrived and of course neither James nor the twins can wait to set it all up.

It's going to be – double quotation marks in the air for this, even I'd agree on that – a recording studio in our garden room. Slaves to their newest project, James and Harry have already spent hours and hours making the space as soundproof, and as comfy, and as creatively inspiring as possible.

Once, I'd hoped to write a bestselling novel in the garden room, but I only ever got as far as having a snooze on one of its sofas, my laptop remaining firmly shut beside me.

I rather suspect that long-term the intentions about to be hatched in the garden-room-slash-recording-studio – which is how James now describes the posh shed we installed behind a privet hedge towards the bottom end of the lawn – will similarly end up on the scrapheap of lost dreams. I'll keep these thoughts to myself though.

My family is not totally bereft of musical talent, even I can hear that, but I think they'll find ultimately that they are average to fair, rather than outstanding. Not that talent is necessarily a requirement of success. Who knows, they might even have that bit of luck that making it requires. More importantly, I do think it's a good thing for James to be spending some quality time with his children as he's not always done that.

Before they all head down the garden, I start to gather our dirty plates and say as enthusiastically as I can, 'Great idea, fam. Go for it! So you guys do you, and I'll do me in the kitchen, and you can show me the big reveal later. Unless anyone fancies giving me a hand here?'

That question is designed to buy me time. As I thought would happen, I have no takers.

Then I have an ancillary thought that perhaps I can work to my advantage. 'James, if this recording studio does the business, maybe you ought to move the grand piano in there too? A baby grand might be exactly the sound you need.'

James and I rarely bicker (and we never argue as such – James is quite stubborn when he wants to be and so I nearly always let him have his way, which I view as his reward for being insistent on actually very little), but the baby grand piano has been a small bone of contention between us for a while now.

One of James's aunts left us the dratted thing in her will, and since then its dark bulk has dominated our living room, to the extent that we barely use it these days. I love the idea of us having a baby grand in theory; in practice, not so much.

And it would be nice to have the option of us piling into the living room on high days and holidays. Thank goodness we have the kitchen extension, to tide us over the rest of the time.

'We won't disturb you,' says James helpfully. 'And you shall have the honour of being our first audience, Cat. Nice idea re the piano.' I can tell by the tone of his voice that he doesn't have any intention of moving it. 'We'll have to see how much space we have left once the mixing desk is set up,' he adds, just in case I hadn't got the message, 'and if we need a bigger drum kit. I don't want to lose the sofas there; if anything I think we'll need more seating.' He gives me a cheeky grin as if he's outsmarted me and this means the piano staying in the living room is now a done deal. Ordinarily it would be, and so I can't fault his optimism. He doesn't realise he has a new Caitlin before him, a wife who's no longer content to bend to everybody else.

I smile at my husband sunnily as if he's just said something brilliant. I'm going to need to be very clever to get my way. 'Oh right.' I keep my voice upbeat.

He knows me well enough to understand that I've not rolled over. 'It's important, Cat, that we have enough space that a band can play in,' James adds in a voice for dealing with someone of very little intelligence. 'Once this is all over, Harry and Ellie will want to jam there, and I might want to have some mates over too.'

I know the 'this' he's referring to is the pandemic. I like it that he thinks it will be over at some point. For myself though, I'm not so sure.

'Yes, the neighbours will be hoping you have enough space for a whole band to practise, especially if you can do it late at night,' I reply.

James looks at me seriously, gauging whether I'm serious. And I can't decide either whether I am being my normal go-to ironic, or if I am trying to irritate.

Honestly, everything in my life seems to have gone out of kilter, and now I can't even work out if I mean something when I say it, or not.

'Deal,' I say then to appease them all, ''re the space for a band, as long as I don't have to do any of the setting up.'

They all look horrified at the thought of me helping.

'I'm inspecting later, to make sure everything is as tip-top as poss.' This should buy me time to get to Daniel's home.

Then I make sure I high-five Ellie and say 'you betcha' when she says this studio is going to make her a star, just as I am walking past to the utility room where I bung a couple of towels in the washing machine to seem busy.

Harry looks at me as if he wants to ask me something, but then he doesn't say anything, and with his mouth still open he turns instead towards his father.

Once they've gone, I give it ten minutes, and this is just as well, as James comes back in search of his retractable knife for yet more opening of boxes. I have no idea where it is and so off he bumbles again.

I wait a while longer and once I've checked that they are deeply engrossed in whatever it is that they are doing, which they look to be when I take them fizzy drinks and crisps to stave off kitchen visits for nibbles, the knife has been found, and as the end-of-day shadows have darkened and lengthened, I dress in my darkest running kit.

I creep out of the front door with the car keys in my hand so that I can say I'm getting something from the car if I am seen. But I daren't actually drive it over to Daniel's – losing our parking space would be really suspicious.

There are moments these days when I feel as if I'm having to think like a master con artist. It's because I love my family I'm going to these lengths. I need to protect me and, by extension, them.

My feet pound the pavement, sending small electric shocks to my shins as I run the short distance to the house I know so well. These shocks feel like punishment.

At Daniel's front door I almost go to enter the code into the pad. But then I think better of it – his security system might log the door opening and shutting. I pull on the latex gloves I've brought with me and go round to find the side gate is only pulled to – thank you, me, for being so lackadaisical – and from there I can slink around to the back and slip in unobtrusively through the bi-folding doors, where I call Daniel's name to a void of silence.

He doesn't answer.

The first thing I notice is that the smell of Daniel's blood has grown a tiny bit more pervasive since this morning. The same somehow, and still very, very faint, but I detect a slight fungal edge to it now, although that could very likely be my imagination working overtime.

Obviously, Daniel's death wasn't a dream, then, and my spirits dip, and I feel that panicky flutter flare that I'm becoming used to.

But this result shows I'm not doolally, I suppose, and so I wonder what I'd have felt if he was alive and just sitting on a sofa. Happy he was there and clearly hadn't wanted to contact me, or upset that I'd hallucinated him dead? Embarrassed that I had let myself in unannounced, wearing rather sinister disposable gloves, I imagine then.

I decide not to go upstairs, even though ostensibly that's

why I'm here. While words such as de-comp and bloat do a jig around my brain, I decide that I don't need to see him again. He wasn't looking fantastic first time around, and I doubt the sight will have improved, although he won't yet be at the stomach-turning stage.

I hear a little bump, but then I realise it's that pesky grey cat again, at the bi-folding door. I see the inside of his mouth in his mute cry for attention. I ignore him, even though he has a paw raised in salute, and then he shoots me an if looks could kill yowly face.

Daniel's laptop is open on his large table near the back doors. Maybe there are answers there? It seems foolish to leave already, after everything I've had to do to get me here. Now I'm here, my thoughts have gone again to the question I had been avoiding all day – who killed Daniel and why? Perhaps if I find this out I can head the police off when they do eventually become involved, before my family hear of my involvement. And part of me is just desperate to know what was going on in Daniel's life, a man I thought I knew, that could result in him being killed in cold blood.

I slide on to a chair, and enter his password.

It's the number plate of his scooter, followed by a 1, I'm fairly certain, as I remember teasing him about it.

That doesn't work. I try the 1 before the number plate. And then I try the number plate with other numbers either before or after it. Nothing succeeds.

Damn.

My phone beeps in my pocket, and it almost makes me jump out of my skin.

It's Ellie, Harry and James WhatsApping me a selfie of them standing in front of a huge stack of flattened cardboard boxes (the recycling men are going to hate us), and they have various keyboards and widgets laid out in front of them. They all gleefully hold up tools they've used for the unpacking or the putting everything together and their smiles look very self-congratulatory, and I know this means they expect me to WhatsApp them back my equally pleased reaction.

I have to swallow my heart back down, so panicked is my initial response to the arrival of their message.

I jump up, noisily scraping the chair backwards in my alarm. Every sound feels deafening in the silence of the house.

I wrench off my gloves and stand in front of a patch of generic light-coloured wall and take a close-up selfie of my face with a pantomime wide grin slathered all over it, and my thumb sticking up alongside my jawbone.

'Way to go!!!' I type with fingers made awkward by my duplicity, and then I add three emoji of the dancing girl in a flamenco dress as if I'm shimmying in happiness at their achievement.

I check that my clothes can't be seen in the photograph and the bit of wall to either side of my head looks like all of ours at home. I resize the image slightly and fiddle with the brightness and the filter as the 'old' Caitlin would, and then once I'm happy I save the photo, and then add to my reply and press send.

Still in the old-me mode, I send immediately a second WhatsApp to them: 'Where do I buy my concert ticket from?!! A guest list? Chris Hemsworth as my plus-one?' accompanied by the laughing face emoji that has tears of joy spurting from both eyes and is angled to the side.

I must go. I look at Daniel's laptop, as I slip on my gloves again.

I'd love to have a poke around on it, but it's not the time now. I should have brought a bag with me to take it away. I could go through his belongings to find a holdall or something, but I realise I don't know if Daniel has a family – I've never asked him – or, if he does, how familiar they might be with his possessions. And so it could be foolish of me to remove either of these things.

And for me to carry the laptop home without it being hidden feels the sort of thing that somebody might notice and feel suspicious should they later be questioned about it, especially in my running kit. Who carries a computer when out for exercise?

I decide I'll come back tomorrow, dressed very unobtrusively. I'm convinced there is some sort of answer for me in the flat, if only I can work out what it is.

And it's only when I'm safely at home once more and back in my ordinary clothes and am heading down the path to the garden room to take James and the twins some celebratory low-alcohol lagers that it strikes me also that I know surprisingly little about Daniel.

I don't even know if he has any family, or who the pals he hangs out with are.

Indeed I can recall almost nothing Daniel has told me about his life prior to meeting me.

What has overwhelmed all my thoughts and time with him has been spectacular sex and then post-coital chats about what I was interested in. Clearly, I've been seduced by his lashings of attention, and in turn this has totally clouded my curiosity about him.

He's been brilliant in deflecting any personal questions, I realise, so brilliant in fact that I never noticed his lack of answers when I was dazzled by his encouragement to talk about me.

Nearly a whole year spent hankering after Daniel, and other than his favourite sexual positions (about which I feel qualified to go on *Mastermind*), next to nothing else to do with him has remained with me.

I should have wanted to hear him talk about himself, I feel, and his hopes and his fears. But I never made that happen. Whatever must he have thought of me that I wheedled out of him so little?

Not much, I would think.

Not much at all.

Ali

What is she up to? I ask myself, as I watch that bouncy woman – now looking very unbouncy – sneak cautiously around to the back of Daniel's flat. I log the time of her arrival in the notebook I keep on my table for expressly such jottings. I'd expected that she would come back to Daniel's, but she's ahead of my reckoning on when she would do it, which is annoying, but there you go ... Murders make people act in odd ways. I'm really glad I didn't have that glass of wine, as that might well have made me miss her.

She'd crept up on the place very stealthily, dressed in an equally foul but quite different running kit.

Her gloves – powdered nitrile rubber, I guess – gave a blurry ghost of paleness in the final shivers of daylight as she pulled them on, and my attention was snared.

I fancied I could hear a small snap of the gloves as she let go of the bit across the wrist, but I know this is merely my imagination working overtime and nothing more than that. My windows are shut and my hearing, like the rest of my senses, is no longer what it once was.

I study Miss Ponytail's gait. Strong and quietly confident still, even though there is a tinge of something else I can't quite identify to it. Guilt?

What does it all add up to?

I only have a tiny glimpse as she heads across the garden on her way in, just a couple of steps, and so I'm not sure.

But I want to know for definite her state of mind, as although she looks a bit flat it doesn't seem more than that. It doesn't quite seem to signify what I suspect she should be feeling, having killed a man.

Yes, there's more to this woman than meets the eye, I think. I'm beginning to see her as a worthy opponent.

I exaggerate.

Of course we're not opponents as such, it's more that I see her as deserving some serious time and thought expended by me.

I know the woman won't be able to see me as the lights in my front room are not yet on, and so I feel quite confident in staring in the evening murk from the safety of my lofty bay window.

She is full of surprises. She comes back out quite a bit sooner than I'd anticipated – a fleeting visit that's a bit too long just to leave something there, but not quite long enough for much else. I see that she's sliding what looks like her phone back into the pocket on her hip, and then she scoots off down the road the same way she arrived, presumably heading for home.

Pusshkin trots down the garden path in her wake. That is such typical behaviour for him. He always wants to be where he's not welcome, and as far as I know Daniel never encouraged him inside. I think Pusshkin's cattitude may have been learnt from me.

Initially I suspect that maybe Miss Ponytail has been downloading something from Daniel's laptop. Then I realise she was pocketing her phone and although she could have been taking photos, more probably it means that she's just received a message and she needs to return home at once.

Her business at Daniel's then is almost certainly unfinished. And it's very likely that she lives nearby, close at hand to Daniel and me.

I feel without a shadow of doubt that Miss Ponytail will be back.

To me, she didn't look like she got whatever it is that she came for. There was something in the narrowed lips I glimpsed under the streetlight that suggested this, a slight peevishness I would say, and perhaps of moue of indecision as to why she was there at all.

Join the club, I think, as frequently I find myself doing things that don't make much sense at the time, and precious little more later on.

And I am fairly certain she plans to return early tomorrow, as I doubt she'll sit around on seeing through her plans – she looks the type that once she's made up her mind to do something it all happens quickly. I expect she's the sort to be up with the larks rather than to be a-bed with the owls.

I'm reverting to my earlier plan. It's a good one. I'd better have a shower and put on clean clothes though.

And then I need to get over there pronto to be ready for her, just in case she comes back later tonight. But really, I'm banking on tomorrow morning. I'm guessing she has a family, which might well mean that another absence later tonight could be noticed.

As far as I can tell, Dodi is the only resident still in occupancy in the houses to either side of Daniel's flat. Not long ago I'd noticed a staggering number of those who live in our street had happily ignored the Government's instructions to remain at home. In their droves they had left London to sit out the pandemic in their second homes or in family bubbles elsewhere. The local burglars must be having a field day.

Still, I bet the natives of the villages and the seaside towns aren't too pleased about the influx of outsiders that will have swelled their numbers. I take their point, but I'm not wholly on their side as to me it seems to be quite a complicated issue. Inhabitants in those villages and seaside towns must also be very glad of the money the high-earning DFLs – Down From Londoners – inject into their communities in the normal run of things, probably keeping many fancy pubs and restaurants going, and so it would be harsh not to acknowledge that this transaction of who sits out the lockdown and where, isn't totally a one-way street of the rich abusing the poor. Although I daresay there are elements of that.

But this emptying out of residents buys the woman with the swingy hair a bit more leeway to do what she needs to in Daniel's flat. They won't be peeping out of their windows and noting strangers or wrinkling their noses at an unpleasant pong, not in this street anyway. I wonder if she's twigged that.

It feels good to have a sense of purpose, a plan again, I think, as I force myself to drink three large glasses of water and head to the shower to scrub myself clean. I'm not dirty by any means, but I realise that I don't wash my hair as much as I should as there is no one to see it. Also, the smell of Daniel's body seems to have clung to my skin and mingled with my own scent.

Tomorrow I'm going to be ready and waiting for Miss Ponytail. I've every intention of being at the top of my game for her return. I want to be on her side, I do, but I need to know more.

There's something about her that makes me feel energised. I know I've only snatched the odd glimpse, but there's something there, I just know. I like the look of her tonight more than I did this morning, I decide, as she seemed thoughtful and careful in a way I'd like to be. And, frankly, I'm curious about what could have gone on between her and Daniel to lead to such an outcome.

I pack a little kit bag of items that might come in useful, not forgetting some bottled water and a snack or two, some hand sanitiser, which I am trying to take with me wherever I go, and some throwaway gloves. I don't forget Daniel's hold-all either. As an afterthought I put in a couple of rolls of paper towel and some microfibre cloths, and some spray bleach cleaner. I might as well make sure my fingerprints are thoroughly erased.

As I do this, I start to think about hiding places in his flat from where I shall be able to watch what this woman is doing. Nothing obvious comes to mind, but I'm sure there will be somewhere. I think I'll decide once I'm there. And I hope that what I'm about to do will reap rewards. I rather think it will.

Showered, packed and wearing my dressing gown, I chuck some penne into some boiling water as I don't want to have to come back to eat.

Pusshkin looks at me quizzically.

I realise I'm humming a tune.

He creeps backwards until he's mostly under the sofa, still keeping an eye-to-eye contact with pupils large and mother of pearl as his tail slowly and uncomfortably lashes from side to side, clearly not used to my good mood.

His behaviour makes me laugh, and I realise I feel better than I have for ages.

Good humour is something I haven't experienced much lately.

And then I realise that it's not often I have the chance to rub shoulders with a bona fide murderer. Well, never, in fact.

A tiny thrill snakes through me. It's small but intoxicating all the same, and I like the way a sense of danger seems to sharpen my sensations. In fact, I rather wish that I was friends with Miss Ponytail – she's much more to her than dull old Daniel.

For the first time in a long while, I see that I'm happy about having something to plan and plot for as well. Something to feel enthusiastic about, despite the possible dangers that might come with getting involved with murder.

I look around my home.

Stay Home, Stay Safe.

SHSS, my arse.

Get Out, Get Dangerous, I say.

GOGD.

That's a good slogan, a better way of feeling alive than all that stay home malarkey.

I run over everything in my head, checking to make sure I've thought of everything. I think of the woman's stealthy approach this evening. I barely saw her but I feel inspired. I have so many things to learn from her, I'm sure of that.

I'm shocked to look down and see a glass of wine clutched in my hand. I can't remember how it got there.

But I don't need my wine, and I set it down in the sink.

Pusshkin looks at me with the sort of expression I think he'd have if I'd just slapped Bambi in front of him. 'Quit your blathering and eat your food, cat,' I say out loud.

I go back to the bedroom and look for something dark to wear, all the better to merge in with the shadows inside Daniel's flat. I change into some old black jeans that faded to dark grey and unearth a dark brown jumper. Perfect.

My pasta is ready and my humming is growing louder.

Things are about to happen.

I need to calm down.

But I'm excited at the thought of what the next few hours might deliver.

I have to make myself listen to a recap of the Government's daily briefing to calm down and make sure I've sobered up, and then I watch the news.

It does the trick, it's so depressing, with bungled PPE deliveries, disputed figures of infections and new symptoms being announced daily. And that's not to mention the rapidly rising death rates.

And to think that when Pusshkin and I saw the reports of the raging bushfires in Australia, it felt the bleakest possible start to the year as we cried at the sight of those traumatised koalas and roos. Now, that hideous tragedy seems an age ago, and a deeper tragedy is unfolding around us all.

I glance at the unopened bottles of wine that I took from Daniel's flat, standing in a cluster on the draining board.

I feel ashamed for my earlier excitement, as well as for the open bottle sitting there, like it's judging me.

I get up and push the unopened bottles to the back of a cupboard, behind my tins of soup and half-used bags of sugar, and I tug the cork off my corkscrew and push it into the final bottle, and then I stick it in the fridge.

I need my wits about me, and I have bigger fish to fry.

Caitlin

The next morning all hell breaks loose at home. I'm really not in the mood, for obvious reasons, especially as I had to turn off Radio 4 this morning as the world news was making my already-heavy heart race and I felt I couldn't catch my breath.

The true enormity of Daniel's loss is really striking home now. I feel torn to pieces with sadness and regret, tempered with a strong sense of feeling ashamed.

I'm ashamed because I realise quite how much this last year has all been about what I've wanted to make me happy, rather than – and this is a shock – about either Daniel or James in any sense. I thought I'd grasped this before, but now I see I was only just scratching the surface of true understanding.

My urge for Daniel was rooted in making me feel carefree and devil-may-care, and as a sop for meeting James in my first year at uni and thus having my wild and irresponsible years pulled back.

I think I may have been blaming James for this a little over the years, as if it's his fault that I've maybe missed out a little on the fun things about being a single woman. And of course it's not his fault; it's mine for stopping looking for the fun I could have as part of the life I've got, and me settling too easily for book club Prosecco-fests, and girlie evenings at the Marksman.

Poor James has never tried to stop me enjoying myself, but when Daniel came along I suppose I wanted to inject a little playful risky excitement into my marriage, fool that I was. I have friends who have failed to find a partner or can't get pregnant, which is hideous for them, but I must have stopped telling myself to be grateful for having these things gifted to me on a plate and instead I was restless as if my life was too comfortable.

And now I'm just so damn sad that a young and vibrant life like Daniel's has been cut down before its prime. And that mine is in freefall.

I see too I was so stunned by what I saw when I found him lying there that it divorced me from my emotions.

But this morning, today, I feel more in love with him than I realised, probably because I've never experienced anything quite like it before. But I also feel more in love with James too, as the realisation of what I've been doing to him for the past year, of what I've been risking, what I've been doing to us, is also really hitting home.

Maybe it's something to do with my age and being on the cusp of forty, but as the months passed since I first saw Daniel at the lido my experiences with him never strayed into the all-consuming type of love I first felt for James, with my desire that he be the father of my children (and actually still do feel quite often, as I rather fancy the idea of another pregnancy before that window of opportunity totally slams shut).

But I never wanted Daniel's baby. Instead, with him I found a heady sort of love, as if his pretty eyes and firm body were part of a fast-track romantic highway for me that I enjoyed being on, all big sighs and flirty looks. Of course it was also intensely passionate, and I was immensely flattered by the attentions of such a handsome man, and all of this combined to mean that for a long time I was able to give myself the get-out clause that I was only there for the sex.

My bruised senses feel cloudy still, but I think ultimately, whatever I told myself, I've pinioned myself between a rock and a hard place in the emotional sense. Daniel treated me as a woman and a lover and nothing more, and without the intrusion into our time together of all the responsibilities that someone like me has with a long-term marriage and family, it meant too that I had permission almost to rebirth me. And I'll never forget it was Daniel who gave me that new me, I see now.

But the rose-tinted glasses have fallen off too, and I totally accept in the cold light of day that it was an idealised relationship. We never spoke of money or children, or mundane things like loading the dishwasher, and I doubt very much our relationship would have survived those discussions.

I don't quite know what's changed in my head overnight but this morning I have a pain piercing deep within my chest.

I understand now what the romantic poets mean about heartbreak, as I feel mine has been wrenched in two. There's the loss of Daniel, of course. But slowly this anguish is giving way to another deeper, more potent sense of mourning, which I feel is the abrupt slaying of my younger-feeling self, making me sorrowful and self-punishing. I feel old, and emotionally desiccated.

My emotional landscape is further frayed by thoughts of my feelings for James, in the light of Daniel's death.

And my feelings about my husband are more complicated, but then I suppose they would be. We've had a lot of water pass under the bridge in our twenty years together. I do love him of course, and have never stopped doing so – but in his eyes I can't help feeling that I'm his wife, his children's mother, the chief bottle-washer at home, and rarely just the Caitlin who caught his roving eye above the rim of the shot glass at that party where we met.

I wouldn't want to be without James and the children, that's for sure, but I wish I could stop the world for a little, and give myself a chance to get used to the shock that I've had this week, in the knowledge that Daniel and I can never again spend another heady hour together. And to give myself the chance to return to Daniel's to find whatever it is there that I'm looking for, once I've sorted out in my mind what that may be.

I've barely slept, and so I'm up early and finishing my large espresso, mulling this over while looking out on the back garden and soothing myself by looking at the intricacy of the dew sparking diamond-like in the elaborate spiders' webs on the bushes.

Then out of the blue, I notice a young man I don't recognise padding down the lawn, away from the house. He is carrying some satsumas and what looks like a hunk of cheese as he keeps close to the edge of the grass, and he's moving in a cartoonish way, a bit as if he's Jerry sneaking up on Tom.

'Oi, you there! You, over by the bushes!' I yell from the back door in my most authoritative tone, noticing the window beside the door has been slid upwards and left open. I almost smile at myself for the daftness inherent in me clarifying to this stranger that I meant the intruder over by the bushes, as if there were more than one of them in our garden.

Amazingly – as there wouldn't be anything I could do to hold him back – he stops dead, although he angles his body towards the shrubs, which gives the absurd impression that he thinks he might still blend in.

I hear movement behind me and I look round to see a sleepy-looking bed-headed James poking his head around the bannister, as he must have been on his way downstairs anyway and is curious to see what I'm making a fuss about.

Now that I know I have a bit of decent back-up close at hand, I scream as forcibly as I can at the intruder as I march out of the back door towards him, 'Wait right there, laddie! What do you think you are doing, pal?'

Laddie? Pal? Jeez, I sound like an angry character in an episode of *Shetland*.

There's an answering mumble from the stranger, which is drowned by Ellie appearing from what feels like nowhere to say right beside me, 'Chill, Mum, chill. It's all right. I know him. He's a friend. Don't get het up.'

If there are ever three words guaranteed to ensure somebody already cross becomes apoplectic, then I think they have to be 'Chill, Mum, chill'.

Nobody is going to 'chill' at this point, least of all me, especially when I see my daughter is clutching some chocolate and a carton of orange juice, and so I know that she and this person are partners in crime.

I stick out my hand in command that the stranger stay where he is and angrily turn my head in the direction of my daughter. I can see by the warning cast to James's face – he's now lurking behind Ellie in his bare feet on the garden paving stones – that I should go carefully as we don't know this stranger, nor what he could be capable of.

Sod James. Sod Ellie and this friend.

'Explain yourself, my girl,' I say to Ellie, who has backed off now that she has realised that I'm not playing and in fact am really quite angry.

'And you, come here!' I fling towards the stranger, who shuffles a couple of yards forward and then halts again.

Now that I can see him properly it's a bit of a surprise to see how young he is. He's quite cute though, with green eyes and a honey-coloured floppy fringe.

Ellie tries once more a plea of placation, 'Don't get upset, Mum, I beg you. There's nothing bad going on, I promise.'

No matter what Ellie says, I feel it in my bones that there's something not right – if there was, there'd be none of this creeping about outside.

I study my daughter for a moment or two. She is wearing her PJ shorts and a tee-shirt, but there's a rosy look to her cheeks and her hair is tousled, and her lips enviably bee-stung. She looks defiant too, and actually a little like the cat who's had the cream. I'd bet my life on what they've been up to. I recognise that look. It's one I've seen in the mirror when I've got back from Daniel's. Well, not the last two times I've been in his flat. But all the times before that.

'Come right here, both of you,' I command Ellie and this boy in the sort of jabbing voice that brooks no argument.

'Mum, stop making a fuss. Please,' Ellie says, suddenly not sounding quite so confident. 'This is Harley – he came over early to drop off some, um, school stuff.'

'No, Harley didn't come over here early,' I announce firmly to the garden, and possibly any neighbours who might be staring out of their windows as they wonder what's got my goat first thing. 'I've been up for ages and nobody has entered the house in that time. One hundred per cent I know for a fact there's been no one come in through the front door since I've been up, Ellie.'

I'm so certain about this as both our front and back doors are alarmed and give a chime when either is opened, which was a godsend when the twins were small and I could hear if the doors were opened from anywhere in the house. Clearly this feature has its advantages now they're older too.

There's been no chime from the front door this morning.

Ellie and Harley glance at one another. They know they are rumbled, I can see it.

'Ellie, has Harley been up in your room all night?' I ask. 'Or alternatively have you both been in the garden room for the whole night – together – and then felt like a snack and so crept inside?'

My daughter's glow deepens to a blush and she tries to muddy the water with the usual teenage flim-flam about Harley coming over to see the recording studio the previous evening, and it got late without them realising, and Harley was sleepy, and so it was a good idea that he stayed over, and although they were in the garden room all night, she vows on my life that nothing happened.

I don't believe a word.

'Harley, have you been having sex with Ellie in what I am going to describe as under our roof?' I ask directly. 'And if it is all so innocent, Ellie, why did you open that window? The satsumas that tempting, eh?'

James is beside me now and I see him trying not to smile at my prudishness.

I sound exactly like my own mother, which is something I always promised myself I would never do. I know that James and I will very probably laugh about this satsuma comment later and he'll teasingly imitate me, once we're alone and it's all calmed down.

'Mum!' Ellie sounds panicky now.

Both she and Harley go bright pink, and I hear Harley gulp nervously.

He has the look about him that shouts he wishes he was anywhere but here.

'Are you aware Ellie is only fifteen?' I ask, and I stare at him until he looks me in the eye. I don't care to think about my own antics when I was fifteen with a married neighbour at the bottom of our street called Mr Rowse, back in the day.

Harley gives the smallest of nods. I look to see if he's contrite in any way. But from what I can see although he's sorry he's been caught, he's not especially regretful about what he and Ellie have been up to. Though I would suppose most teenage boys wouldn't be.

I twist in James's direction. He's watching but clearly is disinclined to get properly involved. I frown to let him know it's time he stepped up to the plate a bit more obviously.

'We're in the same class,' squeaks Harley then, as if this will make it better. He blinks rapidly and I see that he's a bit scared now that I am quite so up-close and personal.

Christ on a bike! Harley's voice isn't even properly broken.

'Jesus, Ellie,' I groan.

'Chill,' says Harry, who is now outside too, blinking in the sunlight as if unused to it, which to be fair he probably is these days. 'Harley's cool.'

I practically growl.

At last James makes his move. 'Well, we can't have it going on like this, as it's early and we'll be annoying our neighbours,' he says. 'Let's move it inside.'

Nobody takes any notice.

'Harley and I have been going out for a while,' whispers Ellie, as if that's any sort of defence.

'I. Do. Not. Give. A. Toss,' I say. 'It was technically a school night, not that that makes any difference. It's more that I don't want either of you sneaking around doing things you know we wouldn't approve of, or sanction' – I look between Ellie and Harry at this point – 'or strange people staying overnight in our house or property without our permission. Lockdown and no school is certainly not open season on you having sex under our roof, Ellie. In fact, you shouldn't be having sex at all, as you well know. And we are all supposed to be *isolating*, remember. It's fucking lockdown and we're all supposed to be fucking isolating!'

Pot-kettle-black.

But this is what you have to do when you are a parent, although most people probably wouldn't be flinging the F-word around with such abandon. Personally, though, I'm beyond giving a shit right at this minute.

'What about Harley's parents?' I say.

'His parents are doctors and were working last night on a hospital COVID ward, and they're sleeping in staff quarters anyway, and so Harley's older brother is in charge but he's a policeman and he had to work too,' Ellie sighs.

She's trying to distract me with the necessary jobs that Harley's relatives do.

Oh Jesus! How wrapped up in my own life have I been? There are things going on around me I have no idea about, and it unsettles me. I look at Ellie, and then Harry, and finally James, and right at that moment they all seem like total strangers.

James starts to say something about honesty and dishonesty to Ellie, but my attention is interrupted by an incredibly subtle two-hander of Harry signalling some sort of silent message to Harley, who responds with the minutest twitch that it's been received and understood.

I grab Harry quite roughly by the arm, speaking over the top of James, 'Out with it, Harry.'

Harry turns his face away.

I give his arm a firm shake and then he looks at me imploringly.

Although no words are spoken, he couldn't shout any louder that there is something he doesn't want me to find out, something that's between him and Harley, and in a teenager's world is deemed to be more serious than a sexual peccadillo.

If I still had any vestiges remaining of being the unshockable and ever-cool mum, it's at this point that they disappear totally. I will find out what is going on, or sodding die in the attempt.

'Harley?' Even I quail a little at the steely sound of my words.

Both boys remain tight-lipped.

'In that case,' I say, 'I am going to go to your room, Harry, and then the den, and I will turn everything upside down and rip everything apart. And I will take your laptop, your phone and your iPad and go through everything until I have discovered whatever you don't want me or your dad to know about. Don't you dare think I won't, Harry. And when I have found whatever it is, I will then be in touch with Harley's parents to let them know what you've all been up to.'

Feeling shaky with spite and a little out of breath, I let the silence hang, and even James looks at me with what I'd like to think of as respect, but is possibly more of a tinge of dislike. I'm sounding shrewish, and I know he hates it when I do this, and it couldn't be further from the sort of wife I always try to be. I think I'm angrier than I might be in ordinary circumstances, but to be fair to me I was already running on empty.

I think back to yesterday when I was staring at Harry's huge trainers and thinking he was still a sweet boy. Now I'm not nearly so sure. Every instinct is telling me I've been complacent, and the twins and my husband have all been taking advantage of that.

Ellie squints at her brother with a certain sympathy.

I feel Harry go a bit floppy as I've still got his arm in a vice-like grip, and I know I've won, at least as far as Harry trying to stand up to me is concerned.

My son's voice is weak and wobbly as he whispers, 'It's only a few nos upstairs, Mum. And just a touch of weed. Harley didn't bring much over.'

James and I exchange looks. We've done quite a few drugs in our time, but that was when we were at uni. And a little bit now and again at dinner parties since. But nothing serious.

Then James gives Harry a really frowny look, and I think at last, he's stepping up to being a dad.

Harry is much younger than we were and, anyway, this all feels so unlikely, coming from my lovable dopey son. My son with the suddenly huge feet and an obsession with computer games.

I mean, I'm not surprised at Ellie having sex as such, just mostly irritated she has the gall to be doing it in our house when we are there *and* during lockdown.

But Harry, although obviously the same age as his twin, has always felt the younger of the pair somehow. His Call of Duty fascination aside, he's always been much more the innocent of the two and generally inexperienced in the ways of the world. For instance, I would think Harry is pretty much still in the starting blocks as regards actually having sex with another person. And as for drugs, I hadn't had the slightest suspicion up until now that he might even have started down that route, aside maybe from the odd toke at a party.

In fact, I guess that we're so dumbstruck at the speed and intensity of the unravelling of the transition from child to teenager to what feels in this moment like proto-lout on the part of both of the twins that neither James nor I can immediately think of anything to say, or what the appropriate parental response should be, or any of the other things we probably should be thinking of.

Thoughts of Daniel swamp my mind for an instant the moment I open the wormhole in my mind to what I shouldn't be thinking of, and then I have to force my attention back to the problem before me.

'Anything else we should know?' I ask Harley, who shakes his head.

'How long has this been going on, Harry?' I add, just to be sure.

His voice is so soft he's hard to hear as he says, 'Only since before Christmas, Mum, I promise. And this is the first time with Harley – we only did a little last night, and actually it was mainly me giving a little weed to him rather than him giving it to me. And the good thing is that we've finished that now.'

This means that as I was enjoying my long-term liaison with Daniel, my son was busy morphing into one of those boys that other parents are relieved is worse-behaved than theirs. I daren't ask Ellie about the start of her sex life, as I fear I might not like the answer.

It's as if the echo of my own poor behaviour has blighted both of my children.

'Anything else we need to know about what might be up in your room, Harry?' James's voice is downbeat, as if he can't imagine there possibly could be anything else.

There's a pause and I think that getting information from a reluctant teenager is like trying to get blood from a stone.

'Only a very little packet,' mutters Harry.

I have no idea what 'packet' is, but I'm not going to show my ignorance, and when James flicks his eyes my way I know he hasn't a clue either.

Harry grasps this. 'Gear,' he says then quite loudly and as if he is talking to someone very stupid, as if this is going to make my muddy waters clear again, although I am still confused as way back in my day (which feels a very long time ago right at this second) 'gear' would only mean heroin, although I think probably that's not the case now as Harry is just a bit too calm for it to be quite that.

'Flake,' Harry says even louder, as if that is going to help me, and then he sighs in exasperation at my stupidity at not knowing what he means.

I hear one of the neighbours' sash windows open, so either they want to hear more about the drugs supply in Hackney, or possibly they want to take a photo so that they can report me and James for having a stranger in our house, a drug-dealing stranger to boot, which would be the absolute cherry on the cake.

James and I catch each other's eye.

For fuck's sake.

'We need to have a talk,' we say in unison, and although the last few minutes has been tiresome in the extreme I can't quell a little flutter of pleasure that both of us seem to be thinking of one another as a 'we'.

As I walk over to Daniel's much later than I'd meant to, I'm ostensibly on an outing to the supermarket. I have all of Harry's drugs stash in my pocket, except for the Nitrous Oxide canisters and the accompanying balloons, which James has taken charge of. I'm not sure what he intends to do with them, but I don't really care to be honest. I didn't want to leave the rest of what we'd confiscated at home, and I haven't yet decided what to do with it.

Harley has been ordered home in disgrace, and James and I are yet to decide whether we should speak to his parents.

The twins were sent to shower and dress, and while they were doing this James and I took coffee down to the garden room, where we had a serious talk about Harry and Ellie, and what they'd been up to.

It was nice actually – well after I'd tossed the blankets Ellie and Harley had mussed up behind a sofa – and I'd apologised for being a grumpy old cow lately, and James had said he was sorry for working so much and he intends to pull his hours back.

It was nice, just the two of us there with no other distraction, and I realised that work and COVID and shit times have really got in the way of James and me. I guess there are a lot of other couples who have been struggling in these respects too.

James looked at me with full concentration as I spoke, and I did the same to him. And after a while we even had a little snuggle where he put his arm about my shoulder and I leaned into him as we relaxed for five minutes and drank our coffee in a companionable silence. It was the best I've felt since finding Daniel's body. The best, by miles.

The upshot is that we concluded that lockdown is the ideal time for us to spend more time with the twins as, clearly, they need more of a guiding hand. They're not bad kids, but they've just been behaving as many of their age will when their parents are preoccupied by other things.

We're going to have a family night tonight, and then James and I are going to come up with some sort of a project where we can all bond and spend time working towards a single objective. Although not the recording studio – James spending time in it with the twins can happen alongside, but it would be too obvious for me to get involved and they might feel patronised, which wouldn't be what we want at all.

'Nice PJs,' James says to me as we stand up to go back to the house. I love it that I can tell by the tone of his voice that he's about to say a punchline, and sure enough he adds, 'They're not as alluring as those satsumas though.'

It's not really at all funny, but it does make me smile, mainly because I knew already that this was what James would remember about what I said, and I knock his arm with my elbow to show my appreciation.

As I head over to Daniel's, I think that it's tempting, so very tempting, to bury my head in the sand. To throw myself into repairing my family, which I know is important. But I also know that once the police find Daniel's body and our connection, my family will implode. James won't forgive me. I need to stop that from happening. If I can. And I feel I'm missing something obvious that I can only find at Daniel's, something that I should know and that is the key to finding his killer.

We've decided not to ban Ellie and Harley from seeing each other. I'm conflicted, to be honest, as while Ellie hasn't covered herself in glory and she really should be concentrating on other things like her schoolwork, I can see that Harley is definitely not the worst boyfriend Ellie could have, and actually he seems quite sweet. I don't feel he's a likely Mr Big in the drugs world, that's for certain.

Teenagers take drugs. Fact. I know this. And they have sex.

And I suppose part of a parent's job is firstly to try not to encourage this sort of behaviour, and secondly that if it is inevitable this is going to occur, to make sure they do it as safely as possible.

After all, lockdown isn't bringing out the best in any of us, is it? And so it seems we are living in strange times, and as parents it's probably best we don't make a mountain out of a molehill. It's important we don't drive them to even worse behaviour.

I do appreciate how miserable it would be for a teenager at the moment, unable to hang out with friends and do all the usual stuff. Ellie and Harry must be feeling the constraints on daily life just as keenly as I am, and now I've calmed down, I'm not as cross as I was.

In theory I absolutely should speak to Harley's parents, of course. Any parent deserves to know about potentially dangerous behaviour, I really believe that. But the fact there's a brother in the police force does complicate matters, as for me to wade in might cause intense family ructions. And as Harley's parents are both NHS doctors, I guess they'll be exhausted and have matters more pressing to think about than underage sex and a few drugs, that are to do with really important things like saving lives and helping those who have gone down with the virus.

Jesus, life is just one long series of compromises, isn't it? You try and do your best, then something happens, and your best just becomes pitched lower and then lower than that.

Isn't life unpredictable and complicated? I never expected to have an affair, yet I did. And I never thought there'd be lockdown, or that what began as a casual fling would end like this, or that I'd be struggling so. And I never thought I'd be shocked by my children in the way I have been. Or that helping them be better people would come with such a lot of contradictions and unknowns attached.

Then I perk myself up a smidgen with the thought that I've managed to negotiate all of this until now.

That has to be an achievement of sorts, no?

I turn my thoughts to the here and now.

Last night felt like unfinished business, I suppose, and maybe I convinced myself that if I knew what had happened, or I could find a solid clue, it would put the whole business to bed for me. Or maybe I'm here as I feel that in some obscure way I owe it to Daniel, to pay him a sort of private remembrance in the place where we shared so many happy times. As I say, I don't really know. It makes no sense, but I'm getting used to that feeling.

But what I do know for certain is that today is the last time I'll be here. I'm not going to come again.

I stand and stare about after I've slid the bi-folding door to, trying to decide what, precisely, feels different. For sure as hell something does.

Eventually I tell myself that what is so disquieting is that although it's not been long since Daniel died, already the place is empty and unloved, and bleak, a little as if Daniel's beautiful home is already starting to decay.

Maybe my imagination is in overdrive, but it's as if there's a faint layer of dust on the surfaces, and a dimmer sense somehow about the place, almost as if the loss of Daniel himself has sucked a little light away from the flat.

I wander about aimlessly, picking up this and that, and then putting whatever I've lifted down again. Sometimes my disposable gloves give a little squeak as I do this.

I sit at Daniel's laptop, but the battery is now dead and it won't start. I can't find the dratted cable to plug it in and nor can I find his phone either, and there's no answering ring when I dial it from mine.

I try to think through things logically.

But the longer I sit, the more I realise it's hopeless.

There's no point in me taking the laptop with me. I'm clean out of ideas now that I know that the password I thought was right doesn't work.

I've already realised that I know very little indeed about what I should. I know every inch of Daniel's body but next to nothing about him. If I can unravel Daniel, maybe it will help me feel differently about me, I tell myself.

And then I realise that I do know something important about Daniel or, more exactly, I know two important things.

Firstly he was very secretive, and secondly, this probably meant he was hiding something. And as I've learnt, secrets have a way of coming back and biting you hard. Maybe Daniel had a secret that angered someone so much that they killed him.

I look around me as I sigh. Yes, it's show-house bland. Expensive and attractive at first sight, but without the personality that knick-knacks add. Rather like the picture of himself Daniel carefully presented to the world, me included.

It's discombobulating. And suddenly I find him hard to conjure properly in my mind.

Well, I can remember him clearly, but it's not the nice things about him any longer that are springing to my thoughts, but increasingly some less appealing aspects of his nature. His pedantic way of going about things sometimes, say, or the odd snide comment or over-eagerness to laugh at those less well off than himself, or his slightly sniggery, high-pitched laugh.

I yearn to think well of him. But thoughts intrude of the tiresome way he'd spend an age working out what to wear and then laying it out far too precisely, as if he were sixty going on thirty, or how he'd insist on giving me a blini with horse-radishy crème fraîche and caviar when he knew I don't like caviar or horseradish.

These most definitely aren't the memories of him that I want to clutch close to me.

I loved him after all, and so I would like an echo of our passion to be what I'll always recall with ease, and not these other, intrusive things that the more I think about them, don't seem very nice at all.

I notice that my ears feel as if they are almost hurting with the thick silence of Daniel's flat.

Then it strikes me that what is unsettling me is there's the sense of something other about Daniel's home that feels a bit different to how it should, although I can't put my finger on exactly what this 'something' is.

It feels almost as if I'm under scrutiny.

It's an intense sensation and increasingly so, to the extent that it makes me shudder involuntarily, as if someone is walking over my grave.

My throat constricts and my back tenses unbearably as the hairs stand up on the back of my neck. I've read about this happening in detective novels but have never before given it credence. But it is true, the hairs really do stand up as if they have a mind of their own.

And then I see what would be anyone's nightmare.

In the shiny black glass of the wine cooler's door, reflected back at me, is the white of an eye and the shadowy outline of a man. He is crouched behind me in the dark where he thinks he can't be seen.

Staring.

Ali

I'd almost given up on Miss Ponytail.

She doesn't arrive until well past the time I expected, by which point I am completely stone-cold sober. It feels novel, and not wholly unpleasant.

I'd eaten all the snacks I'd brought across the road with me, and then I'd investigated Daniel's store cupboard, fridge and freezer, all of which offered pretty slim pickings, unless one is particularly fond of jars of preserved lemons or kimchi or Thai red curry paste, or powdered Huel 'nutritionally complete food', which I suspect I'm not.

I'd scoped out several unsatisfactory hidey-holes, and then moved a few chairs an inch or two in a darkish alcove in the windowless centre of the floor and wedged myself in behind them.

It's not a great place in which to hide, but it's almost definitely the one that best suits my purposes. It affords a good view of most of the lower ground floor, the bi-folding doors, the entrance to the cellar and the stairs. Not much is going to escape me from here as regards any comings and goings, and I've taken out the spotlights nearby to put me in a bit more shadow.

And once I'd done all of that and the laptop had finally given up the ghost and died, I spent an age cleaning everything on this level and in the basement and upstairs that I think I may have touched, leaving the bag of used microfibre cloths and the cleaning spray in a carrier near the back door ready for when I leave. Before dawn I'd risked opening some windows for an hour on the kitchen level to encourage, hopefully, the bleach smell to fade a little.

When Miss Ponytail arrives, she jolts me awake from a little doze. Who knew that doing a stake-out is so tiring when basically you are doing nothing but keeping still? It's a bit like travelling or sunbathing. Totally energy-zapping when you've done nothing at all in the physical sense. I make a face and try to yawn silently. Then I insist to myself that I am totally awake and raring to go.

With Pusshkin staring in through the bi-folding doors behind her, looking shocked to see me, I watch this woman sniff the air, and zip up her jacket all the way to her throat – it is a bit chilly in here now I've turned the underfloor heating off – but she does both of these things in a distracted manner as if she's not really noticing that she is doing them nor how things have changed in the flat. She's not obviously sniffing and so I guess the smell of the bleach isn't too strong.

Slowly I crouch down as she's looking out at Pusshkin and make myself as small as I can, but as I stare and she starts to move about, increasingly I find Miss Ponytail's haphazard behaviour thoroughly perplexing. It looks aimless to me as she wanders back and forth in the kitchen area, and without any method or real intention about it. What on earth is going through her mind?

Curious. Very curious. She doesn't strike me as an aimless sort of person, and it's obvious she hasn't come to clean up. She doesn't have anything with her.

Usefully, I have the charging cable to Daniel's laptop

curled neatly in my pocket, alongside Daniel's phone which I've turned off, and its charger, as I think this might force matters rather if she can't plug the laptop in, as I wonder what she'll do in that case. As I like computers, I realise that I'd sort of assumed that Daniel's would interest her too, and so far I'm not seeing anything that dissuades me of this. And I want to see her response once she realises that she doesn't know where his phone is.

I've already downloaded nearly everything on his laptop to my own system. All those hours of sitting in my window with Daniel as my subject have paid off, as through my binoculars I watched him enter his password on the laptop so often that, although it took me a few goes, eventually I was able to mirror successfully the pattern his fingers had made, and I was in. From what I've seen so far on his laptop, everything looks pretty boring to me. But I suppose I might change my mind once I start going through everything with a fine toothcomb, up in my window bay. I will do this carefully. I am convinced that the secret to Daniel himself will be on his computer; it's where he spent so much of his time. But, right now, it's hard to connect Miss Ponytail with the body upstairs, with what might be on the computer.

I read somewhere once that facial recognition and, especially, fingertip ID sign-ins only work when someone is alive. I think this might be true as I wasn't able to open Daniel's phone through his face or his finger.

However, I tried the same code that he used for his gate and front door keypad, and voilà! I was in, although again this bit of my snooping is going to be picked up when I am back in my flat.

For far too long Miss Ponytail wanders about as if seeking divine inspiration. She is clearly searching for something, but

I don't think God is listening though, if the increasingly vexed sighs she's letting out is any indication.

For a heart-stopping moment I realise that I forgot to move the bag of cleaning supplies that I'd left near the bi-folding doors, but she seems oblivious. Some detective she is. With all honesty, I think Pusshkin could do a better job of this than her.

At last she sits down, pushing her hands into her pockets and letting out a deep sigh. She opens the laptop and then closes it when she realises the battery is dead, her shoulders slumping. She puts her head in her hands, the picture of utter dejection, although after a while she straightens and then stares ahead with what look to be unseeing eyes.

She sits like this for a long while, but then the feeling eddying in the air around us both suddenly begins to shift and tilt.

And this is how I understand that she has seen me.

I stare back at her, not sure of quite what I should do. I hadn't imagined quite this scenario. I thought we'd confront each other most probably, but that it would be in a more action-packed way. Maybe that's only how it happens in films.

I definitely want to speak to her, if only so that I can grow old knowing I'd had a day when me and a murderer were in the same room and spoke. I don't want to hurt her or anything, more just see what she'll do.

Her eyes are unblinking. I can see them open large in trepidation, reflected back at me in the shiny black of the cooler door – the mirror of each of us to the other.

The stillness of the moment stretches. Her watching me watching her watching me. She looks horrified, maybe because I haven't moved, even though it's obvious that she has seen me.

There's a sharp intake of breath – hers, I think – but this alters the atmosphere in the room once more, pushing it this time towards something distinctly more extreme.

For the first time, I realise that this all seemed a better idea when I was a bit drunk yesterday, than in fact it is. If this goes pear-shaped and I end up hurt, I'll only have myself to blame. And fuck knows what I'm trying to achieve anyway.

She doesn't look much of an adversary, but that's probably what Daniel thought too, and look how that worked out for him.

I don't feel frightened of her as such. Well, there was a little tremor of something akin to fear, I admit. It's more that I feel wary.

All the same, I can't pretend that it's not gratifying or empowering to see how terrifying she finds me as slowly I unfurl and stand up. It's certainly heady for me, realising as I do that I have the upper hand, for this moment at least.

I extend my right hand and move a little stiffly towards her, announcing in a deliberate attempt to wrong-foot her, 'How delightful to meet you.'

She springs up in a manner redolent of those YouTube clips of cats that leap a mile in the air when they turn around to discover a cucumber has been placed beside them. Pusshkin, even in his most jumpiness of heydays, would have been hard-pressed to match this woman's jolty leap backwards.

And then she scuttles rapidly in reverse all the way over to the wall near the wine cooler where she stands with her back pressed hard against the plaster.

She stares at me quite panic-stricken, and I can see the rapid rise and fall of her chest as she breathes.

I probably should try to defuse things a little as I don't want her to have a heart attack.

'Hello,' I say, trying to make my voice sound reasonable. 'My name's Ali. And yours?'

She gives a small moan, and I see then that for me to speak in what is almost a friendly manner is even more intimidating than if I were shouting out an overt threat. That's a bit unexpected.

I take a step back to give her a bit more space.

It was the right thing to do, as she appears to be calming down a little, although then she starts to peer at me in confusion.

'You . . .' she murmurs in the way we all do when unexpected things suddenly align and are slotting into place in our mind.

And then she yelps, 'You. *You!*'

Realising who I am is obviously not very comforting, although I can see that she no longer considers me to be any sort of mortal threat. In fact, her reaction makes me feel a bit ridiculous.

'Should we sit down and talk this through, woman to woman?' I suggest. 'Tea?'

'Fuck off.'

I'm not offended, although I don't take my eyes off her as I decide that long-term I must reduce my own swearing. If middle-class Karens such as Miss Ponytail are resorting to foul language used at the drop of a hat, as I hear tell that they increasingly are, the poor things struggling to deal with their anxiety and over-spilling emotions during lockdown, it must be time for me to move in the opposite direction and clean up my act.

I sidle a little closer to Miss Ponytail, very obviously placing myself between her and the bi-folding doors. The

front door in the opposite direction is deadlocked and the
key is also in my pocket; this donkey jacket of Daniel's that
I'm wearing now may be ugly but its pockets are usefully
roomy.

Helpfully, I slide the front-door key halfway out for her to
see. She's not an idiot. I can see she knows what it is, and
understands at once that it's not worth her hoping to make
her escape out through the front of the house.

And so, after a silent battle of wills as we face each other, I
glance to the seat from which she'd sprung up with such
alacrity, and eventually Miss Ponytail jerkily lowers herself
back on to it.

I place another chair not three feet away, still between her
and the bi-folding doors, and I then allow myself to sit too.

Right now I don't think either of us gives two hoots over
the niceties of the correct two metres of social distancing,
which according to Government guidelines we shouldn't be
doing at all, even if we were outside and wearing masks.

It feels like stalemate as we gawk at each other without
saying anything for quite a long time.

'Okay, time out,' I say, the weary tone in my voice not
deliberate, wobbling slightly in my chair as I cross my legs. I
think the long wait has led to a sense of anti-climax. 'Let's
stop messing around.'

We both give a little start when there's the sound of an
ambulance careening down the road that the houses to the
back of Daniel's look out over.

'I'm Ali. Shall we get down to business? What's your
name?' I say.

When she doesn't answer me I remind myself that she
might well be terrified still. She has been caught where she
shouldn't be, and she has no idea if I'm on her side. And she's

no idea if I mean to harm her, or not. For all she knows, the police could be on their way.

'What's your name?' I say again. 'I'm not going to hurt you. And I haven't told anyone. About Daniel upstairs, I mean. But I really am most interested to know why you killed him.'

Caitlin

'I beg your pardon?'

The mad woman doesn't respond to my words. Perhaps because, I hope, I sound both sharp and a little scary. Or maybe it's the incredulous tone of my response that shocks her into silence. She appears to be swaying slightly on her chair and I wonder if she's been drinking.

I sit there with my jaw clenched.

The truth of it is that I'm totally knocked for six by what's unfolding. This is not at all as I saw my visit going.

She honestly seems to believe that it was me – me!– who killed Daniel.

I'm shocked. How can she think that I have anything to do with the mess of what happened upstairs?

In fact, I'm so dumbfounded that it takes away some of my alarm, just for a moment or two. And then I force myself to get a grip. This woman could be a murderous loony for all I know, with a knife in her pocket. And what the fuck is she doing here? Is it possible that she killed Daniel, although for what reason I couldn't begin to guess? I look at her again. She doesn't seem like a killer, or somebody who wants to pin her crime on me, but then again, maybe that is the mark of a successful murderer.

I do understand of course that it's not too great that she saw me sneak in here. It's obvious that Daniel and I must have a prior connection, and I know she saw me leaving Daniel's house yesterday, right after I found his body.

But, still, I'm almost offended that she must take me for being a right simpleton if she honestly believes I'd kill Daniel and then be so daft as to revisit the crime scene and, just, wander about.

I try to imagine how I might come across these days to someone who doesn't know me already, but I'm stumped frankly.

And, of course, if I shouldn't be here, then neither should she.

I look hard into the eyes staring intently at me. There's something beady and intelligent there that I really don't care for much at all.

Their owner gazes a bit too calmly back at me, although I wonder if I also see a tinge of excitement – or is it fear? – throbbing there. I'm increasingly thinking she'd be easy to under-estimate.

I would probably do well to bear this in mind, I tell myself.

And the minute I think this, it strikes me that she – Ali, was it? Yes, I think so – could be correct in her assumption that Daniel was a bastard. Those sharp eyes might have seen him for the man he was more clearly than I ever saw him.

But whether Daniel was a secretive bastard or just incredibly private doesn't really matter now. There is nothing that I can do to whitewash the fact of what I've done with him. And if one believes in karma, this crazy situation with the possibly drunk woman before me right now is very likely some sort of karmic payback for my shabby treatment of my family.

Maybe dealing with Ali is the price I have to pay for how very much I have let them and myself down.

If this woman will let me, of course. And provided I'm still alive.

What is her game? She's very hard to read. And, annoyingly, she doesn't actually seem drunk at all the more I look at her, I was wrong about that. Before, I'd pegged her for being an out-and-out alcky, one of those rank lost souls you feel sorry for when you see them wandering the streets always drunk, looking as if they are hobbling over the ruins of their life. Now? Well, I don't know what the fuck she's about.

I sigh.

It all fucking beggars belief. How did I find myself centre-stage in such a shitstorm of a shitshow?

My best plan is to go on the attack.

I snap at her, 'Shouldn't I be asking you that? I know I didn't kill Daniel. And from where I'm sitting, wouldn't you say that it's looking much more likely that you did it? What the fuck are you doing here, Ali?' I try to appear threatening and confident, though the thought that I'm only feet away from someone who could well be the main suspect as Daniel's murderer is daunting.

'And I'm sure that the police, and everyone else are pretty likely to think the same, aren't they?' I add. 'You creeping round his house when you have no business to be here at all!'

She doesn't say anything. And disconcertingly, she doesn't look particularly put out or worried by what I've just said.

And so, in temper I add something I've no intention of following through on, but which is verging on the kamikaze. 'In fact, I think I'll ring the police right now!'

'Nice one,' replies Ali quite quietly, and then she salutes me with a single finger at the same time as letting out a brief, unamused guffaw. She adds, 'And tell me precisely why you think it is that I should do away with him, Miss Ponytail?'

'It's Caitlin!' I snap in frustration before I can stop myself.

'Caitlin,' she echoes quickly.

I really don't like this woman. She's got a knack for wheedling me.

I go to rise but Ali raises her eyebrows in an insidiously menacing way as she places the flat of one of her hands firmly on the table in a sit-down gesture that is done with such authority that I doubt this is the first time she's made it. I almost feel jealous of her technique, her power.

And although every fibre in my being is screaming that I should be doing my best to get out of here, I find myself sinking to the chair again as I blurt out the first thing that I can come up with, not that I believe it at all, 'Jealousy, if I had to guess. If you couldn't have him, then nobody could, and that's why you murdered him.'

She snorts quietly to herself and I regard her in silence. She rubs her elbow over the table where her handprint would be.

'Daniel and me? Oh priceless. But please don't let me stop you phoning the police to report me. Or yourself. In fact, do be my guest.'

She nudges her battered telephone a few inches across the table in my direction and then waits to see if I'm going to reply to her or, presumably, ring the police. I push it back.

'I thought not,' she goads. 'Now, let's begin again.'

Ali

I suggest to Caitlin that we should head over to mine, saying it's obvious that neither of us wants to leave more physical evidence of our recent presence in Daniel's home than we already have, and we have things we need to discuss. Well, the word suggest probably makes it seem as if she has choice in whether to do this or not; she doesn't, I make it clear.

There's a bit more of a stare-out between us before she caves, and at last she dips her head as if in supplication. Although I don't believe she is particularly smart, she's clearly not an utter fool.

Before we leave I scoop up Daniel's laptop, and then I remember the carrier of cleaning stuff.

'Come on then, I haven't got all day. I've had a shit morning dealing with under-age sex and drugs, and I'm feeling very over being pleasant or nice,' she says bad temperedly as she stalks ahead of me out of the bi-folding door, and she and her ponytail then stalk around the corner to the side of the house, and I pull the door shut and hear the lock click into place.

Caitlin won't be able to get in again through the back door now, and if I want to go in again, which I doubt I will, I'll have to go in through the front door, unlocking the dead-lock and then using the keypad.

Up in my flat I indicate with a toss of my head that she should sit at the table in my window bay.

She chooses my chair and lifts up a novel I'd left open on the table. She gives the sort of shrug that tells me she's read it too, and looks my way with more of an appraising expression; the fact we have a point of similarity clearly surprises her.

She stares about, her brow wrinkling when she notices my stuffed bookshelves and the overspill of paperbacks piled everywhere.

There's not been anyone else in my flat in a very long time, and I notice that it's not very tidy.

Caitlin is here illegally of course as we're all supposed to be not letting anyone in who doesn't already live in the property these days, but this latest indiscretion can just be tacked on to our other misdemeanours, I don't doubt.

Pusshkin jumps up on to the table, ready to make friends. He must have raced us back.

'I might have guessed this would be your cat,' says Caitlin tetchily as she lifts Pusshkin up and places him firmly down on the grubby carpet.

Affronted, he moves a few feet away and then plonks himself down without taking his eye from hers, before showily Pusshkin lifts up a hind leg so that he can wash his bottom.

Caitlin makes a tsk noise.

But then her attention is diverted by the sight of my wine glass from yesterday, and her chin tilts.

It's as if her mind has suddenly changed gear, and it makes me feel a bit cautious of her.

'Was the wine why you were at Daniel's in the first place?' she asks. 'Have you been raiding his wine-cooler?'

That's a whole lot more perceptive than I'd given her credit for. But what the heck. I have no reason to lie to her.

'At first,' I confirm.

She nods seriously, as if pleased that she was right. 'A lucky guess,' she says. Her tone of voice tells me she likes to be proved correct in her assumptions.

I elaborate, 'I was waiting there just for you today though.'

'Me? What for?'

I nod towards the steps down to Daniel's front door, the top of which are clearly visible from where she is sitting. At first she doesn't understand, but then her eyes narrow and I see the penny drop.

'How long have you known?' says Caitlin.

I've no idea whether she means about her and Daniel, or whether she's referring to Daniel's murder. 'Not long,' I say as the answer is the same for both.

She presses her lips together, and says, 'It had been going on a while. But I had nothing to do with his death. I found him that way.'

I can't sense any sort of edge about her, such as a hair-trigger sense of anger, or jealousy poised ready to bubble to the surface. Though maybe she just hides it well.

Caitlin seems too used to being spoilt and cossetted, and life always going her way. Try as I might to imagine it, this woman before me in her expensive clothes just doesn't seem to have it in her to be a murderer.

I'd rather hoped Daniel had met his end at her hands. He was very proud of himself, and probably thought himself invincible. The thought of a thin and nervy woman having the upper hand in the final moments of his life, would have been dispiriting for him, and a firm example of poetic justice in my opinion.

Caitlin, despite the gloss, has something that's a little bit limited about her. By that, I mean I don't get the sense that she is used to putting herself in somebody else's shoes. I'm sure she'd disagree heartily, but the unobservant way she wandered around Daniel's home gave no sign that she is guilty of anything else other than being an adulterer, although I can see that she's sharpening up now that she is in my flat, if the way she is running her eyes over my possessions is anything to go by.

'Okay,' I say, 'I admit it's unlikely you murdered Daniel.'

Her shoulders quiver a little, she's so tightly wound.

'But it doesn't really matter what I think,' I point out, 'it's the police you have to worry about. They will be wanting to speak to you, seeing that you two were involved, and they won't find it difficult to get to you.'

Her body wilts as she sees the truth in this. She's so abject that I think she's forgotten to heed the thought just at the moment that if she didn't kill him, that on the basis that I was in his flat, then I'm also in the frame as an obvious candidate.

'Caitlin, I'm assuming you'd like to know more about what happened before the police turn their suspicions on you? Especially as, and I'm guessing too, that might also . . . harm life on the home-front,' I add.

She tries to stare me out, but there's something in her face that tells me I'm right, and that she's seeking some sort of get-out clause from somewhere deep within her.

She needs to know evasion is a waste of time, and that from now it's only the truth that passes between us.

I lift my phone and waggle it before her to reveal a surreptitious recording I made of her and me when we first spoke.

'Already on the cloud, location and dated,' I whisper, 'just in case you have ideas, Caitlin. And of course the police would be able to triangulate our two phones to prove we were together. It wouldn't be especially incriminating but it might give the police pause for thought, as your biggest hurdle is that if you are so innocent, why were you back in Daniel's flat?'

'Well, that puts you at the scene too. And why would you want to get involved?'

'Fair comments,' I acknowledge. 'But when Daniel is discovered, as he undoubtedly will be at some point, the police are bound to come here with some routine comings-and-goings questions.

'And I'm just a drunk. It's most unlikely the police would ever take me seriously as a murderer. I have no motive at all. Whereas you . . . Well, you do!

'Of the two of us, you and me, only you would be deemed likely to have a convincing motive for being Daniel's killer, in that he could have made life very difficult for you, should he have chosen to do so. Don't forget that I could too, if I were to be arrested now.' I'm rather proud of the clear way I've set everything out for her.

Caitlin stares disconsolately at Pusshkin, who returns her look now with his topaz eyes unblinking, as she digests what I've said.

She sniffs loudly as she twizzles the wedding ring on her left hand. She may have cared for Daniel more than I had bargained for, to judge by the sad look in her eyes when I mentioned his name, but she is aware of hubby sitting at home and the need for her to play it correctly from here on in so that she doesn't make what is already a bad situation worse.

Suddenly I start to feel a bit sorry for her, and I surprise myself.

'Don't panic, I'm not about to go running to the authorities telling them about you two. But, and I'm not being rude or trying to be funny, having seen your aimlessness in Daniel's flat just now, I think you need someone like me to give you a snowflake's chance in hell of finding some evidence that will clear you of suspicion if the feds do come calling, if that's what you were planning to do.' She sighs as if that's a bonkers thought. 'I might seem dim and stupid, but I'm not,' I add.

She's not convinced.

But I know that I need a project to perk up my life, and so it's a happy coincidence that also I am bored and nosey enough to want to know what happened to Daniel.

None of what I've seen about her is adding up properly, and frankly I'm intrigued.

'Suspicion is not the same as the police really thinking me guilty of murder,' she counters at last. 'And why should I believe for a moment you have anything that I need?'

'Try saying that to your husband when the police are unpicking your affair, maybe, and your comfortable middle-class Hackney life.'

Caitlin's eyelids flicker. She can imagine this scenario all too well.

'Or your children, when they find out,' I rub it in.

The eyelid nearest me positively vibrates with horror.

Bullseye.

'And perhaps ask yourself, that if I have nothing you need, quite how come it is that you are sitting in my flat. Remember, Caitlin,' I say, 'I really don't give a toss what people think about me. And compared to you, I have very little to lose, and these two things about me make me . . .' Actually, what do they make me? 'I'm a loose cannon, and I'm quite happy to be so. Trust me on that,' I finish a bit lamely.

Caitlin grunts nervously, and her knee jiggles furiously.

I may have over-played my hand and I need her to calm down.

And – I know this already! – I must rein in this inclination to be mean; she doesn't know me, or that I'm toying with her because, well . . . mainly because I can mess with her head a little if I want to. But it's not nice, I know. Just ask Dodi about that. The heady feeling of having someone to interact with while I'm almost sober – for the first time in, quite literally, months – has gone to my head a bit too much. Heck, I need to get a grip and start acting a bit more rationally, otherwise I'm going to end up more loopy than this Caitlin.

She's not going to be any good to either of us if she gets panicked all over again.

I say in a much more conciliatory way, 'But I'm not threatening you, Caitlin. I really do want to help you. Please believe me on this. I'm not so irredeemable that I can't see that you need a new start in getting your home life back on track, or that your children need you. This Daniel issue needs sorting as quickly as possible. I know it's a truism and all, but two heads are better than one. I'm bored. Also, I doubt very much that Daniel utterly deserved what happened to him, and even if he were killed randomly it's not overly reassuring to me that I live directly opposite, alone. And so, to me it seems obvious that the best thing is if we pool our thoughts, and try and come up with what really did happen.'

She's putty in my hands after that.

Privately though I reserve my opinion to change my mind over what Daniel utterly deserved.

Naturally I follow Caitlin home. I feel light-headed at having had such a long conversation with somebody; it's been months since I've done that, and I rather like the sensation.

Caitlin isn't as chirpy about our chat as I am though. She's distracted and heavy-footed. You'd think she'd be keen to make sure she is looking after herself as much as possible by keeping an eye out for what is going on around her. But, no, she's meandering along lost in thought with a mask dangling from a forefinger. She appears as if she has the cares of the world on her shoulders. And she doesn't look behind her once. She seems to have remarkably little sense of self-preservation about her, which is, I guess, a consequence of a pampered upbringing, where there'd always be a layer of money and privilege to cushion any blows. But this isn't a good thing out in the real world.

But my more street-smart attitude isn't so brilliant either. I grew up on one grotty kitchen-sink estate after another around various parts of London, which is going to give anyone pretty low expectations of what life throws out, and so I think my own tip into self-sabotaging behaviour springs in part from me somewhere along the way giving up on the struggle to keep going. It felt pointless, and I felt pointless, and I guess I just wore myself out in the end by thinking everything so depressing.

In contrast, and in spite of what's happened to Daniel, Caitlin seems to have a more optimistic view of human nature than me and what life will do to us all. So deep in thought is she that it doesn't seem to even enter her mind that I'd do something such as trail her down the street.

It didn't even take me long to find her. After she left my flat, I forced myself to wait two minutes before nipping out after her. She had stopped at Mehmet's to buy some cigarettes and a lighter, lighting up immediately outside. It's been a while since she smoked, I can tell from her inexpert way of cupping the fag from the wind, and a couple of seconds later, her cough.

It's not long before she pulls off the band holding her hair up, and I see her checking in a distracted way her reflection in the window of a car, running her fingers through her hair and then glancing at her phone. She hesitates and looks to be practising the sort of expression I suppose she thinks her family will expect of her. For a moment I think she is getting ready for a selfie, but she doesn't take one. I think she's just overwhelmed by what's happened, and is worried about whether she can carry off at home her impression of innocence.

Yes, I see that she does have a lot to think about.

But nobody said that new starts don't cost a lot, and I'm not talking about money.

She turns into a garden only a few streets away from my flat. I'm about ninety per cent convinced that she will turn up tomorrow back at mine as we arranged. I'll bet my bottom dollar though that she'll be an hour late on purpose so I'm shown I can't boss her around.

Instead of returning home, on impulse I sneak into Caitlin's neighbour's back garden. I manage to find a position behind some bushes where I won't be too obvious if they look out of their window, and I get quite a good view inside Caitlin's house.

Caitlin and her partner have lavished money on the property, that's obvious. It's actually very nice. I think I could be happy living there.

Two slouchy teenagers leave the garden room at Caitlin's chirrup to them from the back door. I tuck their names away in my mind – Ellie and Harry. I guess these were responsible for Caitlin's bad-tempered comment about underage sex and drugs. Be that as it may, they seem like nice, decent kids to me.

I hear her speak in a voice that unless I knew the truth I would swear was happy, suggesting that they put what happened earlier aside to be dealt with another time and that this evening they all have a Tiger King 'mega-sesh', with everyone dressed as either Joe Exotic or Carole Baskin.

Bless her, she is trying hard. I hope she doesn't overdo it – if anyone is suspicious already, this might seal the deal for them.

Caitlin proves herself a better actor than I would have thought though. She makes it sound such a tempting way of spending an evening that I'd like to be there too, almost.

A rather striking man who is clearly the children's father, and whom I presume is Caitlin's husband, saunters up the garden in the wake of the kids saying he'll only watch it with them if he can be a tiger or better still, a lion. He also has the attitude of middle-class privilege that Caitlin does. He doesn't stop to lock the garden room door, apparently secure in the thought that nobody is going to take whatever is in there. Or that if they do, it can all be easily replaced.

As Caitlin calls 'hurry up then, Mufasa' and he smiles back at her, I can see that indeed she has a lot to lose should her affair come out.

I know that it's easy to make incorrect assumptions about family life from what one sees on the surface. But even with my most cynical gloss on this, I'd have to admit they seem a blessed family. They're good looking and with everything they could possibly want – I mean this in terms of their relationship to one another, and not in the material possessions they've cocooned around themselves. They seem close and pleased to be together.

And although they look like an advertiser's dream of the sort that usually has me reaching for the sick bag, and while I know there is a maggot of dishonesty wriggling away underneath it all as far as Caitlin is concerned, suddenly I get an ache in my jaw and a pricking behind my eyes, as if tears are threatening.

I know this idealised image of family life is in some ways a sham and a façade – the presence of Daniel attests to that – but there is something nice and heart-warming about it all the same, and my own secluded life seems the dark side of the moon. I've never had a particularly happy home life and so I don't have much to compare it with, but I guess the jury's out on whether I should have taken a few more risks and opened my heart to the possibility of finding love.

Despite the affair, despite the secrets, I sense something strong and good is beating at the heart of this family before me. Something it's well worth Caitlin working hard to protect.

I slowly inch a bit further down the neighbour's garden, and then with my face almost poking through some trellis I watch for a long time, hearing snippets of laughter from those teens larking around in the kitchen as they pour lots of things into a huge jug, and then the father's voice gets their attention and I think the Tiger King telethon must be about to begin on their giant telly.

It's time for me to go, otherwise I'm going to risk depressing myself over this glimpse into a future I never allowed myself to be open to.

All the same, as I walk back home, I realise that the sight of a family looking as if they are pleased to spend an evening together has lifted my mood, despite the tinge of sadness I feel about the snake of deceit twisting from Caitlin's heart. Even so, and while it's a shitty world, it's not all bad to judge by the joshing between Ellie and Harry. I find this a comforting thought.

Even when I'm back in my empty flat, my mood remains upbeat. So much so in fact that my usual large glass of wine offers little appeal, and so I reach for a small one. I can't remember the last time that at this point I wouldn't have been climbing the walls in angst at the thought of such a small little leveller.

Pusshkin and I stare at each other.

'Roll on eleven o'clock tomorrow morning,' I say to my cat, who gives a little beep of a mew back to me. He meows again when I tell him, 'I bet she's late.'

I find myself smiling, and then I add, 'I'd best get a bath and good night's sleep in as I want to be on my mettle.'

I look around, noting the dirty dishes by the sink and the piles of old post on the table. I'd felt a fierce sort of pride in my mess when Caitlin sneered. But now it's closer to a stab of shame, and I start scooping rubbish into a bin bag just as the Thursday night Clap for Carers cacophony erupts.

Stay Home

It's eight o'clock, and I swear to God that Pusshkin's ears are flattened in suspicion. It's been a long time since he's heard me contemplating having a bath and going to bed early. And as for housework, well, frankly he can barely believe his eyes.

Latest

Caitlin

The next morning I get up feeling jittery.

Each day I seem to feel a little more weary, a little more frazzled, more unravelled, and I've just about given up any pretence of working. All of which is apparently happening anyway right across the nation from what I can tell – everybody I know seems to be finding it hard to concentrate, what with the normal rhythm of our lives so twisted out of shape. Although, on top of what I'd be feeling in any case, the abrupt entry of Ali into my life has made every little nerve misfire today feel of catastrophic proportions. Smoking yesterday hasn't helped my sense of well-being either. Most definitely not. I haven't done it for the past couple of years, and frankly I was a fool to think I'd get off scot-free for dipping my toes back into that particular murky pond.

I could shake Daniel until his teeth clacked against each other, if he were alive still, because if I'd never met him I wouldn't be in this mess. So while obviously I blame myself for the trouble I'm in, and rightly so, childishly I want to wallop him too.

Luckily the Twittersphere is awash with other people moaning about feeling exhausted through general pandemic anxiety and so I'm going to allow James to assume that's what has happened to me, rather than I'm suffering an intense sense of impending doom and chickens coming home to roost, or that increasingly I seem to feel a huge need to anaesthetise myself to take the edge off the harsh brutalities of the world about me. It's not easy just making it through, hour by hour.

Catching Harley in our garden hasn't done anything for my confidence either. I think this is because that altercation has come to feel like the tip of the iceberg of what I – or in this case, what I don't – know about things. It hints at a slippery slope of horrors lurking beneath the outwardly calm veneer of our lives.

While what Ellie and Harry have been up to wasn't in itself the crimes of the century, those few short minutes in the garden got me thinking about us all, which I realise I haven't really done very much of recently. Once I started down that path, it wasn't long before I had to slough off quite a few assumptions that I'd been making happily for all these years about James's and my parenting skills, and our comfortable existence.

But even though everything the twins have been up to is now out in the open – well, I hope it's everything – I can't stop feeling that both Ellie and Harry seem to be acting oddly through appearing so normal. Although they're amenable enough in the aftermath of the Harley debacle, I don't know, I seem to sense deep within their uncharacteristic docility there might be secrets and subterfuge at every turn, just waiting to burst through out of nowhere and trip me up.

Perhaps my own guilty conscience is clouding my view of my children but I feel uneasy about our home dynamics.

I said as much to James last night in the bedroom as we changed our clothes and the twins laughed and joked in the kitchen. I chose head-to-toe leopard print and James opted for double denim and my wide Western belt with tassels for our Joe Exotic extravaganza.

I'd just dumped the wraps and some tobacco and Rizlas I'd confiscated from Harry on the linen duvet cover.

'Let's just get through the next few weeks, Cat; I really don't want arguments all the time. But chuck all that down the toilet,' James said with a deep sigh. 'Other than the weed.' He raised an eyebrow at me. 'Oh, and packet stands for cocaine these days, so Google tells me.'

I haven't done drugs since the twins were small, and even then it wasn't much. But James's idea to save the weed was a good one. He rolled a spliff, his hands still somehow as expert as they had been in his university days, and we smoked half of it while lying on our clean, white bed. It worked, making me feel less tightly wound and like I might be able to get through the evening in reasonably good cheer. We all need a bit of a break. Maybe it was the weed, or just that there was so much else going on in my life, but I gave myself permission not to worry about the twins for just an evening. I also told myself that I wasn't, under any circumstances, to think about either Daniel or Ali.

Before we joined the twins James and I cleaned our teeth and washed our hands, and then to take away any lingering whiff of weed I squirted hairspray on both of us and styled our hair appropriately.

We had a moment of the sort of larking about that we always used to do, playfully pushing each other out of the way as we jostled to see our reflections in our large freestanding mirror, and the weed kicked in and made us laugh as we realised how ridiculous we looked.

'Good to go?' James asked me, with a final squirt of the hairspray.

'Good to go,' I answered, and very much hoped it was true.

The evening was much easier than I had expected it to be, with our uncharacteristically unsweary and well-behaved kids (the sort of offspring in fact who would love 'a den' – success at last, perhaps).

While we'd been busy upstairs, Harry and Ellie had invented a drink they named Tiger Brew. It seemed pretty much to decimate all the fizzy drinks in the fridge, but I thought I'd worry tomorrow about how all of this would be replaced, with supermarket home-delivery slots non-existent for ordinary folk.

'That looks amazing,' I said as I peered at the jug of neon drink, and my heart felt warm when I noticed Harry's bashful smile at my praise, and Ellie's grin.

With what I hoped looked like a playful raise of my eyebrows I added a sizeable splash of tequila to the brew that I poured for me and James, shaking my head when Ellie hopefully pushed her glass my way for a shot too, with a 'what are the chances, Mum?'

James and I smiled a no, and as Ellie gave in gracefully my husband and I clinked our glasses together.

For that moment, as James looked affectionately into my eyes, I saw again the young man I'd first fallen in love with. A little older perhaps, but just as attractive, just as wonderful. It was a good moment.

I microwaved a ridiculous amount of popcorn, and then the four of us settled down to binge-watch Tiger King. Daniel and Ali never felt far away, to be honest, but luckily I didn't need to concentrate too earnestly as what was on our large screen was all so wild and hard to credit anyway, and so I think my family all thought I was enjoying it as much as they were.

I snuggled close to Ellie, and James plonked himself near to Harry. The sight of James checking to see if his son was having a good time was sweet, and I put my arm around my daughter to pull her close, as I allowed her the occasional sip of my drink.

I know that only that morning I'd wanted the twins to feel bad about the sex and the drugs and breaking the lockdown rules, but as we laughed along at the bizarre antics on-screen, in the dim light of our telly area I felt all I needed just then was to have my family around me, and us to be having a fun time.

I know that kids of this age are that weird blend of trying to push at the boundaries, and yet they're also – just now and again – children still. And as we sat together I thought there was something terribly touching with just a tinge of heart-ache about James and me acting as if we were the parents I'd always hoped we'd be, while the twins behaved as the children that they no longer were. It was almost as if we were all saying goodbye to something, but I prayed it was in a way that was going to usher in a new and better version of our nutshell family.

I told myself too that if my world was about to come crashing down, it would be good for Harry and Ellie if I'd banked a recent good memory of them having a great time with James and me. I knew our life all together might be about to take a hideous downturn.

My determined mood continued when we called time on the evening, and as neither me nor James felt ready to sleep once we had closed the bedroom door, we shared the rest of the spliff, hanging out of our bathroom window as we muffled our giggles like teenagers do. And then in bed, we had sex, urgent and needy, him more urgent and me more needy.

It drew a natural conclusion to a most peculiar few hours. While I never quite was able to stop myself feeling melancholic over Daniel, this brief sojourn ended up as something that I found almost unbearably precious, in spite of everything.

In fact, I think this odd evening of having both my grief and my irritation with Ali muffled by an unexpectedly nice time, ended up giving me a bittersweet experience in my husband's arms, the like of which I've never had before. I know that I felt full of love for my family, and I wished I was worthy of their love for me.

As I went to turn off the bedside light I thought I caught James looking at me, just for an instant, as if slightly confused. He didn't say anything though, and not long afterwards he was asleep.

Within what felt like minutes of James dropping off, the dawn chorus became very loud outside, the sound jarring, and I found my mind suddenly swamped with a whirl of problems to do with this (the stuff going on here at home with the twins) and that (Daniel and Ali).

I got out of bed and closed the window, and when I lay down besides James again, I tried to decide what I should do.

And then it struck me that it's almost as if out of nowhere just a tiny sprinkle of the dust from Ali's hedonistic nature rained down on me, and I wondered if perhaps she had more to offer than I'd given her credit for. The very thought of her suddenly seemed calming. She's a nuisance and a pain, but at least having her know about me and Daniel, means that I'm not stumbling about in this quagmire of emotion totally alone.

I remembered how James and I had laughed in the bathroom a short while ago, and I smiled to myself.

That sneaky spliff had brought us closer together than I could remember for a long while. The irony of this wasn't lost on me, considering how witchy I'd been in front of Harley and the twins. But sharing that moment with James was such a boost, and for once I was pleased to have double standards.

I realised then that 'fun' was something Daniel and I had never experienced together. I'm glad it's with my husband I've rediscovered this forgotten side of me.

Or maybe Ali's refusal to give a fuck has shown me that sometimes it is fine not to care, as I seem to do, about what others think of me. Normally, keen not to seem out of step, I nod along with the parents at the school Ellie and Harry go to about ways to censure and control, but this last evening I've done it my way. Not necessarily the best way, but my way, and I think my children and my husband liked it. I know I did.

I force myself to take a deep breath and tell myself that this will be okay. With Ali, I think, on my side, we will find a way to get out of this. If we can find out what really happened to Daniel, I can save my family. Maybe I can even create this version of us as our new normal.

The twins are dressed and downstairs by eight thirty in the morning. Off their own bat, and as if they are on their best behaviour still.

'Three decent hours' schoolwork with no dicking about,' James bargains with them over breakfast, 'and then we can get stuck in making our first recording. Deal?'

'Deal!' they say as one.

And I text Ali to say I can't get there before noon at the earliest, although I can't quite make sense of her laughing face emoji in reply.

Then I remember something I'd already agreed to do later on, which is Zooming Dukie as we watch Sophie Ellis-Bextor's Kitchen Disco and drink too much Prosecco. Not at all what I feel like doing later. I mean, I know I need to keep up the pretence of normality, but in the cold light of day with undiscovered murder on my mind, dancing and laughing is the last thing I feel like doing. I can't even claim a cold or a headache to get out of it as then everyone will be thinking I have the first signs of COVID. Honestly, in some ways a week or two flat out with Corona virus sounds almost tempting right now.

But first I've got to go over to Ali's and deal with whatever she has discovered on Daniel's laptop, and that may be a bumpy ride too.

I make sure there's a huge pile of sandwiches for the twins and James to take with them to the studio (which I'm becoming rather a fan of as it is diverting so much attention away from me) and then I check that nobody needs me for anything.

As I stand in the hall looking at my messages and fiddling with my trainers, I can hear James on a last-minute call with the irate head of year from the twins' school.

It sounds like there'd been an important Zoom lesson earlier in the week that Ellie and Harry had missed, not that either of them had mentioned anything to James or me, or written it in one of the boxes on the large calendar I've hung on the kitchen wall for precisely this sort of thing, which would have meant that I could have given them a nudge.

Over the weekend I'm going to go through their timetable with them, I resolve. This is not the first time they've been missing in action, I know, and clearly the school is most unimpressed.

James sounds calm and very reasonable, and I am sure he will soon have whoever has rung eating out of his hand, as he's good that way. The last words I hear my silver-tongued husband say before I leave is him laying the blame for the twins' oversight firmly at my door – I've been 'busy', apparently – and then he apologises profusely on my behalf.

I don't believe he does this for any reason more sinister than he wants to end the conversation as quickly as possible.

Normally I'd be irritated and want him to share the blame, but now I think this blame he bats my way is my due.

Ali looks a different woman when she opens the door to me. She's trimmed her hair and is wearing a perfectly respectable skirt and jumper. She may have even spritzed herself with scent.

As I step into her flat I notice that her living room looks tidier too and has a fresh Zoflora smell wafting about rather than the stale must of the previous day.

I'm taken aback at how nice she has made the room look, with her books more organised and the clutter gone, and when I appraise Ali herself I realise – rather to my shame, as I had categorised her as a no-hoper – that actually it wouldn't take much at all to make her really quite presentable.

The cat is curled up dozing in a sun puddle, and he opens an eye, but when he sees it's me, closes it dismissively and promptly goes back to sleep.

Ali prepares us a cafetière of coffee, while I sit in the chair by the window. The atmosphere feels a bit tense, a little as if we are circling each other once again as we calculate what the other is thinking. We are just two very different women, basically strangers, brought together by Daniel's death.

I see Ali's hand shaking a little as she pours the coffee, but she seems sober.

I don't much like the woman but she is making an effort and that's more than I would likely do in her position, if our roles had been reversed. And from what I've discovered by myself, she's probably correct to assume that she has more snooping skills than I have.

For a moment I feel a tingling of hope – we might even find out who did this.

'Right, where shall we begin?' I ask. 'Have the police been there? Or anyone reported his body?'

She shakes her head to both of my questions, and then adds, 'At least as far as I can tell.'

I wonder if she got drunk yesterday evening though.

Ali seems able to read my mind. 'I didn't have so much as a mouthful of wine last night,' she says.

I feel caught out. But then Ali smiles and my caution suddenly seems no big deal.

'Shall we say what we know about Daniel?' she says in a changing-the-subject voice.

I shrug and tell her I don't know much, taking a sip of my coffee.

'Well, I'm not sure about him,' she says, 'but I did have some ideas overnight for what we should look for, and I was up early poking around on his electronic footprint, just to see what was there. The thinking and the putting it in place can come after that. To me, he seems a lonely man, with something very soulless about both himself and his home, as if he tried incredibly hard not to give away clues about who he was, which perhaps is a clue in itself. It was the first thing I noticed about his flat, but maybe I made what I saw fit that picture, mainly because I'd watched him so much from this window, and it was the story I told myself about him.'

Ali sounds a bit too enthusiastic, I think, as she talks, and I wonder if she is quite all there, or whether she has some sort of underlying mental health issue that leaches into mania at times.

But when I study her carefully, all I see is someone who merely seems focused and observant, and who knows what she thinks. These are all qualities I'm short of, and so I decide to concentrate on what she is saying, rather than how she is saying it. It feels the right thing for me to do.

I haven't really thought previously about what Ali is saying, and I'm a bit wrong-footed. I suppose I'd always been so eager to fling myself into Daniel's arms that I'd been too busy concentrating on him, rather than how he lived, I see now.

But now that Ali has sown a seed of suspicion, I understand instantly what she is driving at. There was an empty feeling about Daniel and his home, tasteful and expensive as everything was that he surrounded himself with so showily.

I nod thoughtfully. 'I don't know that I ever really noticed this when he was alive, but I think that's right, Ali. At first I thought he had only just moved in, but it never really changed and then I got used to it and stopped expecting it to change. And he was clever at moving the subject away from him and back to me if I asked him much.'

'What else did you notice?' Ali asks. 'Anything, no matter how inconsequential.'

'I'm cross I didn't pay more attention. I was never there for long and I didn't ask him many questions – he was incredibly good at listening though.'

'I take it you liked the sex?'

I nod. I don't feel as uncomfortable admitting this to Ali as I would to anybody else.

'Well, it might not mean anything. But he kept you coming back for more, and that might mean something too. We have to wonder at precisely what it was that made somebody want to kill Daniel. And sex means a certain passion, I guess. Although we mustn't blind ourselves. There are other passions too. To me what happened didn't look particularly premeditated, although I'm not sure why I think that. Perhaps the door to the garden left open means something too, unless you left it like that,' says Ali.

'I did leave it like that, but it was open already when I visited and found his body,' I say.

'Right, I see. How did you two get together?'

I describe seeing Daniel at the lido when I was sunbathing, how it was a chance meeting and how hard he'd tried to get the women lying about to look at him.

She listens without commenting. But there is an air about her as if she is accepting of human nature, and so I don't feel particularly judged.

It's comforting, I find, and a relief I don't have to lie.

I've spent so much time being dishonest to everyone else since I met him, even if the lies have often been omissions about what I've been up to rather than verbal untruths, and it has been a huge strain.

It's reassuring that Ali feels to me to be lifting some of the burden that I've been hefting along.

I stare at her with more attention, and she looks targeted and in a positive frame of mind. I wonder if the fact that Ali and I are sitting side by side in her window bay means something to her too, although I don't kid myself that I can understand precisely what it is that she is feeling.

We glance at each other, and then we smile and say 'more coffee?' at exactly the same time.

We look through the files that she'd downloaded from Daniel's computer, and the multitude of screenshots Ali made on her own computer from various documents and so forth. Or more precisely, she scrolls through, concentrating quite obsessively. While I watch over her shoulder, she flicks from file to file like lightning.

She reads and absorbs information at a tremendous speed, certainly much more quickly than I do. I suppose that shouldn't be a surprise considering how many books there are in her flat, as she must have had lots of practice in getting her reading speed up. There's a lot to go through, but it would feel much more onerous if Ali weren't leading the way. There are bank statements, and websites, and some work stuff, Ali says, and of course his browsing history.

I'm impressed that she was able to get into his computer so easily, and I ask her about how she cracked his password. Ali looks awkward when she admits to watching him with binoculars, so much so that it makes me laugh. And then she smiles in what appears to be relief at me laughing, and I like that I can make her smile. But it's the way she seems able to grasp the meaning of something in just a few seconds that totally staggers me.

'Honestly, Caitlin, this is child's play,' she says when I tell her I'm impressed. 'His weakness was that he never thought anybody would be looking at his digital life. Over-confidence simply made him sloppy.'

She moves on to Daniel's social media.

It's when she's scrolling his WhatsApp, which he had linked to his computer, that she gives a low whistle.

I look at it with more attention, and it certainly is revealing, although not in a way that makes me happy.

To be sure, we cross-reference the names to his Facebook (which he'd more or less stopped posting on about eighteen months ago) and his Instagram, his photos and all the rest.

I've already realised what it is that Ali is uncovering, but it's not long before she says cautiously, 'Caitlin, it's clear that he has – for want of a better description – a girlfriend called Nikki. Actually I think I saw them having a bust-up out in the road, a while back. Did you know about her? I didn't realise he still saw her, but her partner seems to be on night shifts, and these last months late in the day hasn't been me at my best . . .' She shakes her head and sighs. I think she may be realising what a lot she loses when she's drunk.

I shake my head to show I didn't know about Nikki, not trusting myself to speak, but I can't prevent a tear splotting on the table and my lower lip beginning to tremble. To give myself a moment to get back under control, I angle the screen my way and trawl the private messages between them. There are numerous naked pictures of her, and sometimes him too. She has a small tattoo on her ribcage. I think it's of a bee. Fuck it, I'd always thought that if I ever got a tattoo it would be of a bumble bee, but now that cow has taken that from me too.

Daniel is undeniably warmer and more chatty in his messages to Nikki than he ever was to me. With me, he was almost business-like in comparison. It seems clear he cared for Nikki quite genuinely, certainly much more than he cared for me. I don't mention this, and neither does Ali, although presumably she has read what Daniel and I wrote to each other.

Ali awkwardly hovers while I pull out my phone and start to scroll through my calendar, comparing dates on my own exchanges with Daniel. Once or twice when he said to me that he had had to work it seemed that he was seeing this woman.

I put my phone down on the table and stand up abruptly. Ali points wordlessly to where the bathroom is without me asking, and I go and stand in front of her hand basin running cold water over my hands as I try to compose myself.

What really sinks my heart though is that it is painfully clear that often he'd have both of us over on the same day, but with her quite often staying the night, if her affectionate messages of the day-afters are to be believed. I've no reason to believe they shouldn't be, as they don't seem to have been written for public consumption.

I never spent a night with Daniel, and that this Nikki had this privilege hurts, very badly.

I had honestly believed I was special to him, in the way he was to me. What a mug. I wasn't in any sense 'the one', and it's obvious he had someone in his life he felt for more than me.

I am a hypocrite.

I mean, I know this already. But although I know I have James, and was never really available to Daniel, and he knew that, the presence of Nikki still really kicks me in the gut. Of course, I never hid from him that I was married or that I love my husband. All the same, Daniel was important to me. And that he clearly never reciprocated the level of my feelings wounds me deeply, it really does.

I return to the living room, and I can tell instantly that Ali has more bad news.

'Caitlin . . .' she begins, but then I don't hear her any more as I stare at what she has uncovered.

There are explicit messages to other women too, and so while initially I'm pleased that Nikki wasn't getting it all her own way either, in the end it just adds up to one big shitshow.

He seems to have been obsessed with sex in a way that thoroughly unsettles me. To see the evidence of his proclivities laid out quite clinically makes me feel used and dirty.

While there's no suggestion he met these women in person, he certainly was involved in active – very active, on his part – online relationships with them.

I stare at Ali's cat, who is now sitting up, and he gazes back at me with what I feel is compassion in his golden eyes. Fuck me, even a tragic cat is finding me even more tragic than him, I imagine.

I wonder how much Daniel actually enjoyed any of it, for to be doing it so often and to have so many people in his life, it feels so desperate, so cruel. He had no compunction in ghosting women once he'd had what he wanted, once he made them preen and pose for him.

He was never cruel to me, I hadn't thought, not until now. But now he feels very cruel.

I lean back in my chair, overcome. This is the man that I fell for, that I was risking so much for. But I never knew him at all.

There's been a murder. And suddenly I'm not surprised there has.

Meanwhile Ali has gone into Google Maps, and is looking at his account in the timeline section where the calendar shows every place Daniel's phone has been and for how long, and this electronic profile of his stretches back, quite literally for years.

And, should I doubt what I've just been thinking or the pictorial evidence I've just seen, then the map timeline will set me right. I can even see the exact hour when Daniel and I met at the lido.

'Ali, this is terrible, that there's this information just sitting there,' I say, feeling quite queasy. I'd never heard of this sort of thing.

'It's just information, Caitlin,' Ali replies firmly, 'think of it like that. Information, in itself, is neither good nor bad.'

'It's so invasive though,' I say.

Ali raises her eyebrow, and then she adds matter-of-factly, 'I expect there are a lot of parents out there quietly watching what their kids are up to, and a whole lot of teenagers who just give their phones to their friends to look after if they need to go off-grid and they know their parents monitor their digital footprint.' She doesn't need to say that there must be spouses too who take advantage of this.

I stare at my phone. There's something so pitiful, so insignificant about the hour and seventeen minutes Daniel spent the day we met, showing off at the lido, before talking to Dukie and, finally, me, that it feels as if a knife in my gut is twisting.

Ali senses I'm struggling. But she doesn't say anything, and instead she shows me how to bring up my own Google map history, and it reveals each and every time Daniel and I were together, even down to his house number.

'How long were you seeing each other?' she asks.

'Getting on for a year.'

189

'Goodness,' she says. 'I can't believe I didn't see this Nikki coming and going, and now I didn't clock you either. I know I've not been in a good place, but I'm not much of a snoop, am I?' She sounds deflated and sorry for herself.

Suddenly I feel overwhelmed with fury.

That fucking Daniel – he's messed with my head, and now he's messing with Ali's too. I mean I don't like the woman, but we're all supposed to be kind to each other at the moment, and Ali is clearly vulnerable, and Daniel has been really unkind, both to me and to her. A lesser extent to her, but it won't stop Ali feeling a bit more kicked about by life, all the same.

'I feel such a twatting idiot,' I spit out, and then I sob, my snotty-sounding 'fucking fool' a minute later applying to me, and Nikki, and Daniel, and all the rest.

'I know what being made to feel a fool is like, and it stinks,' says Ali gently, and she fetches a box of tissues. Putting her hand on my arm for a moment, she says, 'Caitlin, steady. You're no more a fool than anyone else. Be a little gentler to yourself, eh?'

Full marks to her for not saying a big fat I told you so or you deserve this for being such a harlot at heart.

I'm not sure I'd be so magnanimous in her position, should the roles have been reversed, as doesn't everyone yearn to say this sort of thing in situations like this. After all, I've been cheating on my husband for the past year. How can I expect pity?

Is Ali another person I've got wrong? Is the mistake I made in getting involved with Daniel going to spread out and engulf us all?

A memory of the night before flashes into my mind, me and James giggling together while rolling the joint. Poor James. Poor me. Poor Ali.

'I'm going to run to the shop for some cigarettes,' I say once my tears have reduced to the level of wet snuffle, as I've left the ones from yesterday at home.

Before I leave, I gulp down a glass of water, and I can't help but notice when I see my reflection in her newly cleaned kettle that I've been doing ugly crying and my face is all blotchy.

'You'll have to hang out of the window if you're going to smoke,' Ali says in a mock-scolding voice but with a soft expression, 'my home being such a temple and all.'

By the time I return, Ali is compiling a list of times and dates.

'Right now, Nikki seems to me to be the obvious candidate as Daniel's killer,' I declare showily as I spark up. 'I don't care if there is evidence or not. But I know I didn't kill him, and I'm ninety-five per cent sure you didn't either, and so I'm going to pin the blame on Nikki just because, well, just because . . . Just because I hate the very sound of her.'

'Crazy logic. And you're being petty in your reasoning. But you might be right, all the same,' Ali says. 'The last time Daniel saw Nikki was the evening before he died. They had a furious argument at his, the aftershocks continuing after Nikki got home, as she left text and voice messages that he was a bastard.'

'What did they argue about?' It's like picking at a painful scab but I need to know the details. I feel irrationally jealous.

'It's not clear. What is certain though is that she was really riled with him.'

I inhale as deeply from the cigarette as I can, riding the wave of dizziness this causes.

'Does Nikki know about me?'

'Not that I can see as I've not noticed you mentioned, but that's not to say she doesn't.'

I don't know whether that makes it better or worse, and I take two deep drags on the cigarette, which has such an effect that I need to clutch the windowsill as suddenly I feel a bit too light-headed from the nicotine rush.

'Men can be very disappointing at times,' Ali points out sympathetically.

Ali doesn't seem at all shocked by either me or Daniel, and I suppose this is because she has a rock-bottom opinion when it comes to human nature generally.

She looks at Daniel's search history, and then I don't really listen as she rambles through a meaningless hotchpotch of Reddit and a debt collector trying to repossess the Vespa, together with suspicious VPN sites, Bitcoin trades and dark web users bouncing around VPN sites so that their digital footprint is hard to trace.

I get that Daniel is pretty shady all around, but all of this pales into insignificance as I'm too busy thinking about the shabby way he treated the women in his life. None of us deserved it. Nobody should be treated so badly. I am an adulterer, but I could never be so malicious as he.

I'm so lost in my thoughts that it's a while before I realise that Ali has stopped talking.

Ali is staring in a distracted way out of the window.

'Um. No,' she mutters to herself in a most peculiar voice that is for her benefit rather than mine.

She turns to me. 'The police have just parked opposite, Caitlin. They are about to find Daniel.'

I don't have the words. For an instant I imagine a car-crash spool of horrific images of me being hauled off in a police car, the shrill of the plastic wrist restraints being tightened ringing in my ears, followed by me standing in a dock watching the judge's gavel pounding down, and it's a series of scenarios that I can conjure up with alarming clarity.

Although I've known this would happen at some point, now that it has, I feel as if I might faint. I clutch at the window-sill once more and don't say a word.

What can you say or do when you are living a nightmare, and there is no way to wake up?

Ali

Jesus, for a dreadful nanosecond when I tell her about the police arriving, Caitlin looks about to croak on me right then and there.

I've never seen anyone go scarlet and then icy white in what feels like less than a second.

'You have to go,' I say.

She looks as if she can't move, that she's a rabbit caught in the headlights. 'Why?' she whispers.

'Use your imagination, Caitlin. You mustn't be found here,' I say. I grab her bag and jacket, and I manhandle her out of my flat, frogmarching her down to the front door.

'Make sure you look as normal as possible as you go past the police car, and don't you dare look back,' I hiss at her as firmly as I can just inside the front door to the whole house as I don't want my fellow flat owners to hear.

She's in shock.

I give her arms an abrupt jiggle in order to try and get her to concentrate. Her head waggles a little as I do this, but then she looks at me with her eyes dark with apprehension.

I say right into her ear, 'For goodness' sake, go, as they may well be coming over here in a minute to see if us in these flats have seen anything unusual, and it's not going to be helpful if they find you and me on the doorstep. You must act normally when you go past the car, as even though they may track your phone records in time, you're gambling that this might not happen and they might not find you, remember, which is why you must behave as any ordinary person would.

'There'll be a camera running that will be at the front of the police car, and maybe another at the back too. Turn your head their way as you get close, and obviously crane your neck as if you are trying to look down towards Daniel's front door, as if to see what the police are doing – it'll be too suspicious on those cameras if you don't look at all at what they are doing. Caitlin? Got it? Then get home and stay put. I'll be in touch, but it may not be until things are quiet.'

I bundle her outside as she murmurs to herself 'innocent'.

Goodness knows if she has taken any of what I've just said on board, but it's the best I can do.

As soon as I'm alone back in my flat, my eyes flick over to the fridge and I think about pouring myself a glass of wine. It's so tempting. But what I do instead is snatch up Daniel's laptop and phone, and hide them in the loft above the hatch at the very top of our communal staircase.

And then I wait for the knock of the police on the front door.

Sure enough, it's not long before there is a rat-a-tat-tat downstairs.

None of the other residents ever answer, and so taking heart from the persuasive way Caitlin rallied her twins and husband to bring them in for Tiger King, sounding so much as if she didn't have anything to be furtive about that even cynical old me was almost convinced, I make sure I have as bland an expression as I can manage before I open the front door. If Caitlin can act well, then so can I.

I expect the police, but instead, as Pusshkin and I discover, it's Mehmet who is standing about eight feet away down the path, with a gaudy floral mask on that makes him look ridiculous. There's a plastic carrier bag on the doorstep. My mouth opens in surprise, but I can't think of what to say.

He's here to check up on me, I realise. To see if I'm all right.

'It's not like you, not to come,' he says awkwardly and in a slightly muffled voice, as Pusshkin entwines his body bendily around and between Mehmet's legs.

'I know,' I say, flustered. 'And I'll be back, but I'm, um, just having a . . . breather, you know. Sorry about the cat – he's very friendly.'

Mehmet looks at me anxiously to see if I am offended by what he's done.

In the carrier I can see some butter, pasta, a carton of milk, a small box of tea bags, some broccoli, a couple of apples and some pet food.

'My pleasure to bring you this,' Mehmet says. 'No charge.'

'You are keen I have some vitamin C with that fruit,' I tell him squeakily, my throat so constricted with emotion that I can hardly get my words out.

'I am.'

We smile at each other. It's the first time we've ever done this.

I'm beyond touched by his gesture. I can't help but compare Mehmet's quiet thoughtfulness and his generosity, with my unnecessary treatment of Dodi with the SlimFast.

What a total bitch I was. She didn't deserve it, even if she had made me feel slighted when she'd barged in front of me. I've had far worse done to me, and in no way was I then justified in stooping so low to take my own general unhappiness and dissatisfaction out on her. I must make amends at the earliest opportunity, police willing obviously.

Talk of the devil.

A policeman in uniform and a disposable mask and gloves comes down the garden path while talking into his radio, and Mehmet's face becomes his normal level of inscrutability once more as he turns to go.

'Thank you, Mehmet. I do appreciate it,' I call to his retreating back. 'See you tomorrow. Or the day after. Sometime soon anyway. Thank you!' I'm saying the last bit quite loudly to make absolutely sure the dear man hears.

He doesn't look back at me but he lifts his hand in acknowledgement as he heads back towards his shop.

And then I plaster on what I hope is my most helpful expression and say to the policeman in a more formal voice, 'Good afternoon, officer. How may I help you?'

'There has been an incident in the house opposite,' he says. 'Might we go inside as I'd prefer not to discuss it on the street?'

He and I look around. We are the only people in sight, and the windows to the other flats in my house are all firmly closed.

'Even with social distancing?' I reply.

'In this case, even with social distancing.' He sounds quite firm.

I take the policeman upstairs and indicate he should sit at my seat in the window, as I put on a mask as I'm not quite sure what the rules are on this inside one's home when there is a police officer present. Better safe than sorry seems a sensible approach.

I offer him some tea, which he refuses, and I go to stand on the other side of the room well away from him and he points out that I have a good view of the street, and I agree that I do. Maybe I should have made him sit somewhere else.

'Have you noticed anything odd going on lately across the way, that house directly opposite?' he says. 'Or strangers about? Or people you know going to that property who wouldn't ordinarily be doing so.'

'I spend quite a lot of time sitting there, but the whole street has been very quiet since the start of lockdown,' I say. 'A lot of people who live around here have gone out of town, and during the day there are a few joggers and dog walkers about, but practically no vehicles and generally it's much less busy than normal. And hardly anybody is about at night. It's been totally quiet across the way as far as I can remember, and so I thought everyone in that house was away. What's happened?'

To my ears I sound convincing, and the policeman doesn't appear to think that anything I've just said to him is suspicious.

He asks me for intel about the neighbours, and makes a few notes as I fill him in on who lives where. I say that the other residents in my house might have seen something, but he shouldn't expect too much as all of their living rooms overlook the back garden as their layouts are all different to mine, and they have their bedrooms in the front of the house. I don't say I know Daniel's last name or anything like that. I just call him Daniel and that I've not seen him for a fortnight. And I add I think the top maisonette is between tenants.

'Are you able to tell me what has happened?' I try again.

'There's been a death,' he tells me, 'a young man.' And then his face goes blank in the way that people do when they are not intending to elaborate any further on what they have just said to you.

'Oh,' I say in a way that invites him to add a little more. 'Is it Daniel, do you think?'

After a silence as he looks at what he's noted down, I add, 'Daniel lives on his own. Was it an accident? If it's not him, has somebody else died in his home? Should we in this house be worried for our own safety? Was there anything special that alerted you to the situation?'

I think these are the sort of questions that a concerned citizen who doesn't know about there being a murder in the house directly opposite would be asking.

'I hope he hasn't killed himself. That would be tragic,' I add, as if that thought has just struck me.

As I thought would happen, the policeman instead thanks me for my help, and he says he'll be off, and I tell him Beryl is definitely in upstairs. I know she hates 'the filth', as she belongs to Extinction Rebellion and was arrested at the protest at Oxford Circus not that long ago, and so she'll give him short shrift.

When I have my flat back to myself once more I make a mug of tea, and I put away the shopping that Mehmet has brought me.

Then, with Pusshkin sitting on the table beside me, together we watch the policeman who came to see me, along with a female colleague, also in uniform, knock on several other doors in the street, as I drink my tea. I was the only person they demanded to come inside to speak to, I notice.

They spend over an hour doing this, but they don't look as if they are particularly excited about anything they are told.

Eventually two other people turn up and put on disposable forensics suits and, carrying metal boxes, they disappear into Daniel's flat. And a couple of hours later what to me look like a pair of plain-clothes detectives arrive, although they don't stay long at all.

At dusk a mortuary van arrives, and I see Daniel's corpse, now zippered up inside a black bag, being wheeled down the garden path on a gurney and into the unmarked dark-coloured van.

And then it goes quiet.

It might change tomorrow, but it all looks a bit half-hearted to me.

'Pleased to report no further problems, so thank you for giving me that feedback,' I email Caitlin, as if I am one of her clients. 'Speak next week? But if I run into any problems in the meantime, I'll be in touch.'

I think the police might be back over the next few days taking more detailed statements, and so it's best Caitlin stays where she is for now.

There's the sound of an email arriving.

'OK', it says.

She understands she must stay home. As the Government is reminding us each day to do. Stay home, stay safe.

Caitlin

I throw every ounce of my energies, yet again, into appearing as normal as possible.

The more I do this, the stranger though it all seems, as deep within my heart and in my thoughts I feel disconnected from just about everything and everyone.

Still, I wing it, just about, in large part because the recording studio has caught James's and the twins' attention in the evenings and so I get a bit of respite while they are down there.

And then Ellie has a totally ridiculous idea that ends up proving a godsend. She thinks that as a family we should take on the 'Shuffle Challenge' TikTok stylee in the hope that we might trend, as apparently I can 'make shapes'. Who knew?

Ellie had taken a short video of me as Dukie and I pranced about as we Zoomed ourselves drinking our wine and strutting our stuff to Sophie Ellis-Bextor's Kitchen Disco. I'm sure that Ellie only did this originally because she thought it would be a laugh at my expense that she could share with her dad and brother, and probably her friends too if I was very embarrassing, although not in a way that reflected on her. But when she played it back she decided I was a better hoofer than she expected, and soon she came up with a way of exploiting this.

And although initially it felt like the last thing I wanted to do, I quickly came to see Ellie's request as a gift.

James and I had said we wanted to do something with both the twins to reinforce the family bond, though I hadn't thought for a moment it would be anything along these lines. But once Ellie suggested the challenge it seemed very organic that we all do it and it gave us something to work towards that had a clear, achievable objective. James and I had wanted it not to be obvious that we were slightly skewing a new direction to our parenting and, as James told me, it really was an ideal opportunity. As far as the twins were concerned, it was as if Ellie was in the driving seat.

And if I am about to be arrested, I want to squeeze every second out of my family while I can.

Obviously I haven't mentioned to my daughter that as I was dancing with Dukie and had a smile plastered on my face, really I was obsessing privately over what was going on with the police at Daniel's and wondering what I would say should the police come knocking on the door that evening, and so I was barely aware of any of the shapes I was making. I really was dancing as if nobody was looking.

Watching Ellie's short video later, it was a shock to see that I look really quite happy, if perhaps a little pissed, which actually I wasn't. Dukie is thoroughly sloshed and all over the place, and so that probably makes me appear a bit more together than I felt. It's spooky how things are so rarely exactly what they seem, isn't it? Anything could be happening behind somebody's smile. The very thought of this makes me shiver.

Anyway, barmy as it is, this TikTok idea of Ellie's quickly takes root and then proves to be an excellent fillip for family mood – even Harry doesn't go all teenage boy about it, although I think James might have bribed him to go with the flow.

Whatever, it's a wonderful way from stopping me dwelling on all the shit that's gone down. And I discover that although I remain worried about what is going on opposite Ali's, it's soon at a lower level than I suspect it would be without the challenge.

I'd be lying too if I didn't admit that me and mine having something to occupy us all that we can do at home does make me feel better, as it feels so honest and so innocent somehow, as if our dancing feet are trampling away the lies and subterfuge. Honesty and innocence are what I crave, and so I encourage Ellie all the way.

So, taking up the dance challenge becomes a done deal between the four of us. I'm keen on it because it distracts everyone else from me, the twins (I suspect) because it diverts me and James from their sex-and-drugs naughtiness, and James wants to do it because . . . Well, I don't know – to show he's still got it? (He has.) Or, more likely, I smile to myself, because it's a surprisingly effective means of absorbing my attention and stopping me from going on about moving the baby grand.

The upshot of this commitment to the challenge means that for what feels like hours and hours Ellie drills us on running man, reverse skips, Polly Pocket, and reverse Spongebob dance steps, among others, including her bullying us in shuffling in formation and at a ridiculous speed sideways both up and down the stone steps to the lawn, all to Rawston's 'Don't Worry About It' belting out.

The neighbours must be wishing us further away with all the racket, but we're making happy noise without any fractiousness, and so until somebody says something unpleasant about what we're doing, I'm not going to call a halt.

Thank goodness James and I did a lot of dancing at uni as it was our thing when we first got together. James proved to be a fantastic leader, guiding me in the dark through many styles of beats. My favourite back then was the high kicks and back-drops and spins in old-skool Northern Soul. And later of course James and I had a routine taught us by a choreographer that we performed at our wedding reception as the first dance.

So it's gratifying for us olds to discover that we haven't lost the ability to learn a dance routine that is at once eerily similar and yet peculiarly unlike anything that we've ever attempted before.

All this leaping about stills my over-active brain too. Discovering Daniel wasn't the man I thought he was has to some extent cauterised my grief, I begin to think. Although there are moments I feel sad still, these are more tinged with melancholy than grief. And as for the police coming knock-ing? Well, sometimes fear paralyses me at the thought. But when I'm dancing with my family, I increasingly let the atti-tude take over me that there is nothing I can do for now. They come, or they don't. And they aren't here yet.

I regard Harry secretly, and Ellie too, as I can't help but be a bit suspicious about them, given how they've shocked me. But no matter how hard I try to catch them off guard, I don't seem able to, and it's almost as if James is taking extra special care of them. I see him and Harry having the odd father-to-son chat, with Harry nodding earnestly, and Ellie beaming when James jokingly tells her 'You go, girl!' when she is being particularly bossy. I'm thrilled that without me having to be a drag and point out to James that Harry especially needs a bit of fathering right now, James has done this off his own bat. Bless them all. I watch them laugh together, and I almost feel my heart could burst.

I won't contact Ali for any updates about what she can see the police are up to until she gets in touch.

And the more we dance, the more I'm able to exist in the moment, with James encouraging us all the way. And, while I feel a black cloud of anguish hovering above me it doesn't descend, and I'm content to let it all rest at that.

When we break for drinks, James and I stand there sweatily as we tell the kids funny stories of when me met and how we'd go clubbing, or to a Northern Soul weekender at some Pontins holiday camp or other, with the twins only looking slightly mortified on our behalf. I think it's the first time they've realised properly that me and James had a life before they came along, and that once we were young and we liked to let our hair down.

Then we make our clip, and although I say so myself, it's not bad at all.

Ellie agrees, and uses it as her first post on TikTok.

After it's live, we high-five each other in celebration, and although it is a silly achievement, it does feel like an achievement all the same.

Then a miracle happens. The twins agree without us demanding it that they will from now on knuckle down to their schoolwork a bit more seriously, which, I remind myself, is proof that if you allow some responsibility, then most times kids will step up to the plate and do the right thing.

By the time I set off for Ali's when finally she summons me, I hear Ellie and Harry cheerily greeting their teacher via Zoom. Or it might be Teams. But no matter what it is – the point is that for once they are doing what they are supposed to be doing.

Result.

A result as far as the kids go.

But this upbeat feeling only offers a nano-second of respite for me though. And then I'm almost paralysed with the returning thoughts that tumble through my mind of all the shit that is going on right now and that I wasn't the only woman in Daniel's life.

'Can we go and do a little spying on Nikki?' I say to Ali not long after I arrive, and I've clarified the police haven't grilled her especially hard on what she knows, or visited other than that time they first arrived.

I feel a bit too fired up and impatient, I can hear it in my voice but I can't hold it in. I need to do something physical, and this offers a task that is achievable, rather than me sitting and fretting and wondering how long I've got before the police come calling again, which is the likely option if we don't do this. 'I really want to see that woman up close if we can,' I add. 'I'm thinking about her too much and I think it might help.'

'We could, I suppose,' Ali says cautiously as if she is considering the pros and cons, 'Nikki lives quite near Tesco, and so we could make that our designated shopping trip for today.'

I get the impression she'd had other ideas for what we should be doing, but although I give her the opportunity to say something, she doesn't, and so then I think maybe I've got something wrong. I look at Ali carefully to see if she's had a drink but she seems pretty together. At least as much as I am, at any rate, which I don't suppose is saying a whole lot as I definitely feel frayed around the edges.

As she changes out of her slippers and faffs about with a bag and purse, I say, 'Tell me again about what happened with the police.'

'Two words sums it up,' Ali replies. 'Not. Much. Very little, in fact. A young officer with no more than bum fluff on his face did spend a whole five minutes with me, as I gave him the names of the neighbours, and told him who I thought was away. I said I'd not seen any suspicious activity, and then off he toddled, after I'd directed him upstairs to speak to Beryl, as I knew she'd give him short shrift and would tell him at great length precisely why she feels the police should be defunded. And a couple of detectives – or that's what they looked like – arrived ages later and were in and then out again to Daniel's quickly without even looking up at mine, and earlier what looked to be a forensics team visited. After which his body was taken away, and nobody has been back since, not that I've seen, and I've been pretty much glued to the window. There's hardly been anything about him on any of the news feeds, other than a report that said nothing more than the basics the police give out that a young man's body was found in a Hackney house.'

'Really?' I say. I feel incredulous that Daniel's death has caused nary a ripple of interest. 'That's all? I've been deliberately keeping my head down and not scanning the news websites while awaiting the knock at the door.'

Ali nods. 'Yup. Total anti-climax. But strange times we're in, so maybe we shouldn't be surprised.'

Even so, I'm shocked about how perfunctory the police investigation seems to have been so far.

Then I remind myself, as before, that Ali could have been on a bender, and her not seeing any further evidence of activity since the hours immediately following their discovery of the body might of course merely indicate that she is mistaken. She has missed much more in the past than she thought she had. But I decide it's not useful to point this out to her. We seem to be working together, and so I don't want to sour the mood.

And I look across the road at Daniel's flat, and it does indeed appear to be already forgotten about and desolate.

'I guess it's because all the public services are probably really stretched right now to breaking point, and so there is a limit on what they can do here,' Ali says, as if she is reading my mind.

She repeats, 'It's strange times and I know there's been a huge rise in mental health issues and domestic violence, and so I guess all the systems are under pressure. Presumably the police have a lot of people off sick too and non-essential backroom staff furloughed, and they must be having to throw a lot of manpower into making sure people stay home and how they are actually running police stations, and so they'll be massively over-stretched. I looked again through Daniel's messages and emails, getting in through my laptop, and he doesn't seem to have any family, and so I guess this means that there's no one making a clamour on his behalf, which might well have whipped up the case into a bit of more obvious activity.'

All of this makes sense, and so I nod to show that I agree.

'But Daniel's loss is our gain, remember, Caitlin. Our best bet is to hope that the station is really busy with other things, and that eventually this investigation is downgraded, if it hasn't been so already.'

I pass Ali her gloves.

'The other thing I've found is that it was Daniel's workplace who almost definitely raised the alarm, as they were infuriated at his radio silence,' Ali says. 'He was late on delivering a report, and they were trying to contact him, and so presumably said something to the police when they couldn't get hold of him.

'I know you've fancied her for the murder, and so I

wondered for a while if it was Nikki who raised the alarm as a way of giving herself an alibi, but she's still trying to WhatsApp him, I noticed this morning, and so either she has to be setting out evidence she is unaware of his death as a cover for her being the killer, or she really doesn't know yet that he has died. In that case she really must be wondering what is going on. As far as I can tell, the police haven't visited her yet, so I'm thinking the mobile companies will be likewise squeezed for staff and so are being slow to pass his records over, which can only help you. And Nikki too, who would be looking probably even more guilty than you in their eyes. Of course, the longer it goes on, the more chance there is of the investigation getting derailed and being superseded by other things.'

Ali spends what feels like an age putting on her coat, and then she says tentatively, 'Caitlin . . .'

'I'd definitely like to see Nikki, all the same, as I want to see what's so great about her,' I cut across her, as I fiddle with my clothing in impatience. 'Let's shoot.'

'Ah, um, okay then . . .' says Ali, and we make our way out of her flat.

'How are you?' I ask her as we go down her stairs, wondering if she had been going to confess something to me.

'If this is you enquiring about my drinking,' she says in a good-natured way, 'I'm trying not to think about it and I'm managing. Otherwise I'm fine.'

'It's got to be hard on your own,' I commiserate. 'Although actually I was asking about you in general really.'

She snorts.

'You could try online AA maybe,' I suggest.

'I could. But I doubt I will,' she tells me firmly. 'I prefer to do things my way.'

'Of course,' I say as encouragingly as I can.

'Shut up, Caitlin. You're going to make me want a drink at this rate.'

I don't know if she means this or not, and so I just say, 'Buck up, let's get a wiggle on then.'

We head towards where Nikki lives, walking on opposite sides of the street, Ali about twenty feet ahead of me so that to the casual observer hopefully we won't appear as if we are out together.

We don't want to risk getting stopped and questioned by the police for fraternising when we are all supposed to be isolating only with the direct family members resident in our own homes.

Ali and I are on the phone to each other though so that we can keep in contact, even though it's a bit hit and miss trying to speak to her through my mask, and I'm just finishing describing the Shuffle Challenge we completed when Ali goes 'sssh' at me very firmly, and instantly I stop talking.

A woman in running kit is jogging down the middle of the road in our direction.

'We've got a break, Caitlin. Subject a-hoy, can you believe?' says Ali. 'That's a stroke of luck. I bet she's going to Ground Zero.'

My heart gives a summersault as I see Ali risking a quick glance back at me.

I'm gobsmacked as the woman runs by.

Nikki looks so like me that she could almost be my double.

Ali says into her phone as we both turn to watch Nikki as she runs away from us, still keeping to the middle of the driverless road, 'He certainly had a type, your Daniel.'

'You really think she is going to his?'

''Spect so.'

We keep walking for a few seconds so as not to alert Nikki to our interest in her, should she look back, and then Ali nips across the road to me, and together we crane our heads to see where she has gone now.

Nikki is younger than me, from what I could tell as she passed, and a fair bit shorter, I'd say, though she is older than Daniel. The thing that most pleases me about her is that despite her diminutive height, she's clearly a trifle chubbier than I am. I noticed that Nikki has a wedding ring on her left hand, as Ali predicted she would. In fact, this was almost the first thing I looked for.

She is attractive though, and if she hadn't been a competitor for Daniel's attention with me, Nikki seems the sort of person I could imagine being friends with.

Even though Daniel wasn't a large man, I think somebody of Nikki's stature would find it hard to best him in a tussle. I don't think she looks like a killer. Obviously I don't really know what a killer does look like. But not like Nikki, I'm pretty certain.

Ali is thinking exactly the same. 'It's not easy to think of her wielding a knife and sticking it into Daniel, is it? She doesn't seem big enough,' she says, 'or as if she has that sort of temper.'

Ali's voice is very sombre. She sighs deeply. 'I've searched his emails, his diary, his WhatsApp messages. Even though Daniel seems to have pissed off a lot of people, it looks like he had barely gone out for the past three or four weeks, and I haven't seen much sign that anybody feels massively more pissed off than anybody else.'

Ali stops her muddled flow of sentences, and looks at me. She's working up to something.

I nod that she should go on.

'The thing is, Caitlin, I still think that he really doesn't seem to have upset anybody quite to the extent that they look as if they were gearing themselves up to kill him. Teach him a lesson maybe, but no more. Daniel was definitely dealing with some unpleasant dudes, but the last time I looked, being unpleasant wasn't a crime.'

That makes sense, I suppose.

'And while his work colleagues seem pretty grim in a money-grabbing sort of City-trading way, again I can't imagine any of the correspondence I've seen leading to one of the people he worked with feeling so het up with him that they actually went as far as taking Daniel's life,' she adds.

I don't know how to respond.

Luckily Ali doesn't seem to be waiting for a pearl of wisdom from me, as then she says, 'Frankly, I'm rather out of ideas, Caitlin, especially now that I've caught a dekko of Nikki up close. I thought she would put herself into the frame, but – I don't know – it's more that now she seems to have taken herself out of it.'

'I know what you mean,' I say.

This is not good news, I can see.

I have an awful, horrible premonition.

'Are you trying to prepare me for something else?' The words die on my lips as Ali looks at me intently.

I'd assumed that Ali would tell me I was foolish to be so suspicious.

The fact she hasn't, scares me and makes me feel strange. I shiver with apprehension.

Somebody has just walked over my grave.

And for the first time I feel properly frightened, and immediately I get that sick feeling you do when you are incredibly worried and don't know where to turn.

'I'm sorry, Caitlin.'

I can tell by the timbre of her words that I'm not going to like what Ali is about to tell me.

Shit.

But then as she opens her mouth to speak, my phone vibrates.

And when I answer it, my whole world implodes.

Ali

'The police have been to yours, and Harry's been taken off in a police car?' I echo, a second behind Caitlin's incredulous voice as she speaks on her phone.

I can tell it's someone ringing who knows her well, and so I think James must be the caller.

'Did Harry say anything?'

'Was he all right?'

'Where are they taking him?'

'And you're with him?'

'Has Ellie been left on her own?'

'Was she very upset?'

'Are you all right? Tell Harry I love him. I love you too.'

Caitlin's questions to the caller come thick and fast, and as she says each one, the colour of her cheeks blanches a bit more.

I wish I could hear the answers to her questions, but even the fifty per cent version that I'm getting indicates that, suddenly, events are spiralling out of control.

Caitlin ends the call and gives me a desperate look, and then my heart gives a little lurch as suddenly right beside me, she crouches woozily where she is on the pavement.

I don't quite know what to do.

'They're only questioning Harry? He's not been charged?' I ask as I lean over a bit closer to her, so that I'm not looming above. I can't quite make sense of this.

217

'I don't know, Ali. James is with Harry as his appropriate adult, but I don't understand the system,' she moans. She's not crying exactly, but there is the sound of a sob vibrating behind her words.

'Caitlin, you need to go home and do what you have to do. Is Ellie there? Can you get there on your own? It will be good for you to be with Ellie as she'll be feeling at sea. I'll keep an eye on what Nikki is up to,' I say, although it now seems futile to be watching Nikki. What I needed to say to Caitlin can wait.

Caitlin's eyes are glassy now, but she nods at me as I hold her arms and carefully help her to stand.

'Good luck,' I say to her. And I mean it. 'Chin up too – those kids and your husband are going to need their mama to be the backbone of the family, and so you can't go falling apart. You're stronger than you think, I'm sure of that. I know a good criminal lawyer, and I'll text you her number. If you need one, of course, which you might not, remember.'

Caitlin nods at me, and I risk giving her a quick hug of support. And then she turns and runs.

I wouldn't want to be in her shoes.

Nor Harry's. I think back to that awful night when I spent time in a cell, and how scared I was. To be only fifteen and going through that would be much, much worse, and he must be terrified. I think we're all at a low ebb anyway these days, and so I really feel for him.

I sigh. What a total catastrophe everything is.

I had been going to tell Caitlin what I'd found, and I'd been waiting for the right moment. But then, just as I was about to speak, James rang, and everything changed.

Now, I guess it's better if Caitlin doesn't know, at least until this latest drama is cleared up. It would only worry her about having an increased motive in the eyes of the police. I know Caitlin isn't a killer. She doesn't have the look, or the guile. I'm sure of that when I see her.

But when I think about Caitlin dispassionately, when she isn't in front of me, I confess to the odd doubt creeping back. Sometimes I can even see the possibility that she is playing me to help her build an alibi.

That's a thought I find upsetting and disturbing, and if I'm home, it always has me reaching for Pusshkin and I hold him close until his purrs calm me.

I think back to late the previous evening.

I'm back on Daniel's computer and it's close to midnight. Goodness knows what Beryl thinks I'm doing up in the loft each time I go to retrieve the laptop, but I guess the advantage of you being a known drunk is that people find it hard to be surprised by 'out of character' behaviour, as it's all pretty erratic. So Beryl keeps her front door firmly shut.

Back at my table in the window bay, I go through a lot of what I was looking at before. It was all as I remembered.

But then I discover an almost hidden link in Daniel's browsing history, and then another and then another. They lead to a website full of amateur, to-order pornography. I find Daniel's account and discover that his password is the same as his email password. Honestly the oaf can't have used more than five passwords across the whole of his various platforms, apps and websites. Cracking them has certainly been easier than the Codeword games I've become addicted to since leaving work. Has he never heard of hackers and information theft? Of people like me, who love to poke around?

My blood chills. For well over a month he has been earning money, good money, from people paying to view illicit posts of Caitlin. There are reams of them – pictures and videos of her, and other women too, although by far the biggest bulk is of Caitlin. Mostly the images seem unaware, carefree, unselfconscious. And what really turns my stomach is that there are rivers of disgusting comments underneath each post, commenting on Caitlin's body and setting out what these apologies for human beings want to see her do next. And Daniel replying that he'll try to oblige.

It makes me feel quite sick and I want to slam the laptop shut. But my stomach drops even more when I read one of the comments on the most recent picture with a reply from Daniel underneath it. He is promising a live webcam broadcast, with very specific acts from his 'one hot motherfucker with no idea who she's fucking in front of'. Caitlin. Poor, poor Caitlin.

I hadn't thought my opinion of the slimy little worm could sink lower, but it certainly can, I discover. What a complete and utter bastard! The fucker.

It gets worse. Daniel's financial situation was dire. In the days before his death he had messaged several creditors about a windfall coming his way, promising them payment soon. I do a quick tot-up of the money that Daniel would be likely to get from his subscribers to this channel, estimating extra in case he was banking on new followers for the live stream. It's a substantial amount, but only a drop in the ocean as regards his financial deficit.

It's gone three o'clock in the morning when I'm hiding the laptop back in the loft, and the knowledge this is shouting only one thing to me: blackmail.

Caitlin wouldn't want her lovely marriage and family and home to come tumbling down about her ears. I'm sure she'd pay very handsomely whatever he demanded – she had money and he knew it, and so she would have been a cash cow as far as he was concerned.

Still, Daniel looked like he had money as well, and things weren't quite what they seemed beneath the surface. Perhaps Caitlin's fancy active wear, her recording equipment, her spoilt twins' needs had bled her dry to the point that she couldn't pay Daniel what he demanded. What would she do then? Would she kill to keep her perfect life?

When Caitlin leaves me after her shocking phone call, as I retrace my steps to see if Nikki was indeed running to Daniel's, suddenly I feel relieved that life conspired against me saying anything to Caitlin.

I'd thought it was best she know about the potential black-mail, and I had wanted to see the look on her face when I told her. To see if she was shocked, or scared that I know. But with this news of Harry, I'm no longer sure. I'm not really sure of anything now.

I had done some more digging and discovered that the pictures of her weren't contained to the one website Daniel posted them on, but had now spread through the internet. If she doesn't know, I guess it's probably for the best she doesn't find out right now. She'll never have a moment's peace if she's waiting for her son or husband to see her as Daniel captured, doe-eyed and eager, waiting spread-eagled for somebody who was not her husband. Probably the most important reason for not telling her is so that she can be properly surprised if anybody questions her about it.

Of course, the police might find out about all of this, but as I had to look hard to find it, they might not. And should Caitlin not be exposed to what I know, I guess that in time her images, although always there, somewhere on the internet – as I doubt there's a whole lot now she can do to get them taken down – will gradually get sunk back in the search engines, superseded by all those other women's images that are posted daily.

It's a depressing world, but for Caitlin, if she is innocent (innocence being something of a movable feast at the moment), I suppose the greatest chance of her secrets remaining hidden will be safety in numbers, lost amongst all those other poor women being duped by the men in their lives.

I've never seen any sign in Caitlin that she knew Daniel might be sharing images of her. In fact, I'm not sure she's even aware he was filming her at all, to judge by her reaction when she was looking at what he'd filmed with Nikki. She'd looked almost envious then that he had showered such attention on her rival. I expect Caitlin allowed the odd little clip to be taken that she thought was just between the two of them, probably with her being kept unidentifiable, but I don't have the impression it's more than the text of her touching her breasts that he'd often sent her.

I don't think she's realised that if I've seen what passed between Nikki and Daniel, then I'll have seen this clip too, and I really don't want to be the one to point this out to her, not when it's been quite pleasantly companionable between us.

I guess though that all of this is a long way away from what Caitlin is thinking right at this minute.

As I walk up to my house I hear a woman sob, so I turn into my own front garden and pretend to dead-head a few flowers that have somehow managed to grow in spite of all our inattention.

I can make out a husky-sounding Dodi filling Nikki in on an extremely lurid and not very accurate account of what went on in Daniel's flat and how it was that he came to be dead. (Gypsies, apparently.) Dodi sounds like she hasn't spoken to anyone for several days and I feel another pang of guilt. I really must make more effort with her.

Nikki is trying to ask questions through her snuffles and tears. She appears stunned, horrified and devastated.

She definitely doesn't look like Daniel's murderer.

I feel a flash of anger at Daniel as I watch Nikki fall apart at the seams across the street. That man didn't deserve either of these women. The little creep, still wreaking havoc from beyond the grave.

To my surprise, I find I feel a sizeable twinge of sympathy for Nikki.

I'll add this to the heap of mixed feelings I have for everybody else.

Goodness. I must be getting soft. I blame lockdown, as really this isn't like me.

It's Caitlin though who's really crept under my skin, and I worry most for her, although the rest of her family seem to be doing their level best to catch up.

My concern swirls to a level of anxiety I don't care for.

Oh Christ, I'm starting to care about what happens to Caitlin's family, I realise.

I'm not certain that's a good thing.

Time, Gentlemen Please

Caitlin

'Mum!' Ellie screams at me as I run down our garden path. 'Harry—'

'I know, I know, darling. Dad's just rung me,' I say, 'it makes no sense.'

And we stand at the front door with our arms wrapped tight around each other in comfort.

Ellie feels stiff and unyielding as I hold her, and as if she is trembling with hyper-vigilance.

I need to let her know that I am here, and that I've got her back so she needn't worry quite so much.

It will be a lie of course, but that untruth can just get at the back of the long line of lies that I'm already surrounded by.

'It was horrible, Mum. The police car had its lights flashing and they just left it like that in the middle of the road outside our front gate. Some neighbours were standing in their gardens watching as it took Dad and Harry away, and I felt so embarrassed. We were down in the studio and so we didn't hear the front door, and they kicked in the side gate to the garden and came marching down, really shouting. And Dad yelled back at them and when he wouldn't be quiet, they threatened to arrest him. And they said it was Harry that they had come for, and Dad called them cunts and said Harry hadn't done anything.' Ellie starts to cry, and I have to do my best not to join her.

I'm shocked on all fronts. James usually tries to talk his way out of bad situations, so that in itself is odd. But what is stranger still is that never in our nearly twenty years together have I heard him say 'cunt', not in any single situation.

What on earth is happening to us all?

We all seem so unmoored, that I wonder if we can ever come back from it.

But I can't say any of this to Ellie. She's looking to me to make things better.

'Look, Ellie let's go in and have a cup of tea. It's not making any sense to me,' I say, 'and I'll try calling Dad again as there must have been a huge mistake.'

We go down to the kitchen, and I make sure Ellie is sitting on the sofa. She's drying her eyes but I can see that she is still trembling, and so I wrap her favourite wool throw around her.

I change my mind about the tea, and fetch each of us a can of Coke from the secret supply I'd stashed away. I'd intended the revelation of the cans to be a nice surprise in a week or two, but now I don't give a shit about that. Our urgent need for caffeine and sugar is greater than having a surprise in a few weeks, when Harry or myself might no longer be living in this house.

For a moment I want to stick a slug of spirits in mine, but I stop myself. I know I must keep a clear head.

It's hard though. My sweet son has been arrested, and I'm sure it's all going to be my fault in one way or another. So I change my mind and pour in a generous slosh of vodka, I feel so wired.

'Ellie, did you hear why the police wanted to take Harry with them?' I ask.

'They said something but I was screaming and then Dad was shouting and so I don't know what it was.'

'What else did Dad say?'

'I don't know, other than he kept telling the police to fuck off as Harry was totally innocent. Dad was fuming like I've never seen him before, and they said he wasn't helping Harry by making such a fuss, and it was only when they waved the Taser about Dad shut up. It was horrible and I was really scared, and Harry was crying too and you know he never does that. And my phone is in Harry's jacket as I'd been wearing it, but he put the jacket on to get in the police car and the police wouldn't let me get it from the pocket, and so I couldn't call you. And I didn't know what to do.' Ellie's voice descends into a wail.

How frightening it must have been for her, and for Harry too of course. And James wouldn't have been feeling great either.

I pat Ellie's knee as I glug all my Coke down. My throat feels incredibly parched and the drink doesn't seem to be making it less so, but the vodka calms me slightly as I try to phone James. Really, I want to go to the police station but I've no idea where they are.

There's no reply. It's just not my day. Anything to do with me these days seems destined to go wrong.

A knock at the door sends me racing upstairs to answer it, but I find a note pushed through.

It's from Ali, giving the details of the criminal lawyer she knows, and after keying them into my phone, I flush the note away in the loo. I'm not sure why, but I don't think it's a good idea if Ali and I keep hold of evidence that we are in touch today, not now Harry is with the police. I've no idea if this is merely something drug-related, or if the contagion surrounding Daniel and what I have done to this family is now seeping everywhere, and has wrapped my poor son in the fallout.

What I do know though for certain is that it's all one unholy mess. If I thought I'd felt sick previously at the thought of myself being arrested, it's nothing to the fear and the horror of my son being driven away in a police car. Something isn't at all right, I just know it.

The note had also said that every day Ali will be in at eleven o'clock, and that I must visit when I can, but only when it's not going to cause me trouble or make me look suspicious.

Like that is much of an option for me these days.

I ring the lawyer, and she says she'll try to find out some information, and she'll see if she can go to the police station. But for now, it's probably best if I stay at home and look after Ellie, and she'll ring me when she knows more.

Nothing happens for simply hours after that, and Ellie and I drive ourselves nuts trying to imagine what is going on.

I ask Ellie if she thinks Harry has done anything he shouldn't have aside from the drugs I already know about, but she claims not to know anything. I study her face carefully and decide I believe her.

'He did go out early that day though, I've just remembered,' she says then.

'Which day?'

'The day the police kept asking about. When you came in and told us off for arguing as Dad was on a Zoom. Harry had gone out that morning and told me not to tell,' says Ellie.

I remember that morning. Not an hour later I found Daniel's body.

He'd obviously not been dead for long when I went in, as the blood pool was only just starting to go the tiniest bit dry and darker-looking at its edges. I shudder at the image, but push it out of my mind. The affair, Daniel, his death – they are all nothing in comparison to what might be happening right now. That my boy is being questioned by the police, and for what, I don't yet know. But what I am certain of is that what is happening with Harry is putting him at grave risk of being the catalyst that is finally going to pull this family apart.

'Where do you think he'd been?' I ask.

'Out to buy weed. It's been really difficult, and Harry was in a crap mood when he woke, so I think Harley told Harry to go over. But I know something went wrong and it didn't happen, which was why Harley came over to us that, um, er, time,' Ellie tells me. 'I never asked Harry much about it.'

I think back to that morning, when I got up late and the pair of them were arguing in the den. And me, fool and selfish bitch that I was, instead of finding out what all the bickering was about, all I could think about was how quickly I could escape so that I could go to see Daniel.

But I won't allow myself to believe Harry could be involved in anything serious. He couldn't be. It's ludicrous.

And I'm going to hold on to that thought. Hold on very tightly.

When the phone rings I jump. It's James, who is understandably sounding most unlike himself.

I look to see where Ellie is, and I go into the utility room and I shut the door.

He tells me which police station he and Harry are at. It's not the nearest one by far, but not all stations have interview rooms that are being used. The lawyer I rang has just turned up, and they are currently on a break while Harry has something to eat.

Harry is going to give DNA samples and fingerprints after that, and James has given permission for that to happen as the police were very insistent apparently, pointing out that circumstantial evidence could clear Harry. James has also had to make a statement.

I hate the thought of Harry being logged on police files. I start to cry and, once I start, I can't control it.

I need to tell James what's been going on. My lying has gone on long enough. And now Harry is in danger, my husband needs to know what a stupid, stupid woman he's married to.

'James . . .' I begin, but I can't form the sentence. I can only cry harder and the words catch in my throat.

'Don't even bother, Caitlin,' James snaps.

I'm shocked at his voice. I've never heard him speak to me in this harsh tone before.

'You've well and truly fucked over both me and your son, haven't you?' he says.

I don't understand.

'That little fuckwit you were screwing, your Daniel, it turns out the police can put Harry in the vicinity.'

My mind won't compute what James has just said, and so I can only repeat 'What . . . what . . . what', as if I'm a needle stuck in the groove of an old record. My worst fears, the ones I have been telling myself all afternoon couldn't be, are coming true and it feels as though my world is caving in.

'Harry was recorded on a police car dashcam, and the police claim he was acting suspiciously. The police car was in the street for something else, so it was Harry's bad luck to be there at the wrong time,' James says grimly. 'Facial recognition software led to the school, who identified him.'

'Fuck. This is awful. I'm so sorry,' is the best I can manage.

'I bet you are, Caitlin. A tawdry little affair with a short-arsed cocksucker I thought would blow over. Instead it's become a hurricane. I can't bear to think about you, and I think you'll be finding that Harry will feel the same now the police have filled him in. I've had to give a statement too about Harry's comings and goings. But the worst of it is that we need you to come and get us as there aren't any fucking taxis. If they don't hold Harry after this latest round of questioning, that is.'

'You don't think they will hold him, do you? They can't do that to Harry,' I say in shock, before I realise what else my husband has just said to me.

That he knew about me and Daniel.

'I love yo—' I blurt desperately, but James won't let me speak.

'Why, Caitlin?' James is shouting now at me. He sounds bitter, furious. 'Was our life here not enough for you, Caitlin? Not perfect enough? Were you feeling too old in your perfect life?'

'It was nothing like that, I . . .'

'Fuck off, Caitlin. You know, it was fucking everything like that.'

'I love you,' I whisper. He doesn't answer.

'Do you know what, Caitlin?' I sit in miserable silence, as my husband tells me. 'Right now I really fucking hate you.'

I deserve this.

And with that the line goes dead.

Before I can tell my husband that I really fucking hate myself too.

I tell Ellie to stay home and answer the door to no one, on pain of death. Luckily, she didn't hear James and I argue. I guess she was talking to Harley or her other friends online while the rug was pulled from under me.

Her eyes are puffy from crying, and she looks petrified, but she doesn't argue with me.

Later, as I sit in the police station car park before I go to the reception, I attempt to square it in my head if perhaps Harry did do what he's accused of..

Could my dopey son be a murderer?

And if he is, will it make me feel differently about him?

What would it mean for Ellie, if her twin is guilty?

Does my marriage have a snowflake's chance in hell of surviving?

It's then I know what I have to do.

At the police station's door, I find it's locked, and I'm not allowed in. I can see that behind the front desk a woman is wearing full protective gear. In this day and age that means a mask and visor, disposable gloves, standing behind a Perspex screen. But even with all this protection she points to an outside phone that's on the wall beside the door, and she mimes me speaking into its receiver, and she picks up the receiver on her desk.

'Yes?' she asks.

I pause for a second before I respond, but I've already made my decision and I'm going to throw myself into it.

'I want to confess to committing murder,' I say.

The police officer regards me coolly as if trying to see if I'm pranking her.

'Would you mind repeating that, please?' She almost sounds bored, as if what I've just said is something she hears quite often. She certainly is leaning towards not believing me.

My voice is squeaky now as I choke out the words, 'I was having an affair. I tried to end it, and he wouldn't accept it. So, I killed him. I killed my lover.'

She blinks as she looks steadily at me.

'You have my husband and son here, and a lawyer I sent,' I say. 'And you think my son killed Daniel. He didn't. It was me.'

And then the woman behind the reception desk asks me for all of their names, and then my name and address and date of birth and my telephone number. Her face is inscrutable as she taps away at her keyboard, and finally she asks for the name of the victim.

'Daniel Horne.'

'And his address?'

I give it to her, and his phone number.

'And his relation to you?'

'Friend.'

'Did you drive here?'

'Yes.'

'Keys, please. In the tray.'

'Really?' I say.

'Really,' she answers, and then as she stares at me firmly, silently I place them in a little plastic tray that has been pushed out through a gap in the door, and which is sucked back in again. I realise this is so I can't easily drive away again.

'Make and registration.'

This faffing about on small things is torture but I give her the information she wants.

Then the policewoman indicates a bench against the wall that's well back from the door between us, over beneath a window. 'Would you take a seat over there?'

I stay standing where I am as I stare her down in an effort to encourage her to get a move on.

With a put-upon sigh and without saying a word she points firmly at the bench, and I have no option other than to slink guiltily over to it.

Minutes creep by, and then I watch her speak to somebody on the phone, and although I can't hear what she says, I see her laugh and shake her head, and then she looks at me and in my fevered imagination it seems as if she lets out another chuckle.

Nothing else happens for ages, and so I go back to the phone.

'They are very busy upstairs, but somebody will be down to have a word,' she says. 'When they can.'

I get the impression that she doesn't believe that I'm a killer, and CID isn't breaking its neck to speak to me either.

I had no idea it was so difficult to confess to a crime. It always looks so easy on the telly.

'You're not listening to me,' I say as firmly as I can, although I take care not to shout as I know that would only make things worse. 'Your detectives will want to talk to me, and the sooner they do this, the better it shall be for all of us.'

She looks at me steadily through the glass of the reception door, and then she lifts up another phone.

I don't have to wait long.

Ali

I can't stop thinking about Caitlin, and what might be going on. I'm sure it won't be that great.

I follow Nikki back to her home, more for the sake of it than anything else.

She sniffles almost all the way there, and then spends at least five minutes on the corner trying to put her face back together. I assume this means that her partner is inside.

It looks as if Nikki did genuinely care for Daniel. She's certainly upset.

As I watch her breathe deeply in and out, reducing her tears to a snivel, and wipe under her eyes, I realise I am pleased that Daniel did have someone in his life who seems to mourn him from the heart. It would be cruel if nobody really hurt at his death. I'm pretty certain Caitlin is well past that point right now.

Certainly Nikki's reaction is very different to what Caitlin's was, but of course Caitlin stumbled across his body, and so I think she was numbed at first by the shock of that. Now that I know Caitlin a bit, I can see it would have been a difficult sight for her to make sense of. Actually, it would have been a difficult sight for anyone, but I'm sure it was especially confusing and unreal for Caitlin, who is so used to a comfortable world with herself at its centre and everyone else in orbit around her.

Caitlin was miserable about Daniel dying, of course, but only for a while. I'm sure that feeling will at some point decrease in direct proportion to the discovery of the other women he was messing around with.

I suspect that although she'll be regretful about Daniel's passing on some level still, this will be more now because his demise is threatening to implode her charmed world, rather than because she is missing him as her lover. The news of Harry's arrest will have put the last nail into that particular coffin.

As I head back to mine, I realise that I'm more confused about Daniel than I ever was.

I can't avoid the fact there's something desperately sad about him. While I know I never met him, nothing I've learnt about him suggests anything other than him being a creep of the first order. A bit of me wants to pity him, but a much larger bit of me thinks he's got his just deserts, and if he wasn't already murdered, then I'd be quite happy to take a knife to him myself. Almost. He was, quite frankly, scum.

I mean, I didn't have the best start and my mum and dad were pretty rubbish at parenting, although I came across worse during my teaching days. When I was young I felt as if I had to fight hard for each nice thing that happened to me. And I'm all too aware that I've upset a good few people in my time too. But for a while I managed to masquerade as a 'normal' person, and actually for quite a while I did it reasonably successfully. Until I didn't, which wasn't for any dramatic reason or because something awful happened. A feeling of ennui about my life and the world generally just crept up on me, and the rest is history, as they say.

In contrast, Daniel's kicks were all about control – of himself, and others – even if ultimately he was paying a high price. He was essentially isolated, and very probably a narcissist, with psychopathic tendencies. He doesn't seem to have had a conscience or a sense of empathy that I can see, and he went out of his way to affront people, even though to judge by Caitlin and Nikki and all the other women who were pulled into his orbit, he must have had a lot of charm about him when he wanted to. But what those women offered wasn't enough. I don't think he liked himself very much. For him, getting attention from others, even if only sexual or making people cross with him, was better than nobody knowing he was there. He was a cruel man. In some ways perhaps his murder is, just a little, a blessing in disguise.

I shake my head at this thought – it seems a harsh judgement that nobody has the right to make on somebody else, and I feel contaminated that I've even thought it.

I arrive home to see Daniel's Vespa being loaded into a white van, and my mood tips further into the sombre. The police must be seizing it, or maybe somebody he owed money to has just gone and taken it; I doubt it will be a debt collector as they're not working at the moment. Whatever, it's an ignominious end for the thing in his life that seemed to give Daniel his most genuine happiness.

I look around my living room, as I watch the van chug off down the road. I realise that aside from Caitlin and that police officer I haven't had another person in my front room for over two years.

I tell myself that Daniel should be a cautionary tale for me.

As there's still no word from Caitlin, I text Dodi: 'Hi Dodi, it's Ali from across the road. I'm just off to the corner shop

– would you like me to fetch you anything? I'd be very happy to do so.'

Two minutes later a shopping list is texted back, with no please or thank you. The sound of its arrival is welcome as it makes me feel just a little bit less of the cow I know I've been to her, although the abrupt nature makes me think that she's guessed the SlimFast came from me. And while some people might think Dodi is rude, this prickly reply makes me like her all the more.

I realise that I am quite looking forward to seeing Mehmet again – it's days since I've been into his shop, and it's left a hole in my routine, as my daily visits had become such a regular feature of my life.

I add what Dodi wants to quite a long list that already I've put together.

I am going to make sure that the nurse, and the frail old man, and the lesbians all have something to be going on with too.

I've been neglecting them all lately, and it's not their fault that the time I've spent thinking about Daniel has turned out to be so all encompassing, and distracted me from the small efforts I can make to help others in what is a pretty dire time.

I put my debit card in my pocket and remember to grab the Tupperware container of the flapjacks I made Mehmet yesterday from ingredients I found hanging about in my food cupboard. I still feel touched that he brought around some groceries and checked that I was all right.

Everything was out of date, but I ate two of the flapjacks last night when they were still warm from the oven, and I am obviously still standing today, with no ill effects that I can detect. I tell myself it's the thought that counts more than anything else.

And I'll say to him it's just a tiny thankyou and that I won't be offended if he puts the flapjacks straight into the bin.

It's two days before Caitlin turns up.

She looks dreadful, with her hair glossy no longer and looking in need of a wash, and her face an unwinsome combination of dry-skinned and puffy. Her lips are cracked and there are shadows under her eyes. I think I must have seemed taken aback by how she seems.

'I feel even worse than I appear,' she says as we go up to my front room.

I smile, and after a while so does she, even if it is only wryly.

'The Vespa's gone, but no police have been back otherwise, I don't think,' I tell her. 'How is everything?'

'It's rubbish. I was so freaked by Harry being at the police station that I confessed to Daniel's murder,' she says.

'Uh,' I say, 'that was, er, strong.'

She goes on, 'The police knew about me already, but they'd done checks and were still getting ready to speak to me. And when I confessed, they quickly lost interest as I couldn't convince them of sufficient motive, despite what they could see about Daniel and how he lived his life, and I couldn't describe the knife, or that I knew Daniel had been pushed in the chest, which apparently he had. So I was more or less laughed out of the station. The same for Harry, and meanwhile James had to give a statement too as the husband of Daniel's lover, and so the upshot is we have been released by the police and we're not on bail, although our passports have been confiscated, which is a laugh considering there's no way we'd be able to run off abroad even if we wanted to. Apparently there's not enough conclusive evidence regarding Harry, other than dash-cam stuff placing him nearby at approximately the right time. The forensic evidence is compromised, my lawyer tells me, which means there is no corroborating evidence that I did it, and my confession isn't enough, apparently.'

'What was Harry doing there?' I ask, feeling very behind the curve, although from what Caitlin says I think the police can't have found the full extent of what Daniel was promising other people to do with images of her. But then I'd had to dig long and deep to find it, and I guess they might not have had the time or the manpower at the moment to do this. Plus, they obviously don't have his laptop because it's sitting in my loft.

'Oh, I forgot you didn't know. According to Harry, I believe, there's a shortage of weed in the lockdown and so Harry was going to Harley's as he couldn't get it from where he usually did. Actually I'm not one hundred per cent on all the details – other than Harry is innocent, which is the most important thing – as the police confused me with their questions as they weren't in order and I was muddled, and of course Harry and James aren't really speaking to me and since we left the police station they just shut down any questions I ask. And I daren't press too hard, as for the sake of us all being under the same roof, it seems sensible if we all just draw a line under what's happened and try to move on, rather than constantly rehashing what an idiot I've been. But the upshot is that the police don't seem any closer to knowing what happened to Daniel, that lawyer you recommended says – she was very good incidentally,' Caitlin explains.

And then she adds, 'Oh, and by the way, the morning Daniel died there was a police car across the road for ages because of a "domestic", and this is what caught Harry on camera. And that police car sitting there totally escaped your attention, I should mention, Ali!'

I frown in puzzlement. A domestic? Police activity? Drug dealing? How did all of that slip under my radar?

And then I remember the dream I'd had about someone trying to break in through my door, and I wonder if that had anything to do with this, with perhaps the police calling on me to see if I'd seen anything suspicious?

I wasn't in a good place back then, was I?

While I'm a bit rattled by how much passed me by, I do feel generally a whole different person since then, I realise.

It's actually not that long ago, but it feels almost as if I've lived a whole lifetime since.

Caitlin is still talking, and I tune back into what she is saying.

'It's alarmingly difficult to be taken seriously by the police for something you didn't do, at least during a pandemic, I've found. And James has, apparently, known all about me and Daniel since Christmas, so it wasn't a good car journey for the three of us back to home from the police station, I think it's safe to say. And then once we were inside our house all hell was let loose and there was lots of shouting and slamming doors, and that was just me. And now I'm off everybody's Christmas present list,' she finishes.

'I hate to think of it being such a dull old time for you over the past few days,' I say, trusting Caitlin to twig I'm joking.

I stand looking out of the window.

Frankly I'm staggered she confessed to the murder. That was a stupid thing to do, and risky too. And then I remember the way she called those twins to her before the Tiger King extravaganza, and the love in her face for them, and I completely understand her impulse to sacrifice herself, if needs be.

If I had a child, I wonder if I would put myself on the line quite so much for them? I guess I would. It must be nice to care for somebody so much that you'd do that.

Still, it was downright daft of Caitlin. I mean, I get that she'd want to protect Harry, but her confession was a rash action that could have ended up punishing Ellie, and possibly implicated Harry even further than he was already.

I've forgotten my manners as then Caitlin says, 'Do you have anything to drink?'

'Isn't that my line?' And I offer tea or coffee.

'Nothing stronger?'

I shake my head. 'Caitlin, I'm not trying to be funny or rude, but really I don't think this is the time for you to be doing that.'

'There's unlikely to be a better, is there? Everything's so fucked up that I just want to blur it a little.'

'Take it from one who knows, it's not going to help.'

Last night I drank two inches of vodka and it didn't do what I wanted. I feel as if me and an old friend have argued.

Perhaps it's for the best. I wasn't happy before, and while I do reserve the right that I will drink to excess again if I decide that truly that is what I want to do, I know that if I plunge back into heavy drinking once more, it will only end up with the same result again. Me desperately miserable and hopeless. And that is a pretty horrible way of spending precious time. I think lockdown has reminded us all that time is a commodity that none of us should take for granted.

I wouldn't go as far as to say that I'm happy now. But I feel lighter, in my spirits.

In some ways I probably have Caitlin to thank for that. Despite her in theory being the sort of person I've always told myself I wouldn't respect, I realised an hour after I had the vodka last night that actually I was looking forward to seeing her again.

It's been a revelation, that I like her, rather than just feeling swept into the untidiness of her life and then coming to feel worried about them all. She's snuck under my skin in spite of my determination that she's something of an idiot.

I suppose she's shown me there's more to life than the bottom of a wine glass.

And so this morning I told Mehmet that he wasn't to serve me any wine, now or in the future, no matter how much I beg.

He didn't say anything, but he nodded and so I don't think he will.

I make a pot of tea and I pour Caitlin a mug, putting a flapjack on a plate for her too. 'It's better than it looks, so I hear,' I say, nodding towards the flapjack.

Caitlin takes a tiny bite, and then she shrugs in a non-committal way and takes another chomp.

'How did James find out?' I ask.

'Daniel gave me some perfume at Christmas, and I put it in the utility room and not our en suite as I didn't want to draw attention to it. It seemed to make sense at the time, but it was obviously suspicious. And then James went all Sherlock Holmes and found out what I was up to by following me and reading my phone, which I don't approve of, but what can I say?'

I laugh at the smallness of her error. A perfume bottle placed in the wrong bathroom.

Caitlin looks at me as if a trifle vexed, possibly with herself more than me, and then she visibly relaxes. She laughs too, because it's all so ridiculous, the whole god-damned crapshoot.

And the more she laughs, the more I do, until we are both wiping the tears from our eyes.

Her face becomes serious again. 'James rang me from the police station after the first interview with Harry. He – James – told me he "fucking hates" me and Daniel was a "short-arse cocksucker", I think it was. And if I dare to say anything to Harry now, he just tells me to piss off. James has gone totally silent, and Ellie is just generally livid with everyone. She's ordered over £700 of clothes and make-up on my PayPal, presumably just to aim a little extra kick at me via my wallet. I said to them all I know I've messed up big-time, and I love them all. James just stalked out of the kitchen at that point.'

I suppose this has all gone pretty much as it usually does in these situations.

'Have another flapjack, Caitlin,' I say. 'Push the boat out.'

'There is one good thing though.'

'What's that?' I ask.

'The fucking TikTok clip is trending.'

This sets us off laughing hysterically again in a fiddle-while-Rome-burns sort of way.

When we get ourselves back under control once more, we begin to discuss what happens now. Which, unless the police spring into action, seems to be more or less nothing. Caitlin, Harry and James have all made statements, and the lawyer has assured them that something amazing will need to come up before the police will want to speak to them again, as there's not a single shred of firm evidence that would stand up in court against any of them.

I decide that I have been absolutely right not to mention all those images of Caitlin online, or that Daniel was selling them as well as promises of what he could get her to do on camera, or that he was lining up – in my opinion at least – to blackmail her. It could be in time the police will find them, but in these aberrant and strange times, a gambler would think there are good odds that they won't.

'After we'd finished with the lawyer, there was quite a reasonable-seeming detective sergeant who walked us out when me and Harry were formally released, and James was waiting outside to escort us home, and the DS said that they'd only be in touch should new evidence come to light, and so we could go on as normal, as much as we can right now anyway, and our passports should come back in due course. There was hardly anyone about the police station though that I could see, and so I think they are very caught up in a lot of things, which means, I hope, there's a good chance it will blow over in terms of police attention,' Caitlin says in an unconscious echo to what I've just been thinking, although for slightly different reasons. There's a silence, and then she adds, 'Not that I would know how busy a police station is normally.'

I nod.

'What are your thoughts about Nikki?' she asks, after a while.

'She seemed genuinely shocked at Daniel's death, and she cried all the way home,' I answer. 'If Nikki did kill Daniel, then she is a tremendous actress, especially as she wouldn't have known anyone was watching her, I doubt. And I don't think she is.'

Caitlin makes a weary-sounding harrumph.

There's silence for a beat or two, and then Caitlin says, 'I still don't like her though.'

'Perhaps try to think of her as the kind person who helped reveal Daniel as less than you thought he was?' I suggest. 'As if really each of you has done the other a favour, even if she might not be aware of your presence.'

Caitlin sniffs sharply and dismissively.

From this I take it that she's not up to feeling magnanimous about Nikki yet, but I suspect she might in time.

'Do you think Harry did it?' I ask after a pause.

'No,' she says firmly.

But then she sounds much more doubtful when she adds, 'Almost definitely not. But then, I mean . . . Oh, I didn't think Harry did a whole load of drugs either, or Ellie would be having sex at this age, and look what's been happening. Actually, I don't know what to think about anything these days. Pretty much everything I took for granted has been tipped upside down and stomped on, even if I've been personally the agent of a lot of this strife.'

'Ah, drugs and sex – that's teenagers for you,' I say.

'Aren't you shocked? I was, I admit, quite a lot more than theoretically I'd thought I would be in that sort of situation. It just seemed so much. I mean, the quantities were small, but the attitude that this is what everyone does, and Ellie being just so brazen . . .'

I laugh.

'No. I'm not shocked as I was a teacher for far too long. Teenagers get up to all sorts, I'm sure you remember from when you were that age. And drugs and sex will be part of that for many of them. And most of this their parents know nothing about, and never will. And nearly all of them turn out fine in the end,' I say.

'The parents, or the teenagers?' Caitlin replies.

She does make me laugh.

And then she adds, 'I always used to think I was really tolerant. You know, the cool mum. But now I think I'm an uptight witch, but a witch with double standards and loose morals obviously, who can't intuit what is going on around her. And when I first met you, well, I wasn't sure if you were my kind of person, to be honest. Yet you are the only one who doesn't seem to have judged me.'

Caitlin sounds disillusioned. And the tone of her voice shows me she's only puzzled and trying to work out the world around her, and isn't trying to pay me a compliment.

'I suppose I look at it a different way. Is it so bad that you've shown your children that adult life is complicated, that we do the best we can, and sometimes we get it all wrong?' I say. 'It strikes me that generally children are so cosseted and spoilt these days that actually often they're not terribly prepared for the real world when they leave home. You had an affair, Caitlin. They happen. What's important is how you and James move forward from here, surely? He may find it in himself to forgive you, and this could end up as a golden chance at showing Harry and Ellie how adversity may be conquered. Don't you think?'

She looks at me as if she wants something more.

I shrug. 'Look, I'm not really qualified in this area as I know sod all about matters of the heart, but if you want someone to tell you what a despicable human being you are, then you're going to have to find that somewhere else, Caitlin. You made mistakes. We all do. And anyone who thinks they don't is a liar. Your children and your husband, and you, will all come to terms with what's happened in your own ways.

'You might not like what they think of you, but the eventual outcome might not be as bad as you think it will be, once everyone has calmed down. And if your marriage and your family life do all go pear-shaped from here, then I have no doubt that you will handle that well. But first, maybe trust your family a little more to remember that there is more to you than just being an adulterer. I believe they will in time seek an equilibrium that feels positive and makes them feel as happy as they can, rather than one that is only about justice and pay-back. Just allow them a bit of time. It's hardly going to make anything worse, is it?'

'Ali?'

'Yes,' I answer.

'You can call me Cat, if you want. Only James and Dukie are allowed to do that,' she says.

'Okay. If I don't find it feels awkward.'

Then she says, 'I wonder if we'll ever know who killed Daniel?'

Caitlin's voice is thoughtful as she says this, but she looks at me with a tougher look when I reply, 'I'm beginning to think we might not discover what happened, and that at some point we'll decide to look forwards and not backwards. Especially in your case.'

'Thank you, Ali, I do appreciate it,' she says as she stands up. 'You've made me feel that I'd best get back home and stoke the hearth fires.'

'I think that's a good idea.'

After she has gone I make some more tea, and I think about Caitlin as I stare out of the window at the bedraggled-looking police tape strung across the top of the steps down to Daniel's front door.

I am confident that she is better equipped to deal with the wrath of her family than she probably feels right at this moment.

It's a couple of days later when a very different thought strikes me about something Caitlin said.

But by then it's already too late.

Caitlin

I go home, to find an uneasy truce spreading between us.

Ellie breaks the stand-off first, as she can't resist talking to me about the large number of TikTok likes. She re-posts the original, this time with the words 'Thanks to my girls' and 'Thanks to my boys' in lurid neon green and orange lettering that quivers above our shuffling heads.

It takes Harry a little longer. It's quite late at night and I'm perched on the steps up to the garden, having a cigarette. I've given up trying to pretend to James that I don't occasionally smoke, as he might as well know the worst.

Harry comes and sits by me, his gangly legs bent locust fashion up close to his shoulders.

'Mum,' he begins.

'Harry,' I say.

'Would you really have gone to prison for me?'

'Yes.'

There's a silence.

'Did you think I did it, Mum?'

'Not for a single moment,' I tell him, making sure my voice sounds full of conviction.

I do still have a thread of doubt at the core of my heart, but I would rather die than Harry know this.

'Uh-huh,' he grunts, but it's a companionable grunt.

We look at each other, and he seems as if he believes me.

Then his expression changes and I see him wondering then if, in fact, it was me who killed Daniel.

There would have been a time I'd have been either cross or surprised that my son could wonder this about me, but I'm way beyond that sort of thing these days.

I give a little shake of the head, and he gives me back the tiniest of shrugs in acknowledgement. We don't need to say the words.

I'm not going to ask Harry any more. How could I cope if he said something I didn't like or couldn't live with?

It seems that we've all crossed a bridge somehow and the actual details of what anybody has done or felt or said are a whole lot less important than they once were.

We're navigating a bog right now, and we need stability and solidness to give us a chance of looking forward, and so what is the point of risking shaking our foundations all over again when the firmer ground ahead is clearly in view?

It may be me making like an ostrich and hiding my head in the sand, but that is fine with me. Emotionally I am battered and bruised, and I'm not looking to add any more discord or instability to my life.

I doubt I'll ever discover quite what went on, but perhaps the main reason that I don't probe further is that I'm blowed if I'm going to allow Daniel to wreck things further than he has already.

And I think Harry comes to much the same conclusion.

'Thanks, Mum.'

'Pleasure.'

I offer Harry a cigarette and we smoke in comfortable silence.

Then, as I watch Harry walk in that slouchy way that teenage boys have over to the garden room slash recording studio to rejoin his father and sister, I lean back on my elbows and think how complicated it is being a parent. Or an adulterer, come to that.

Nobody tells you any of this when you are just setting out on your adult life, do they? Not that we would have listened for a moment, even if they had, I know.

I light a second cigarette.

The next morning, James bites back a laugh at a quip I'd made, and I glance quickly at him.

I don't think he meant to do it – laugh at what I said. He tries to cover it up, and I make sure I look away quickly enough so that there's not (yet another) awkward moment between us.

But that night he climbs back into bed with me, saying only, 'That bed in the spare room needs a new mattress.'

It doesn't. It was new in October and nobody has slept on it since, other than my husband for the past few nights, but I don't say anything about this, and just wriggle over a bit to make more room for him.

And later, when it's pitch black outside, my husband reaches for me in the dark and I more or less throw myself into his arms.

Afterwards, as we lie together sweaty and sticky, he holds me and says, 'Cat, I don't think I'm ever going to be able to forgive you or forget what you've done, you do know that, don't you?'

'I don't expect you to,' I answer. 'But I'm hoping we can both learn to live with that.'

And James pulls me close, and kisses my forehead.

A couple of days later I'm just considering whether Ali would find it funny, which is the reaction I hope, or be offended and think I'm crass if I put in some ludicrously expensive Drunk Elephant lotion in the gift basket I'm getting ready for her. I'd hate her to think I was trying to score a cheap point when I really do want her to feel thanked and appreciated, and I want to make her smile.

I don't know how I'd have managed without her, if I'm honest.

I think she's been good for me, and I'd like to think of her as a friend.

I toy with the idea of suggesting she join our book group. But I remember the masses of novels she's read, and how honest she is, and I rather think she'd run uncomfortable rings around us. I consider my slightly smug friends at the book group and I'm pretty certain that they would be appalled by someone like Ali. Although, just maybe, Dukie would love her irreverence as I do, and I decide that I will ask Ali after all. Maybe we all are just a bit too comfortable and self-satisfied, and we do need keeping on our toes. I expect Ali will say no, at first.

I've already plundered my cupboard of things I keep to give as presents for the basket – adding luxurious bath oil, expensive soap, and a Bobbi Brown make-up palette. I added some woolly tights too, a leather-covered notebook and a nice pen, and a very plain but cosy pair of cashmere gloves. And the ingredients for flapjacks.

I'm pleased with the card. It says 'Fuck, yeah!' and I've written Ali a note that says, 'Ali, I am so glad we met, even if the circumstances weren't the best. I want you to know I value your friendship, and I'd love for you to think of my dysfunctional family as, in some ways, yours too. Love, Cat'.

I hope she won't think the message is too soppy. I meant every word I've written.

'Mum!' I hear Ellie scream in real panic as I am just re-reading the card, and I drop what I'm still holding into the basket.

I run out of the back door, where I hear furious voices coming from inside the garden room.

James and Harry barrel out of the door.

They're on the verge of fighting, their voices raised as if they are about to go for it hammer and tongs, although I can't quite make out what they are saying.

I try to push them apart, but as they start scuffling, one of them knocks me hard on the jaw, and I'm sent reeling back, landing painfully on my buttocks. I think I'm collateral damage and the hit wasn't intentional. Or this is what I hope to be the case.

'Ellie, what's going on?' I ask as I hold my jaw and try moving it from side to side.

'Harry was talking about Daniel, and he wouldn't shut it when Dad told him to. And then they began shouting and pushing each other, and Dad said Harry should just move on and not talk about this any more, and Harry told him to fuck off, and he shouldn't tell him what to do,' Ellie pants, the words cascading from her mouth in a garbled rush, 'and my keyboards got knocked over and the drums, and I called for you.'

'Stop it!' I scream at James and Harry as I get to my feet.

At the sound of my cry James looks over at me. In that nanosecond James glances away from his son, Harry gives him a last not-very-hard shove to the centre of his chest, sending his father reeling backwards.

I watch as my husband falls as if in slow motion, slowly landing with his body on the grass, but with the back of his head just catching the lip of our garden path with a small thud.

It was incredibly undramatic as a fall, and completely accidental on Harry's part, but James stays still, his eyes shut and his mouth slack.

'Dad? Dad!' scream both Harry and Ellie.

'James, get up,' I say. I go and shake him, but he's out cold.

Harry and Ellie peer over my shoulder at their father. I'm not sure James is breathing. I lift an eyelid, and then the other one. Fuck.

And as I phone 999 and shout 'ambulance' into the receiver I see a little trickle of blood start to leach from my husband's ear down towards the path.

As I wait to be connected I tell Ellie to grab some blankets and Harry to just sit down as he looks as if he's about to pass out. He drops to the ground at once, where he sits moaning and rocking.

Ellie is placing a couple of throws over James, and I am holding his hand as I say to a new voice on the line, 'My husband has just slipped in the garden and hit his head badly. He's unresponsive. His pupils are different sizes and he's bleeding from an ear.'

I'm told to check his breathing, and I answer that I don't think he is. And so I'm talked through CPR, with mouth-to-mouth rescue breaths alternating with chest compressions.

'Ellie, run to the front gate so you can show the ambulance people the way. Tell them Dad has had an accident. Tell them he fell while walking to the house,' I say meaningfully, looking at Harry and then Ellie with my eyebrows raised for the briefest of moments before continuing to pump their dad's chest.

I want them to understand that no mention of a fight must be made.

Not under any circumstances.

I feel focused and deadly calm. I am going to save my husband's life, and I am going to protect my children.

Of course we've been making so much noise that it's possible that a neighbour might have seen the fight. But I can't do anything about that, and for now the most important thing is that we do our best not to alert the first responders that anything suspicious happened in the first place. If the three of us stay firm in telling the same story, we might be able to make it through.

I can't – I really can't – have Harry questioned by the police right now for a second violent act, so hot on the heels of him being interviewed and then disregarded as a potential murder suspect. It would seem too much of a coincidence, especially as both escalated from a push to the chest.

I look into my son's eyes after the next round of rescue breaths, and it's clear he is thinking the same.

Harry looks small and petrified, and my heart goes out to him.

'Trust me,' I mouth at him.

Harry gives one of his infinitesimally wee shrugs and I relax just a little now that I know he's understood what I am telling him, and what we all must do.

I find doing the CPR exhausting and difficult, and I'm almost at the point where I can barely keep going when luckily the first responders arrive. I'm sure my pummelling on James's chest will have obliterated any bruising that Harry's push might have caused.

The ambulance people are wearing full PPE kit and the first thing they do is cover James's mouth so that he doesn't breathe on them. This feels almost an act of unspeakable wickedness to me as I think he needs every bit of oxygen he can get. Part of me understands that on the off-chance he is COVID-positive, they have to take these precautions. I sit back on the grass, feeling weak and spent as I watch them hovering over James. It's almost in slow motion, like a dream. Another part of the extended nightmare that has been rampant these past few weeks.

They work on James for a while, and then with grim faces, they put him on a stretcher and he's wheeled away and into an ambulance.

I drive the rest of us in the car, and we follow the ambulance.

At the hospital we're not allowed near the bit where the ambulances are, and we have to stand outside. There's a wait for what seems an age where we don't know whether James is alive or dead, before at long last we can see in the distance James being taken out of the ambulance and wheeled inside. I think he must have been triaged in the ambulance and there is a queuing system for taking people into the Accident and Emergency department.

We're not allowed inside the hospital either, and so we have to just stay standing outside. I go to light a cigarette but Harry points out there's no smoking anywhere on hospital premises. Ellie cries periodically and Harry looks as if he is on the verge too. I feel beyond tears, my shock at what's happened so intense.

Eventually I suggest we go and sit on a low wall, and I sit in the middle hugging each of the twins close to me. There doesn't seem anything to say and so we sit in silence.

Somebody comes out at one point to say James looks to have a bleed on the brain, and he needs an operation. They stress that head injuries are notoriously unpredictable, so while we should hope for the best, we have to know too that the worst could happen. After I have given our details, we are told to go home and I'm given a number to call so that I can check his progress.

I drive us back. We are all stunned. I can't stop thinking that this is a shit year, and that every time I believe things can't get any worse, immediately they fucking well do. It's a nightmare, and I so hope we're at the end of the road now on our personal traumas in the 2020 shitshow. I doubt it though, somehow.

I put some frozen pizzas in the oven and tell Harry and Ellie they must eat. The pizzas end up in the bin untouched.

I telephone but it's six hours of agony before I am told that James has been operated on, and another half an hour before the surgeon telephones. James has an unnaturally thin skull, it seems, which none of us has known. It was a lengthy and complicated operation, as he also needed to have some stents put inside irregular-looking veins in his head to prevent strokes, and he is now in the High Dependency Unit in an induced coma.

His chances of recovery are put at around twenty-five per cent, with no guarantee that even if he does regain conscious-ness that he won't be badly affected.

I'm so shocked at this grim news that I don't know what to say. My brain doesn't seem able to compute that James and I were in each other's arms during the night, and now he might die through what was essentially a relatively minor tap on the head. It was such an unspectacular fall, such a tiny bump to his head.

The surgeon apologises and says nobody can visit him because of the COVID regulations, and there isn't anything I can do at the hospital.

*   *   *

So begins a new living nightmare with us caught in a horribly repetitive limbo, where the only thing that seems to change each day is how queasy I'm feeling with dread at any particular time.

Day after day James lies in the High Dependency Unit with no change. Then when some of the London hospitals are classified as those dealing with COVID and those not, James is moved once to another hospital, and then a second time.

We're told continually that we're not to give up hope as head injuries are unpredictable, and although they would have liked to see more of an improvement by now, it doesn't mean that James can't come back to us.

What Ellie and I and Harry talk about often is how James's tumble wasn't fast or dramatic in any way. He was caught off-balance and a foot slipped out of one of his clogs. As he lost balance he more or less wobbled himself to the ground, the thwack of his head against the lip of a paving stone being a total surprise.

Yet, James has been left hovering in a no man's land between life and death, with no certain outcome.

I assure the twins time and time again that their dad wouldn't want them feeling bad on his account, but obviously these are meaningless words to them.

The first few days turn out, foul as they are, to be easier than those that come later.

At one point some detectives come around and we sit socially distanced in the kitchen with a cafetière of coffee and our masks on. To judge by their faces, I don't think they get offered a hot drink very often. They seem shocked at what has happened to James, and they speak to me gently. I sit there numbly waiting for the proverbial axe to fall, but after a while I realise that they seem stumped still as to what did happen to Daniel, and that unless we do something very, very silly, then neither Harry nor I are serious suspects as his killer. In theory, this discovery of them knowing very little should have cheered me up, but I find it didn't make much difference to my mood. Once they had gone, I wondered if they'd come back at some point, but they never did. My uncomfortable dreams though have punished me as much as being formally arrested would have, or that is what my bad dreams feel like to me.

And deep in the middle of the night one day when I can't sleep, I realise I don't care much either way about what happened to Daniel, and I'm no longer much interested in who his killer might be.

Odd, isn't it, how things turn out? Once this was what was driving me crazy, and now frankly I give less than a shit. Maybe if Daniel had loved me just a little, I'd feel more intensely about his killer being found. But he didn't care about me, and so to me it's poetic justice that someone somewhere has got away with it.

My days now are spent concentrating on James and how we can best care for him. We can't visit him, and I miss him so much, it hurts.

Ali is a brick though. As we all start to feel worse and worse about James, now that initial numbness of the shock has worn off, she comes over to look after us, and instead of talking about Daniel as we used to do, she and I spend a lot of time researching online about head injuries and possible outcomes.

She spends time with both Harry and Ellie, just chewing the fat or letting them show her around various games, in Harry's case, or something to do with software, or the endless episodes of the *Below Deck* reality TV series which is Ellie's main way of soothing herself, and luckily the twins both seem to like Ali, which frees me up to think of other things.

I know having Ali here is breaking all the self-isolating rules, but that is a very minor worry. As I hoped, she smiled when she saw the Drunk Elephant products.

'If this goes on much longer, I'm going to have to do you another basket,' I say.

'Rubbish,' she replies.

Ali

When Caitlin rang from outside the hospital to say that James had just been badly hurt, I could hardly grasp what she said.

· Since then I've made myself helpful to her, not that I've been able to do much, other than listen to her drive herself crazy with talking about James. And I've been happy to spend time with Ellie and Harry. They're both nice kids, and I hope that one day they get their father back, and everyone can push this horrible time into the past.

The investigation into Daniel's death has remained stalled from the police's perspective. I wonder if when I cleaned my fingerprints that day, inadvertently I took away crucial forensic evidence. At the time I was looking after myself, and I never thought much further than that. But I would gamble on there not being an obvious suspect that looks at this moment more credible than all the others, and the police not having the time or resources, and that the whole Daniel affair will become a cold case before we know it.

To me it seems best that none of us rock the boat from here, and that we allow as much as possible to become water that's already passed under the bridge.

Before

It hadn't been supposed to happen as it did. But that little bastard Daniel just laughed as he stood at his front door, gently rubbing his chest from where I presume he'd already been shoved by Harry.

He wasn't sorry at all, not in the slightest about either of them. He didn't give a shit about Caitlin or that he'd just upset my son. I think it was his attitude to Harry I thought the biggest crime, as Harry was only trying to do the right thing and protect his mum.

And with the sight of Daniel's cruel smirking face, I just saw red – it's true what they say about this. You really do see a red mist descend.

My thrust at him became a shove, and then without quite meaning it to, the shove became, well, just the forerunner to all the rest.

I took the knife out of my pocket that I'd been using to open boxes of what had been delivered for the recording studio, and I just slid it into his flesh.

There was remarkably little resistance.

Daniel looked at me with his brows raised in surprise, and I laughed at his expression.

He hadn't been expecting that.

And for an instant, just for a moment, the earth seemed to halt its spinning.

With the bright sunlight dappling the floor and dust motes playing in the space between us, everything fades from around us and I don't think that either of us can pull away from the gaze of the other.

There's remarkably little blood, although I did get a tiny splatter on my jumper, but I step back anyway as the silence grows and swirls. I wonder if there was more blood there later, seeping from him?

It feels as if God is here alongside us both.

I feel as if I am good. And strong. And right. And righteous.

Then Daniel is on the ground, gasping and groaning unattractively as I watch. Then with one last thrash and tremble it's all over.

I crouch, just to make sure. I cannot turn my gaze away.

And as I do this I am overwhelmed with euphoria.

A surprised tear begins to slide from Daniel's open eye.

And I pop it into my mouth from the edge of my finger. A final insult, a little bit of him part of me now, for ever in me, my triumph.

I stand up and stare at the consequences of bad behaviour.

What Daniel and I have just shared feels the closest I can ever be to anyone, and yet also at the furthest reaches of human experience.

I've crossed a line, and done the worst thing possible. There's no coming back, I suspect.

But I'm not sure I want to.

It is, no doubt about it, the best, most powerful feeling in the world.

I wonder if I'll ever feel this good again.

Stay Home

And as I leave I decide how I'll hide my clothes and trainers, and have a quick shower. Later I'll sneak out and dispose of them in a rubbish bin.

I bet my wife never notices a thing.

After

James

I have a secret, an exhilarating secret.
  Well, more than one, truth to tell.
  I think I've managed it. I think I've got away with it.
  I do hope this is the case.
  I'm talking about Daniel.

Also, I'm not as lost as they think I am. I need to start rejoining the outside world soon, but for today I'm content to lie here, letting the dust settle and my family miss me, as my thoughts ratchet this way and that.
  My head aches a lot and I can't focus easily. Sometimes my limbs twitch, and I give an involuntary groan as the machines keeping me alive blink and beep. I can't move, or keep my thoughts together.
  But each day something loosens, just a little.
  I will get better, I feel it in my bones.

I spend a lot of time thinking about Daniel.
  I became suspicious at Christmas. My wife or her friends would never have bought scent that tawdry. And why put it in the utility room? A schoolgirl error.
  It didn't take me long to find him.
  For a while I didn't do anything.
  I couldn't work out quite what I felt.

It seemed shabby and smutty on the one hand, and destined not to last. Caitlin's a fool, but not that much of one. But I felt an incredible frisson every time I touched her and so I didn't want it over too soon. Each sexual act reclaiming her anew as my own was something else.

I knew I'd confront her at some point, but I wanted it to be a real shock, a punishment, and I found it fun to imagine all the different ways I could land this to the effect I craved.

And then lockdown came, and the more I thought about it, the more I realised Ellie and Harry didn't need to have even more of a bad time than they were already. I do try to put them first.

What a thing for them, to be fifteen and forced to be with their parents twenty-four seven. It's not fair, is it?

Caitlin tried, I think she really tried.

I saw her becoming more and more miserable staying home with us, out of temptation's way.

She struggled.

I knew she'd crack at some point, and my only surprise is that it took her as long as it did for her to fall, and off she went. One doesn't live with someone for twenty years without learning a lot about them.

I hadn't banked on her crumbling that day though.

Harry was so upset when he found me after seeing Daniel, that what could I do?

I never meant to kill Daniel, although I admit it was handy I had that knife in my pocket.

But then he shouldn't have been mean to Harry, or taunted me. Should he?

My wife butched it out well though afterwards, I'll give her that. It can't have been easy.

★　　★　　★

Stay Home

Harry came to me in panic.

He'd pushed Daniel, you see, after finding pictures of his mum online. And he looked at her contacts on her desktop, and there was Daniel's face right beside his address. Harry felt ashamed and he wanted Daniel to stop. But Daniel laughed at him, telling him to butt out of his life, without letting Harry finish. And Harry lost it then and pushed him over. He ran away then, petrified that Daniel was badly hurt, or worse.

Terrified and flustered, Harry ran to me, not knowing what to do.

But it didn't sound so bad to me, when Harry told me what he'd done.

So, I said to Harry that the best plan of action would be for him to do nothing more. He should go to the den and make it look as if he'd been there for hours, and never let on what had happened, not even to his sister or his mother. It would be our secret, just between Harry and me, a secret for all time.

I went to Daniel's and, well, you know the rest.

Ellie helped no end by being just Ellie, when Caitlin went in. Ellie got up from her bed late and I watched her go to the den right after Harry sat down there. She knew he'd been out but she wasn't bothered why.

I snuck back into the house before too long and showered and changed, and not long after that Ellie teased Harry about being MIA in front of Caitlin, I eavesdropped. I'm afraid poor Caitlin was too dim to pull the clues together.

Poor old Cat, she had something else on her mind.

I wish I'd been able to let her know I was teasing her when I'd asked if she'd seen the retractable knife. I couldn't resist, and that was bad of me, I see now. I'd dropped it in a bottle of bleach for an hour to remove every last bit of Daniel and then I made sure it was in the selfie we took, just for a little extra kick.

By the time I got to Daniel's that morning, a police car was just driving away at the other end of the street – I suppose this was where the film of Harry was taken – and Daniel was up and about, if perhaps a trifle groggy.

At any rate, whatever Harry had done to him hardly mattered as that little runt was still well up for being far too lippy.

Totally unrepentant about upsetting my Harry, of course. And when Daniel told me to piss off for the third time, I finally flipped and then I said don't you speak to me like that, and he roared with laughter and then just turned away from me and walked upstairs, not seeming to care that he'd just left me standing there.

Without quite meaning to, I added as I followed, 'And for the record, you can stop pawing my wife with your short-arsed hands, or drilling your tiny prick into her.'

Looking back, I can't decide whether this was an intentional slip on my part, or not.

Daniel stood still in his living room and stared at me in confusion.

This threw me for a minute as I thought it was all so obvious who we were. But now I genuinely think that until then he hadn't twigged who I was, and it's possible that, teens being teens, Harry might not have made it clear earlier that he'd been there about Caitlin.

'What are you talking about? Who's your wife?' Daniel asked, a puzzled look on his face.

'Caitlin.'

'Caitlin!'

He almost wept, he roared so much with merriment as I tried to stare him down.

'That's beautiful,' he wheezed, shamelessly unrepentant. 'How rich! And that boy's mother too. Wonderful!'

Those were the last words Daniel ever said, for I'd had enough of him by then.

They're not much, are they?

I remembered to rub the doorbell with my cuff as I left. It was the only other thing I touched.

Other than Daniel's face when I stole that tear from him. And even then, I don't think I touched him, but more that the tear danced across from his skin to mine.

When the family did the Shuffle Challenge together I thought everything that had happened might only be a hiccup in our life from which we could all recover. We were a family, godammit, all pulling together and relying on each other.

I kept reminding Harry of this, telling him not to worry. Telling him that Daniel had been alive and well when I had seen him, and that Harry was safe and Harley would back up a story about going to Harley's for the weed, as that offer had indeed been made.

At first Harry believed me, I'm sure. There was a lot going on and it was easy to divert my son's attention.

In time he won't, of course, if that's not already happened.

But I know my son, and I'm banking on this head injury I've sustained meaning that Harry will feel guilty, and it shall be this guilt that will seal his lips. And the realisation that if it doesn't, then all hell will break loose at home.

Harry loves his home, and Ellie, and his mum and dad, and he won't want to rock the boat.

The fight with my son on the day of my injury was when I reminded Harry that Daniel was not for talking about. To speak of him could reopen a can of worms.

Harry said he was being careful. With the logic of a teenage boy, he then added in a sulky undertone that it was his mother who should be the one feeling guilty for being a slut.

I said I wasn't interested in talking about levels of guilt or in hearing him call Caitlin a slut (as that's my prerogative), and when Harry said 'leave it, Dad', I felt a quiver and then another sprinkling of that red mist, and so I admit I grabbed Harry a bit harder than I should have. And he pushed me back – he is my son, after all – and I shoved him firmly just a little.

I am heartened by how very hard Caitlin fought to save me though, and how ferociously she's tried to protect the children by insisting what happened was just a simple trip, an accident.

Which I guess it was, as long as I don't recall the look in Harry's eyes just before I hit the ground. I don't for a second think he meant to harm me, just that there's a little something of me in him, something about potential, a little nub of temper that's hard and tough. It's hidden well though, living deep below, but in that instant I saw it flash, and Harry felt it too. I don't think that previously he knew that capacity within himself, and I feel it scared him. He'll have to live with knowing he's not quite the pushover we've all assumed, that there's something deep inside he needs to watch.

On a more positive note, Caitlin's determination that I should breathe again has made me fall for her all over again.

Caitlin and I. We're such a match – both liars, very selfish, and we love our children. Neither of us would argue with this.

Still, Caitlin would do very well to honour her wedding vows from now on. Me being a killer and all.

It's my darkest secret.

The End (Almost)

Caitlin

James is making excellent progress now, I'm delighted to report, really great, and they think he will be allowed home very soon.

Me, and the twins, are so looking forward to having him back with us. I've warned them that James might need allowances making, and we'll have to take his recovery slowly.

They nod their heads, but I'm not sure any of us knows quite what it will mean. There's not going to be any sort of Shuffle Challenge reprise in the near future, that's for certain.

Now and again, late at night, I watch on repeat the short clip that Ellie made of the four of us strutting our stuff. It seems a lifetime ago.

The virile James I see dancing before me is lithe and muscular, and a far cry from the ravaged-looking man he is today, with his thin legs and quite a lot of grey now showing in his hair and beard. I don't think he'll like that grey much.

Still, it will be good to have him back where he belongs.

He's going to be very poorly for a while.

But, as long as he doesn't overdo it when he first comes back, it's quite likely that James will make what passes for a full recovery.

The weather we're having isn't as nice as it was during the first part of lockdown. It was cold then, but the memory of day after day of piercing, relentless March and April sunshine and deep turquoise cloudless skies at the height of the crisis will always stay with me.

It's warmer now, as is to be expected in summer, but it feels more changeable than back then.

Ellie and Harry have really grown up during the time we've all had to stay home. Ellie is quite the young woman now, but Harry has taken it all very badly. I can see it's been a difficult time for him, and when he'll let me, I just tell him to hang in there and give it time as all things pass. He looks at me askance, as if I'm talking rubbish, but then that's a teenager for you.

The latest is they've become politicised and interested in the world outside our home, what with their support for #blacklivesmatter, and #pride and #nonbinary and #trans and all the rest.

They are both more subdued than previously though, more cautious about the world. They don't seem to want to stray far from me.

Ali, who pops over regularly, as I do to hers, claims that these last few months might be a good thing long-term as far as the twins are concerned, as although painful to experience in many respects, it means they are wiser and more street-wise. Which has the advantage, Ali insists, that they know they're not invincible and that the world isn't necessarily going to treat them as special, simply because they are my and James's children.

I know what Ali means, but adultery and murder and the near death of their father touching their lives is a lot to bear.

Meanwhile, the baby grand now takes up pride of place in the garden room slash recording studio. I don't think the twins have been into the studio since the day their father fell beside it. But that's okay too; I expect they'll rediscover it in time.

It turned out we had a bona fide need for the space in the living room that the piano took up, one that even James won't be able to question once he's back.

The living room is going to be his room when he comes home.

He'll need to have a special bed there, for a while at least, and I think to have him on the ground floor near to us in the daytime is better for him than putting him upstairs out of the way. It will be easy for me to keep an eye on him there.

When I had a clear-out of my clothes, Ali seemed pleased with what I took her. These days she's usually wearing something or other I donated, and although I probably shouldn't say, she looks a totally different person. In a good way, of course.

I was right that Dukie has rather taken to Ali too, now that we can all socialise legitimately, even though the Government's rules on social distancing seem all over the place. We are waiting uneasily to see if there'll be a second wave of cases.

Poor Dukie was hit by the virus, quite badly so, although not quite so much that she had to be hospitalised, but she was extremely poorly. I don't personally know anyone else who has had it, although the father of someone Dukie works with has died of it in hospital.

Sometimes I see Ali regarding me with a thoughtful look, but I've told her let's let sleeping dogs lie and not talk about Daniel, and so she never brings him up, and actually she doesn't talk about James much either, other than to point out how much we'll enjoy having him at home again.

I don't think about Daniel much these days. Not much at all, really.

There is the odd moment when I relive the feeling when I was a little in love with him, and I'd hoped he felt the same for me. But any such thoughts are very few and far between.

He really was a total shit.

We are all going on a picnic today in London Fields. Dukie, Ali and I. I've reminded Ali time and again that Dukie doesn't know anything about Daniel and me, and so it's imperative she keeps schtum.

Ali won't let me down, I'm sure.

Harry and Ellie and Harley are coming too. In fact, I've talked them into carrying all the food and the new bamboo picnic plates and the concertina stools and the folding table and all the rest.

Ali took one look at everything heaped together before we set off and said, 'Shall I book the U-Haul now?'

When Dukie said she'd brought her swimmers and I should bring mine, as the lido was now open and we could have a dip, Ali and I shared a surreptitiously raised eyebrow as I replied, 'Not for me. I'm not risking the lido yet.'

Dukie shot me a puzzled glance, but she didn't push it.

A few minutes later Dukie said to Ali, 'Caitlin and I belong to a great book group. Would you like to come?'

'Not on your nelly!' she replied.

Now it's Dukie and my turn to share a look.

I link my arms through those of my two friends, and off we set, Dukie and me trying (and failing) to persuade Ali that she ought to give online dating a chance as she would make someone a lovely girlfriend, although we pull apart when Ellie hisses back at us, 'Social distancing, Mum!' When Ali has gone to help the kids out with what they are carrying, Dukie mouths, 'Is she lesbian?' and I shrug for I genuinely have no idea and neither do I care.

We have a lovely afternoon, and we play some softball, the teens beating us by miles, obviously, and Ali saying to them that if they don't stop effing and blinding they'll all turn out just like her. The youngsters are a bit sweary, but it warms my heart to see Ellic and Harley goofing about, and even Harry getting into the swing.

Ali means them not ending up like her to be a cautionary tale, but I think the twins and Harley find Ali cool, and so they wouldn't mind ending up like her in the least. And actually I don't think I would either, in most of Ali's ways. Well, perhaps not the drinking, but everything else.

We trudge back towards our house as the shadows shift, saying we'll stay in for the evening and watch a film or two.

I've had an 86-inch television delivered with an amazing sound bar, and so we're going to choose something noisy that the twins will love, that we can all plonk ourselves in front of with the volume ramped right up.

I'll probably have to apologise to the neighbours again, but I think we all deserve a treat.

As Ali chats companionably outside Mehmet's with Dodi, whom she's just bumped into, Dodi announces there is a For Sale sign that was put up this afternoon in Daniel's garden.

I don't feel even the smallest pang about this as I slip the loops of my cloth mask over my ears and nip into Mehmet's for a marathon supply of crisps, pop and sweets for the six of us.

Actually, it's going to be seven, as Ali comes inside to say that she hopes it's okay, but she's asked Dodi to join us too.

Poor Dodi, I wonder if I should warn her we'll most definitely be watching something fifteen-year-olds think cool. Then I think, sod it, Ali can deal with managing Dodi's expectations. And, who knows, maybe she'll even love it, whatever we pick.

I smile and nod, and as Ali leaves, giving Mehmet a wave as she does, I turn back to the snacks.

I'm not the only one looking for nibbles it seems. There's a slim young man with curly hair and a black mask also regarding the best of what Mehmet has to offer.

'Excuse me,' I say as I lean down close to him, aware that my face is perhaps a smidge too close to his groin as I reach over in front of him in order to grab a clutch of posh crisp packets.

'Excused,' he breathes, and as I stand up, I notice just how near he is standing to me, and how nice he smells.

He looks unbelievably cute, there in his mask with his dark eyes twinkling at me, the more so when he gives a single lightning wink.

And before I know it, somehow I've winked back at him.

Ali

I know Caitlin will stray again.

No evidence of course, but I just do. I feel it in my waters, I suppose you could say.

I wish she found enough comfort at home, safe in the bosom of her family. But the reality is that Caitlin has got the taste for the excitement of something more, something that will always be outside of her house. She just doesn't know that yet.

The medics have told her not to expect too much from her husband on the bedroom front, even when he has made as good a recovery as he can, and so in time this will become the excuse she needs, I expect.

And if that happens, then I am pretty certain James will find a way to punish her.

Not that I am going to say anything about this to Caitlin. After all, life is unpredictable and what I think might happen, mightn't.

And I wouldn't want to be the one who puts a flirtatious idea into her head, if she really is determined to throw herself into her marriage once more.

I could never prove it, but I know just as surely as eggs are eggs it was James who killed Daniel. How else would he have known with such authority that he was such a 'short-arse cocksucker' if James hadn't confronted Daniel face to face?

The more I thought about it – and I've mulled on this a lot – the more it all made sense, even though I've never ever had a single word with James, and so I don't really know him at all. Regardless, his guilt is the only thing that makes total sense in this whole sorry mess.

If Harry went to Daniel's, it's not hard to believe at age fifteen Harry would run to his dad for help. And a dad who knew about Daniel already, well, you can imagine the rest, which one day Harry will, as well.

And, if James were to catch his wife in a second affair? He has crossed a boundary for revenge once, and once that's done, what's to stop one acting again?

Also, and more importantly as far as I am concerned, I don't want to risk my own relationship with Caitlin. 'Don't shoot the messenger' is a phrase I keep thinking of. I'm certain Caitlin has no idea about James and what he did; I'm sure she'd tell me if she had. I don't believe she thinks much about Daniel these days, and I feel she's got more important things to think about than what really happened.

So for me to tell her of my suspicions that James killed Daniel would be a risky strategy. I don't kid myself that Caitlin wouldn't be horrified she is married to a killer. But, because of her desire to keep her family together, and because she would feel guilty all over again, as it was through her adultery that her husband crossed a line, I think the time would come inevitably when she'd push me away, as every time she saw me she'd be reminded of the final tragedy at the root of her life, the serpent coiled around the tree. These feelings of taint and despair would eventually spread, and tarnish the relationship that she and I have, and slowly she'd start to make excuses about not seeing me.

I'd hate that.

This is a family I want to be around, and until now Caitlin has made me very welcome. I want my place with them all to last very much indeed.

Belonging somewhere is a novel experience for me, and it's something I'd fight to keep hold of.

I'd be disingenuous too if I didn't admit that knowing something Caitlin doesn't, is just a little bit exciting. I feel I'm watching her, in a way she isn't watching me, and this makes me tingle a teeny bit.

Will Cat unravel what James has done, if I don't voice my suspicions?

Unlikely, I would say, as I think for her it's all parked now in her mind under 'Hideous Lockdown', which the other day is how I heard her describe the last few months. It's as if she's put Daniel and the fallout in a neat box, and pushed it deep into the recesses of her mind. The police and the chance of further evidence unfurling that points to her possible guilt have all been banked to worry about another time.

Should she twig though, would she make James pay? I'm not sure. I suppose we'll have to wait and see. He'll be at her mercy, in that living room. Although I doubt Caitlin's realised she's going to put him in the perfect place where he can keep an eye on her every move, as much as the other way around.

Either way, Ellie and Harry might well need a friend. A friend just like me.

Their mum has had a scare, all right.

But she won't have learnt from it, I expect.

I won't say this to her though. What's the point?

And if it all goes pear-shaped, well, hasn't Cat managed to survive the shocks that floor most people? She's come through a little bruised, but still okay.

Heck, I think Cat's big secret is that she likes a risky thrill more than most. And what's more thrilling than a new lover. And what's riskier than a husband who's already killed?

This family needs me, I think, to right their wrongs. IMHO.

And so I'll wait.

And watch.

Stay home. Stay safe!

Acknowledgements

I would like to thank my excellent editor Eve Hall at Hodder, and my wonderful agent Cathryn Summerhayes at Curtis Brown. All mistakes are my own, but Harriet Davis, Louis Rusher, Josie Rusher, Josh Walters, Harley Riman (who I must stress has nothing to do with behaviour like that of Harry or his friend Harley – I just love Harley as a name!), Bailey Wadhams and Julia Hamilton have all been extremely helpful in their different ways, for which I am very grateful.